ROMANCE LOV
Love letter collection :
six romance novellas.

A
TIMELESS
Romance
ANTHOLOGY

LOVE LETTER
COLLECTION

LOVE LETTER
COLLECTION

Karey White
Krista Lynne Jensen
Diane Darcy
Sarah M. Eden
Annette Lyon
Heather B. Moore

Mirror Press

Interior Design by Rachael Anderson
Edited by Annette Lyon and Cassidy Wadsworth
Cover image #153698303, Shutterstock.com

Published by Mirror Press, LLC
http://TimelessRomanceAnthologies.blogspot.com
E-book edition released February 2014
Paperback edition released November 2014

ISBN-13: 978-1-941145-37-1

TABLE OF CONTENTS

Maggie's Song   1

Just Fly   63

How to Rewrite a Love Letter   133

A Thousand Words   197

Between the Lines   247

Blackberry Hollow   303

OTHER TIMELESS ROMANCE ANTHOLOGIES

Winter Collection

Spring Vacation Collection

Summer Wedding Collection

Autumn Collection

European Collection

Old West Collection

Summer in New York Collection

Silver Bells Collection

All Regency Collection

California Dreamin' Collection

All Hallows' Eve Collection

Maggie's Song

by Karey White

Other Works by Karey White

Gifted

For What It's Worth

Ripple Effect Romance Series
Lost and Found

The Husband Maker Series
The Husband Maker
The Match Maker

One

Maggie checked the battery life on the satellite phone, tucked it into a pocket of her backpack, and zipped it closed. She'd never used the emergency phone in the six years she'd guided tours to Havasupai Falls, but if there was ever an emergency, she didn't want a dead battery.

"Dan, don't even think about touching the books while we're gone," Lucas said. His tone was stern, but his lilting Australian accent made him more charming than intimidating. Why did Maggie still have to feel like a Popsicle on a hot Arizona sidewalk every time he spoke?

"And please pay attention to details," she added, eyeing her cousin. "No double bookings. I don't ever want to have to scramble again like we did in July."

Dan put up his hands in surrender. "Don't worry, you

guys. I can handle this. I'll stay out of the books, and I'll triple check the schedule before making any reservations."

"The most important thing is that you get better," Lucas said. "But don't touch the books. Maybe I should password protect them."

"You know, Maggie and I took care of the books while you were gone getting that degree," Dan said.

"Which explains why it took me so long to get them back in shape," Lucas said. They all laughed.

"Fortunately for *you*, you're not a Jensen," Dan said. He and Maggie were cousins who'd been born just twelve days apart. "None of us Jensens are very good with numbers."

"I'm better than you are," Maggie said to Dan.

"Don't get cocky, Mags," Lucas said. "I've seen how you are with numbers."

Maggie smiled and waved him off. Lucas had been teasing her since the eighth grade, when his family had moved halfway around the world to Flagstaff. He'd been a tall, skinny boy with braces, had a mountain bike Dan had drooled over and an accent Maggie couldn't get enough of. The three of them became immediate best friends.

"Sorry you have to take my place, man," Dan said.

"You know I still like guiding tours," Lucas said. "All you had to do was ask. You didn't have to fake appendicitis to get out of a few weeks on the trail."

"Hey, Dan, it's me you should be apologizing to," Maggie said. "I'm the one who has to pick up the slack now that Lucas has gone all soft and desk-jobby on us." She wasn't serious. Lucas was as fit as he'd ever been. Maggie would feel a lot more comfortable about this arrangement if he didn't look so good.

"It'll be a nice change for you," Dan told her. "Between Lucas's guitar and his pizza feast, you'll be begging me to break my leg next."

As great as Lucas's pizza feast was, and as much as the hikers loved it when Lucas pulled out his guitar and sang,

Maggie still had misgivings. She'd done a good job of acting normal when all she had to do was see Lucas in the office every few days, but four days on the trail with his Australian charm, his rugged good looks, and that beautiful, mellowed accent might be more than she could manage.

It had been seven years since Lucas, ever the gentleman, had asked Maggie to senior prom. He hadn't been interested in anyone else, and since no one else had asked her, going together made sense. Maggie had been elated. She'd found a silky champagne-colored dress that complemented her fair skin and chestnut hair. She'd even gone to Aunt Lucy's salon for hair and makeup help. She'd wanted to look feminine and pretty enough for him to take note. She wanted him to think of her as more than a buddy.

At the end of the night, Lucas had pulled her in for a tight hug that had melted her insides.

And then he'd broken her heart.

"I'm so glad you and Dan are cousins," he'd said. "I'd have never guessed I could be best friends with a girl if you two hadn't always been hanging around. You're not even like a real girl."

Maggie had covered her disappointment with a laugh. "If I weren't a real girl, I wouldn't be in this dress or these heels." She waved her hands over the silky gown that had been meant to catch his eye and the dreadful shoes killing her feet.

"Of course you are," he said. "And you look really nice. But I like you better in hiking boots than heels. Those just look weird on you." Her expression must have faltered just enough to tell him he'd said the wrong thing. "Sorry, Mags, but you know what I mean."

"Yeah. Sure. I know what you mean," she'd quickly agreed, and he'd looked relieved.

A few minutes later, behind her closed bedroom door, she'd thrown the dress and heels into the back corner of her closet and cried herself to sleep.

For years, Maggie had buried her feelings, afraid of spoiling the closeness the three friends had shared. She'd worked alongside Lucas and Dan during the summers as the three of them had started Wild Country Hiking Tours. She'd smiled through her devastation as she'd congratulated Lucas on his engagement to Erica, a woman in his accounting program at Arizona State, and then pretended to be sad for him when Erica got a job in Los Angeles and broke it off. Maggie was a pro at pretending to be one of the guys, at never showing any sign that beneath their friendship was a girl who'd spent years hoping that someday Lucas would come to his senses and realize that they were perfect for each other.

"Mags? Did you hear me?" Lucas's voice broke into her memories.

"Oh, sorry. What did you say?" Maggie asked, hoping she wasn't blushing.

"Just asked if you needed anything when I go gas up the bus."

"Oh, no thanks. I think we're good."

"All righty then. I'll see you bright and early. Actually, it's not bright at 4 a.m. It'll only be early."

Maggie watched him walk out to the bus. Why couldn't she just move on?

Two

"Ladies and gents, welcome to The Adventure Bus," Lucas said into the hand mic. The Adventure Bus was a short school bus they'd bought from a school district in southern Utah two years earlier. They'd removed the back two seats to make room for gear and painted it white with *Wild Country Hiking Tours* in dark green along each side. After each trip, they handed out Sharpies to their guests, who signed the bus, marking the completion of their Wild Country experience.

Dim lights gave the inside of the bus a glow and made it possible to see each other. A few passengers smiled. For others, it was too early to respond.

"In about two hours, we'll be watching the sun rise at the trailhead of one of the most stunning places on earth. Since we have a little while before we get there, we'd like to take a few minutes to get acquainted with each other. After that, we'll have a short safety briefing. Then we'll let you catch a little power nap. Since everyone in your group already knows each other, I'll tell you a little about Maggie and me, and you can tell us about you. Hopefully within the hour, we'll be best mates."

From the driver's seat, Maggie rolled her eyes. She'd forgotten how much Lucas played up the rugged Australian outdoorsmen for the tourists. Lucas noticed her expression from across the bus and grinned. Maggie loved that smile, especially when it was directed at her, even though sometimes it felt like it was wringing her heart out.

"Since we want our lovely driver to focus on the road, I'll tell you a little about her. This is my good friend, Maggie."

She looked at the passengers in the big mirror above her head, smiled, and waved.

"She tries to fool you into thinking she's just a wisp of a little lady, but she's one of the toughest guys I know. Once I broke my leg, and she carried me out of the canyon on her back."

A few of the passengers glanced at one another, and Lucas laughed. "I'm just playing with you. But she really is tough, and we're lucky to have her. She knows these trails better than anyone. She graduated from Northern Arizona University with a degree in elementary education. Someday she'll be teaching little tykes how to read and write, but we've talked her into waiting a few years for that. If you're extra nice to her, she might make you the most amazing skillet brownies you've ever eaten.

"My name's Lucas, and I'm originally from Adelaide, Australia, but I've lived here for about eleven years. I graduated almost two years ago with an accounting degree, so if you're bored on the trail, grab me, and we can have a riveting conversation about accounts payable or microeconomic pricing models. Now let's go around the bus and learn a little about you."

The tour was made up of Dennis and Barbara, a couple in their fifties from Fernway, a town outside of Pittsburgh. Barbara was divorced, and Dennis had been widowed. This was the first vacation they'd taken with their blended family, most of whom were adults. Maggie tried to put the names from the reservation information with the faces in the bus, but it was difficult from the driver's seat.

They were a carefully friendly group, and Maggie was suddenly glad that Lucas was here to help smooth over any step-family first-vacation awkwardness. He was good at warming people up and making them feel comfortable.

Lucas shared a few safety precautions, then settled against the window and covered his head with his hat like a spaghetti-Western cowboy. Maggie glanced in the mirror; a few people were watching the horizon as it turned from inky-blue velvet to yellow-tinged lavender. Others settled in for a few more minutes of sleep. Two college-age girls were whispering and watching Lucas. Of course. Maggie watched the road ahead and allowed herself a few minutes to enjoy her own daydreams about Lucas before she locked her heart back up for the next four days.

Three

The sun's rays were warming the far side of the canyon but hadn't yet reached the bus as they unloaded their gear and put it in the small plywood shed at the far end of the parking area. A few men from Supai Village would bring their mules up the side of the canyon in the next hour to pack up all of the gear and haul it down to the campground.

Maggie was locking the back of the bus when Lucas draped his arm over her shoulders. His touch sent a jolt through her, and she jerked up straight.

"Mags? You okay?" he asked, his arm still around her. It was difficult to think with him standing so close.

"Yeah, you just surprised me," she said.

"I was just checking to see if you want me to take the front or the back. I'll do whichever."

Maggie dragged her thoughts away from his hand on

her shoulder and his voice so close to her ear. "Why don't you take the front? I'll take the back."

"Swell. This is going to be fun. I've missed guiding with you."

"Yeah." She wanted to say more—she always wanted to say more—but at the moment, she couldn't trust her voice to sound normal.

"Hey, Lucas?" It was Dennis at the front of the bus. Lucas gave Maggie's shoulder a little squeeze, then joined Dennis. Maggie took a deep breath and leaned her head against the cool metal of the door. When she turned around, she caught Barbara watching her. The older woman winked, and Maggie felt her face flush.

When Lucas finished talking to Dennis, he and Maggie called the group together and ran through a checklist with each hiker. Did they have sufficient water? Check. Had they applied sunblock? Check. Had they used the restrooms? Check.

Maggie lined up the group at the top of the canyon and took a photograph. Several years ago, she'd started a wall of before and after pictures at the office. It was fun to see the difference four days could make. Today the hikers looked clean and shiny and had a sparkle of anticipation in their eyes. In just four days, they'd look different. There were the obvious changes—new hiking boots would be old and broken in, clothes would be dusty and sweat soaked. Men almost always finished with facial hair, some scruffy and uneven, some with the beginnings of a beard.

But the differences Maggie noticed were more subtle. In just four days, some people looked a little stronger; some of their softness turned more angular. Their fresh, eager eyes had a look of satisfaction and accomplishment at having taken on a challenge and won. Maggie had seen the trail change lives and mend broken relationships, and sometimes the camera caught glimmers of those changes. These were things that kept guiding new and interesting, even though she'd traveled the same trails again and again.

Maggie pulled her backpack onto her shoulders and adjusted it so the weight was distributed evenly. When everyone was ready, Lucas led the way down the first switchbacks, already chatting with Dennis's teenage son, Braden. The others fell into line behind them, and Maggie took her spot at the back, behind Dennis and Barbara, who were talking quietly.

The sun slowly moved across the canyon as it rose, nudging its way closer and closer to the hikers. In the early-morning shade, the November air was cool and brisk, but as the sun continued to move across the vast canyon landscape, the temperature slowly moved up with it.

The group moved and shifted order. Braden slowed to have a conversation with his brother, Mike. Barbara's daughter, Jane and her roommate, Montana, the college students, moved closer to Lucas. The only people who kept their spots in the procession were Lucas, who stayed in the lead, and Barbara and Maggie, who remained in back.

They'd been on the trail less than an hour when a rumble moved toward them. "Pack mules coming," Lucas called back to the group. "Move to the wall." Everyone slowed and shifted close to the canyon wall as a short, dark man jogged up the trail with ten mules tethered together.

"Hello, Maggie," he said as they passed.

"Hey, Clifford," Maggie said.

An hour later, it was Maggie's turn to call out a warning. "Pack mules coming down." The group again scooted to the wall. The loaded animals ran past the hikers with Clifford riding the front mule. The animals' hoofs pounded the packed dirt. Jane and Montana squealed.

"They're going to run right off the edge," Barbara said to Maggie.

"Sometimes it seems that way, but they could run this trail with their eyes closed," Maggie said.

"I told Dennis I wanted to ride one of those to the

campground, but if they go that fast, I just changed my mind."

"It's not a very comfortable ride," Maggie said. "About three years ago, I cut my shin climbing down the mountain to Mooney Falls. We wrapped it up, and Clifford hauled me out on a pack mule. I hope I never have to ride one again."

"That fun, huh?" Barbara asked.

"I'd definitely rather walk out of here. Mules aren't graceful like horses." Every step had been jarring. Maggie adjusted the strap on her backpack. "What made you decide on this for your first big family trip?" Maggie asked Barbara.

"Dennis has been dreaming of doing this for thirty years. He and his first wife had booked a trip right before she got diagnosed, so it never happened. I told him we'd better do it before we're too old, and he suggested we invite the whole family. Truthfully, this isn't my kind of vacation. I like hotels and dressing nice and good shopping, but I figured I could suck it up so we could all do it together. Let's hope I make it."

"Of course you will," Maggie said. "The general store in Supai Village may not be quite what you had in mind for shopping, but they do have some cool jewelry and pottery, and they'll ship it home for you."

"I like jewelry." Barbara lowered her voice. "I brought makeup. I was afraid I'd scare Dennis and his kids if I went four days without any. And I brought a sequined sweatshirt for hanging around camp. I may be roughing it, but Dennis is going to think I'm pretty doing it."

"I'll tell you a secret. I always bring mascara, so we're even."

"It takes a lot more than mascara when you're my age," Barbara said. "You're still young and adorable. Too bad Braden's not a few years older. I'd be playing matchmaker. I'm pretty good at that, you know."

"You're a matchmaker?"

"Not officially, of course. But I introduced Emma and

Mike. He sold pharmaceuticals to the doctor's office where I work, and I knew as soon as I met him that they'd be a good fit. And I introduced Dr. Phillips to my neighbor, Donna. They got married four years ago and have two wild little boys now."

"Two for two," Maggie said.

"Oh, and I introduced my niece to a friend of Mike's at Mike and Emma's wedding, and now they're dating."

"Maybe I should hire you. My love life's been stalled for a long, long time."

"Hmm. I find that hard to believe." Barbara said.

"It's true." Whatever Barbara was thinking, she was certainly wrong. A love life required two interested people, not one hopeless woman who'd been pining for the same man for far too long.

The sun warmed everything it touched. Heat beat down from above and curled off the rock walls, wrapping the hikers in a dry, feverish blanket. The jackets and sweatshirts were quickly discarded and stored in backpacks.

"Don't forget to drink," Lucas called over his shoulder. "Dehydration is no fun."

When the trail opened up to a wide, flat area, Lucas stopped for a breather. Dennis and Barbara found a boulder and sat down to rest while the others scattered around to talk and eat the bags of trail mix Lucas had handed out.

"How long have you been guiding?" Mike asked Maggie. He and Emma had found some shade against the wall and had sat down. Emma's face was cherry red.

"We started doing tours during the summers when we were in college."

"We?" Emma asked.

"My cousin, Dan, and Lucas and me. We worked for another guide company, but after two summers, we decided to start up our own." Maggie was concerned about Emma's flushed face. She wasn't sweating like everyone else, meaning her body was having a harder time keeping cool. Maggie pulled a water bottle out of her backpack. "You should drink some more water. And splash some of this on your face. We want to keep your body temperature where it should be."

Emma took the bottle and followed Maggie's instructions.

Laughter caught Maggie's attention, and she looked down the trail to where Jane and Montana were flirting with Lucas. Why wouldn't they? He was outrageously handsome. The frustrating thing was that Lucas was so friendly and open that it was difficult to tell if he was just being nice, or if he was interested back. He probably was. Jane and Montana were both attractive. He could take his pick—tanned and athletic Jane or curvy and exotic Montana. Then Jane reached out and put her hand on Lucas's arm. Lucas must have felt Maggie's eyes on him, because suddenly their eyes locked. He reached into his back pocket, moving his arm away from Jane's touch. Pulling herself together, Maggie smiled and pointed at her watch.

"Let's roll," Lucas said and hoisted his pack back onto his shoulders. Maggie glanced around the group, mentally accounting for everyone. When her eyes reached Barbara, she caught the older woman watching her again. Barbara winked; Maggie felt embarrassed and exposed. She'd spent years perfecting her role as buddy and carefully guarding herself around Lucas, but Barbara's expression made Maggie realize she might not be hiding her feelings as well as she'd thought. She'd have to watch herself a little more closely.

Four

The sun was directly above them. The barren, red cliffs of the upper canyon had gradually given way to weeds and a few flowers. Up ahead was a valley of trees and grass. Fence posts lined the trail that led into Supai Village, a small settlement scattered over less than two square miles. The wood houses looked more like shacks. Some tourists flew in by helicopter and stayed in the lodge, but rarely did anyone stay more than one night. It was tired and rundown, the service so laid back as to be almost nonexistent.

The group had covered eight miles. Between Lucas and Maggie, the hikers walked in an untidy line. Jane and Montana continued to stay close to Lucas, but everyone else was scattered behind them. Barbara had slowed down, and Dennis kept pace with her. The trail widened to the width of a single-lane road, and Maggie stepped up alongside them.

"How are you holding up?" she asked.

"Fit as a fiddle." Barbara smiled a little too brightly.

"It's plenty hot," Dennis said. "Looking forward to the water. It's sure pretty, though. Nothing at all like Pennsylvania."

"It gets prettier and prettier the farther we go," Maggie told them.

"Do we get to stop here for a while?" Barbara asked.

"We'll be here in town for about an hour. There are some picnic tables up ahead where we'll eat lunch, and then we'll stop at the general store so you can check out their jewelry and buy postcards. Be sure to mail them from here. This is the only place in the country that still has the mail delivered by mule. They have a special postmark that's only for Supai Village."

"I should have brought some addresses with me."

"You can always mail one to yourself," Maggie said.

"Good idea."

They stopped at two picnic tables in the shade under a grove of cottonwoods. Lucas pulled out sandwiches and apple slices.

"Peanut butter has never tasted so good," Braden said.

After they finished eating, they left for the general store. Barbara encouraged Dennis to go ahead, and she sat at the table a few more minutes before she and Maggie started out to join the others.

"How are you really?" Maggie said quietly to Barbara as they walked together.

"I'm fine."

"What about your feet?"

Barbara sighed. "They're killing me."

"I thought so. What's going on?"

"My toes are on fire. I'm afraid of what I'm going to find when I take these shoes off."

"Did you go up a size when you bought them?" The information packet recommended that all hikers buy their boots a size larger than they usually wore to accommodate swollen feet and thicker socks.

Barbara looked chagrined. "No. I know I should have. But I've never worn a size 9 in my life, and when I tried them on, my feet looked huge. I'm paying for my vanity."

"How are you ladies doing?" Lucas asked. Maggie hadn't even noticed him joining them until he was beside them.

"We're fine," Barbara said. "I'm just old and slow, I guess."

"We don't have much farther to go," Lucas said. "And you're doing great."

They'd reached the steps of the general store. "Take some pain relievers," Maggie said. "I have some if you need them."

"Thank you, dear." Barbara stepped gingerly up the steps and into the cooler darkness of the store's interior. Maggie sat on a bench against the wall, enjoying a little wedge of shade.

"Mind if I share the shade with you?" Lucas asked as he took a seat. Their arms brushed, so Maggie shifted to give him a little more room and put a few inches between them. Keeping her mind off her feelings for Lucas was hard enough; doing so would be impossible if he was touching her.

"How does it feel to be guiding again?" Maggie asked.

"Feels good. I love these trails."

"Me too."

"I even love Supai Village. For about an hour."

Maggie laughed. "Good thing that's about how long we're here then, right?"

Lucas and Maggie looked out across the most remote town in the continental United States. The only ways in and out were by hiking trails or helicopter. Supai Village was the capital of the Havasupai Reservation, and despite their poverty and isolation, the people seemed content.

If only Maggie could feel content. Sitting beside Lucas was distracting, and all she could think about was how she wished she hadn't scooted over. If only she could lean over and rest her head on his shoulder. It would be so nice if he'd reach out and hold her hand.

Would she ever stop longing for something she couldn't have? She'd thought she could handle Lucas working in the office. It made perfect sense for him to come back full time and handle the business end of the company. But the close proximity had proved more difficult than she'd anticipated. Friendship was no longer enough for her. More and more, she found herself leaving the office frustrated and unhappy. She was tired of working hard, then going home to an empty apartment. She wanted someone to share her life with.

Maybe it was time to move on. Maybe it was time to take a teaching position far enough away from Flagstaff that she could put Lucas out of her mind and begin to meet new people.

"You're quiet," Lucas said, pulling Maggie out of her thoughts. "What's on your mind?"

Maggie couldn't share what she'd been thinking. She scrambled for something safe to say. "I'm worried about Barbara's feet. Her boots are too small, and I can tell she's in a lot of pain."

"If only people would follow instructions," Lucas said.

"She thought the larger size made her feet look too big," Maggie said. "I wish there was a way to let people know before they come that after the first ten minutes, they're not going to care what they look like."

"That cold water is going to feel like heaven."

"I know. I was thinking that if she's having a hard time, I might stop when we get to the stream and let her soak her feet. I can stay with her if you don't mind taking everyone ahead so they can enjoy the rest of the day. Just save setup, and I'll help you when I get there."

"No worries. I can get started. If you're not there by the

time camp is up, I'll come back and meet you."

"Thanks."

Lucas patted Maggie's leg. "Anything for you," he said as he stood up.

Maggie took a deep breath. If only!

Five

"Can you hear that?" Lucas asked.

"Hear what?" Montana asked.

Lucas stopped and put up one hand as the group gathered around him. Maggie and Barbara were the last to catch up. "We're almost to the water. If you're quiet, you can hear it." They all listened, and some nodded. "*Havasupai* means 'people of the green-blue water.' The Havasupai tribe discovered this place more than six hundred years ago. Just ahead, you'll see why they never left." A new energy surrounded the hikers as they started out again.

The bubbling sound of water got louder, and when they rounded the corner, there was a creek on the right side of the trail. The water was clear and cold and tinged with the turquoise Havasupai Falls was famous for. Braden was the first to the water, with the others right behind him, running their hands through the cold surface and splashing their sweat-streaked faces. And each other.

"Everything okay, Maggie?" Lucas asked.

"We're going to stay here a little while and let her soak her feet," Maggie said, and Lucas nodded.

"You want me to stay with you?" Dennis asked.

"Heavens, no," Barbara said. "I'll be fine. I've got my own personal guide. You go on with the kids."

"All righty then," Lucas said. "On to paradise."

Barbara removed her shoes and socks. Her toes were a deep, shiny red, like the skin of a bruised tomato, and were so swollen that her pink toenails looked like buttons in a stuffed pillow. Barbara winced as she touched her big toe. "It feels like the nail's going to fall clear off."

"That's happened before," Maggie said. Barbara shook her head and looked like she might cry. "Hey, if it does, you can brag that you're the most hardcore hiker of the bunch. We'll let them soak for a while. That should give you a little relief and take down some of the swelling. Please tell me you brought sandals to wear around camp."

"I did, thank goodness," Barbara said. "You know, they'd make a killing back at that little store if they'd carry hiking boots for stupid people like me." She lowered her feet into the water and let out a happy sigh. "That does feel good."

Maggie sat with her back against a tree. Just the sound of the water made her feel cooler and relaxed. "We're not in a hurry. You can soak them as long as you want."

"How about until Saturday?" Barbara said with a laugh.

"Hey, once we get into camp, you don't have to put those on again until Saturday unless you decide to hike to Mooney Falls. You can soak and relax as much as you want."

"I watched the video of those guys hiking into Mooney Falls. I already decided I'm leaving that to the young folks. And probably Dennis."

While Barbara soaked her feet, Maggie closed her eyes. She might have fallen asleep if Barbara hadn't been a chatty woman. They talked about the years after her husband had left and how she'd spent over a decade as a single mother. She told Maggie about how Dennis had swept her off her feet after they'd met at Braden's soccer fundraiser. Her best friend's son was on the same team. They visited about the challenges of blending families with mostly grown children and about the differences between autumn in Arizona and Pennsylvania.

After a while, Barbara gritted her teeth, replaced her socks and shoes, and the two women hiked the last mile and a half into camp.

Six

Lucas had claimed a beautiful part of the campground. The trees in this area were well spaced for putting up hammocks, and Lucas had already attached three of them to the trees.

"Good job getting this spot," Maggie said.

"I thought this was the one you liked best," he said.

The rest of the hikers had gone down to the water, and Lucas was working on the fifth of seven tents, which were spaced several feet apart, with the creek running directly behind them.

Barbara took off her shoes and claimed a hammock. She nearly tipped out of the back of it before she got adjusted and closed her eyes.

Maggie pitched in, and together, she and Lucas finished the tents and began working on their makeshift kitchen. They moved two picnic tables to a level area between the hammocks and tents and organized the equipment the mules had hauled in. On the end of one of the tables, they set up the camp stove, then lined one of the benches with coolers. The other side would be the prep area, and the remaining table would be for eating.

Lucas took a cooler to get drinking water while Maggie unfolded several camp chairs and placed them around camp. When Lucas returned, he filled two paper cups with water, handed one to Maggie, and they sat down in two of the chairs. Lucas's water was gone in a few quick gulps, but Maggie drank hers slowly.

"This place is just about perfect," Lucas said.

"I'd like to have a cabin up here," Maggie said. "But I'd want it to be the only one, and I don't think that would go over very well."

"Imagine this place filled with cabins. It wouldn't be perfect anymore."

"I guess I'll just have to be satisfied with a tent."

Lucas stretched his legs out in front of him and laced his fingers behind his head. "Coming up here reminds me that it was good that Erica left. She didn't love this. I should have known it would never work with someone who didn't love spending time enjoying God's handiwork."

"So you're over her?" Maggie asked, careful to keep her voice neutral, her eyes focused on a tree across the campground.

"Have been for a while now. It didn't take as long as it should have, which is another sign she wasn't the one." He took a deep breath and closed his eyes. "When are you going to fall in love, Mags?"

She couldn't tell him she already had. Years ago. "Someday, I hope."

"I'll bet Dan's married by next summer," he said. "He and Rachel are getting pretty serious."

"I'm glad. She's good for him, and he's so happy. I really like her."

"She's a lot better for him than Erica was for me. I like her too." Lucas straightened and leaned forward, resting his elbows on his knees. He was looking at Maggie with a serious expression.

"What?" she asked.

"I was just thinking. We've got to be sure we find people we can all get along with. I know you didn't really like Erica, and that would have made things hard if I'd married her. Dan's got someone we both like, so let's make a pact right now. Let's promise that we'll be sure to end up with people we can all like so we don't lose each other."

Maggie nodded but didn't trust herself to speak.

"I'm serious, Margaret Jensen. I don't want to lose you guys."

She swallowed. "I know you are. And don't call me that."

Lucas laughed, but he kept watching her. "Let's say it. I promise right now that I won't marry someone who doesn't get along with you and Dan. And Rachel, too, I guess." He stuck out his hand, and when she put hers in his, he gave it a vigorous shake. "Now you say it."

"Oh, brother." Maggie laughed as she looked at their hands, still pumping up and down.

Lucas stopped shaking hers but didn't let go. "Come on, Maggie, say it. We're making a pact here. Take it seriously." He still held her hand, and Maggie tried to control her heart, which had begun to flutter like hummingbird wings. His hand felt warm and strong, and his dark eyes were looking at her too intently. "Unless you don't care if we all lose each other." His voice was quiet.

Maggie wanted to hit a pause button. "Of course I care."

"Then say it."

"I promise not to marry someone you guys don't like."

Lucas let go of her hand, leaned back in his chair and closed his eyes. "I should make you promise it'll be someone who likes us back, but of course they'll like us. What's not to like?" He smiled at his little joke, his eyes still closed.

Maggie watched him as his body relaxed and he started to doze. She knew someone she could marry who would fit in perfectly, because he was already in. Lucas was a smart guy, so why was he so clueless?

Suddenly Maggie wanted to see the water. She stood up quietly, not wanting to disturb him, and started toward Havasupai Falls.

"Are you going to the falls?" It was Barbara, and she didn't look sleepy. How much of their conversation had she heard?

"Thought I'd take a quick look before I start fixing dinner."

"I'd like to see it too. Do you mind if I come along?"

"Of course not."

Barbara strapped on her sandals, and they left the campground.

Seven

"This is delicious," Mike said as they ate dinner. Maggie had made stir-fried chicken and vegetables and served it over rice.

"Maggie's the best camp cook you'll ever meet," Lucas said and took another bite.

"Until Lucas's pizza feast Friday night," Maggie said.

"How do you do pizza while you're camping?" Siena asked.

"You'll all be helping top them, so you'll learn my secrets soon enough," Lucas said.

"How often do you bring tours down here?" Emma asked.

"I don't work during December and January," Maggie said. "But the rest of the year, I come down here or on a

Grand Canyon tour almost every week. Lucas only does about one tour a month."

"I guess we came on the right tour then," Jane said.

"Can we request you if we do this again?" Montana asked Lucas.

"Absolutely," Lucas said.

Maggie was scooping left over rice into a storage bag when Lucas put his hand on her shoulder and kissed the top of her head. "A kiss for the cook," he said, then started gathering dirty pans to wash.

"Can I cook tomorrow?" Montana asked.

"You girls," Lucas said, smiling. "I'm not sure what to do with you."

"I'm sure we can think of something," Jane said.

"All right, you two. Leave him alone," Barbara said.

"And as far as cooking goes, let's leave it to the experts," Dennis said. "We don't want to be starving to death when we have to climb out of this canyon."

Jane and Montana giggled, acting more like high-school girls than college students.

Maggie smiled and shook her head. Lucas had always had an easy and affectionate way about him. It was one of the many things to like about him. But tonight, knowing she might soon have to leave, she felt her smile falter.

Lucas pulled out a few card games and handed them to Montana. "Here. This should give you something to do for a while."

"You should play with us." Jane's pouty voice set Maggie's nerves on edge.

"Maybe another time. I'm on the job, remember?"

Jane and Montana looked disappointed, but soon they'd gathered some of the others for an unusual version of UNO.

Lucas and Maggie worked quietly, cleaning up the remains of dinner. "That was good, Maggie. You've become a gourmet cook out here."

"I got tired of grilled sandwiches and hot dogs and

hamburgers. I know the campers probably didn't care, since they're only out here once, but I was sick of the same thing over and over."

"What do we have to look forward to tomorrow?"

"Salmon chowder and biscuits. And rice pudding for dessert." She held up the bag of leftover rice before she put it in the cooler.

"Maggie," Barbara said. "Would you mind showing me the part of the creek you told me about? You know, where I can clean up in the morning?"

"You go ahead and show her," Lucas said. "I'll finish up here."

Barbara's toes were still red, but the swelling had gone down some. The busiest time for tourists had passed, so campers were more scattered. Evening sun slanted through the trees, making long, thin shadows. They'd walked for several minutes before Maggie veered off the larger path and onto a smaller one that led back to the water.

"This is my favorite spot. It's a little deeper, and if you stay out here by the edge, it moves so slowly you hardly notice it."

"Ah, I can see why you like it. Yes. This is where you'll find me in the morning."

"Anything else you want to see before we head back?" Maggie asked.

"Let's just sit here for a few minutes and enjoy the view," Barbara said.

They sat quietly, watching a dog run up and down the bank on the other side of the stream.

"Sorry about Jane and Montana," Barbara said after a few minutes.

Maggie was startled. Had her annoyance been obvious? "They're female. You can't expect them not to notice Lucas."

"But I'm sure it's bothersome, especially since you like him."

Maggie stared at Barbara, who laughed.

"Don't try to deny it. I can tell." She watched Maggie's face. "Well? How long have you liked him?" Barbara was a nosy woman. And far too perceptive. If she weren't so likeable, Maggie would have been tempted to tell her to mind her own business.

"We've been friends since eighth grade."

"When did your feelings change?"

Maggie laughed, but her face was burning.

"Now don't worry. I consider my duties as a matchmaker to be like those of a doctor or lawyer—strictly confidential. I won't announce it to anyone. But I know things. Maybe that's why I'm good at matchmaking. I can tell you have feelings for him."

Maggie looked away.

"There's nothing to be embarrassed about. He looks like a good catch to me."

Suddenly all of the feelings Maggie had kept to herself for so long came spilling out. The stream and the trees blurred together in front of her tears. She wiped her eyes and started talking.

"We've been best friends forever, but our senior year I started to feel differently. At first it was just a crush, but then the summer before our senior year, his mom was diagnosed with cancer—she's cancer free now—but she was so sick. She had surgery and then chemo, and Lucas took such good care of her. Sometimes she said the only thing that sounded good were oatmeal cookies, so he asked me to teach him how to make them so he could make them for her.

"He's good and kind and funny. I love that he reads and that his favorite book is *East of Eden*."

"Did his parents stay in the States?" Barbara asked.

"They live in Phoenix. And that's another thing. He loves it here. He even cheers for the United States in the Olympics." Maggie knew she was throwing out random, crazy facts about Lucas, but she couldn't help it. She'd never told Dan how she felt, and, of course, she'd never confessed her feelings to Lucas. He and Dan were her best friends. Who else would she have told?

Maggie had kept her feelings dammed up for so long that once the dam had sprung a leak, it was only a matter of moments before the whole reservoir flooded poor Barbara.

But Barbara didn't seem to mind. When Maggie had gone on for several minutes, she fell quiet, mortified at her deluge. If she hadn't had a job to do, she'd have taken her backpack and some food and hidden in the little cave she'd found on the other side of Mooney Falls, but she couldn't abandon her job.

Barbara smiled. "You know, Maggie, the things you like about him tell me as much about you as they do about him. I'll bet your mother is so proud of you."

Maggie wiped her eyes again.

"What do you think you should do?" Barbara asked.

"I've been thinking that maybe it's time to move away. It's so hard to see him and not let him know how I feel."

"Hmm. You know, I think that's probably a good idea. You don't want to spend your life stuck in a rut because you can't see beyond Lucas to someone else. You'll end up a lonely old maid."

Hearing someone else say what she'd been thinking was both jarring and comforting.

"I could move to Gilbert or Mesa. It wouldn't be hard to find a teaching position."

"You could always come to Fernway if you want to put some distance between you two. I know the principal there, and I could keep my eyes out for a good match."

Maggie picked up a rock and rolled it over and over in her hand before she threw it in the creek. "I don't think I could ever leave Arizona."

"I thought you might feel that way. I think you should do one thing, though, before you move away." Maggie looked at Barbara, a question on her face. "You have to let him know how you feel."

Maggie let out a gust of air and shook her head. "I can't. What if I ruin everything?"

"Do you really like him?"

"Yes."

"You're sure it's not a little passing crush?"

"More than seven years doesn't feel little, and it sure hasn't passed."

"So how *much* do you like him?"

"I love him."

"Then don't be a chicken. You can't run off scared and start another chapter somewhere else until you close the chapter here. Be brave and go after what you want. If it doesn't work out, you can leave knowing you tried. You can be proud of yourself. If you go without him knowing, you'll always wonder what might have been. Trust me, you'll have a boatload of regrets, and your boat might just sink."

Maggie stared at the water for a long time; Barbara let her think. Finally, she put her hand on Maggie's back. "Maybe he'll love you back."

Maggie shook her head. "I'm afraid he won't," she said softly.

"Sometimes a man's like an egg. Inside are feelings he may not even know he has. But guys like their shell. It may keep them from knowing their feelings, but it also keeps them from being too emotional or too mushy. The shell protects those feelings and lets them look tough and in control. It also keeps them safe from all those scary things on the outside."

"Am I a scary thing?" Maggie laughed, and Barbara shook her head.

"You're not scary. Feelings are scary. Sometimes they're terrifying. But sometimes all it takes is cracking through that shell to get to the feelings inside. Be brave. Crack the shell. You never know what you'll find."

"I don't know if I can do it. If he doesn't feel the same way, I'll ruin everything. He might decide he can't even be friends with me anymore."

"Or you both might discover he loves you. If you're not brave, you'll never know. And really, Maggie, how happy are you going to be working together and being friends the rest of your life when you want so much more than that? Or leaving without ever knowing what would have happened if you'd just had more courage? You think this is hard? This is only hard for a short time. Regrets are hard forever."

Maggie stewed in her thoughts. The sun had slipped behind the hill, and the world had become a dusty lavender. "I'm sure you're right," she finally said. "But I don't know how to crack the shell."

"There's no one way. Look for a chance. Be brave. Surprise him. And don't wait. The longer you wait, the harder it gets."

Shadows were settling in. They hadn't brought a flashlight or a lantern, and Maggie knew if they didn't get back soon, they'd be stuck out in the dark. It was time to be a guide instead of a scared girl. "We'd better get back."

They walked back to camp in silence. Up ahead they made out the lanterns Lucas had lit. Just before they reached the circle of light, Barbara grabbed Maggie's hand and gave it a squeeze.

"Be brave, dear. I don't think you have much to be afraid of. And I'm a very perceptive woman."

Maggie couldn't argue with that.

Eight

Dogs barked somewhere in the distance, and a few campers laughed quietly as they walked by. Maggie had been in her tent for more than an hour, but no matter how hard she chased sleep, it kept darting from her reach. She'd be exhausted tomorrow if she didn't get some rest.

Maggie tried to rationalize away what Barbara had said, but she was right. It was time to face her fears and let Lucas know how she felt, regardless of the outcome. Maggie tried to picture a life in Mesa teaching school. She could do it if she had to, but what about Lucas and Dan? She'd miss them. And what if she *didn't* have to?

For a few minutes, she indulged in the daydreams she'd always cut short. Instead of imagining Lucas saying he loved her, she imagined a life with him. And that life looked good. Maggie was a brave woman. She guided people into canyons and knew how to rough it. She'd camped by herself on more than one occasion. The howling of coyotes didn't bother her, and she didn't panic when things on the trail didn't go according to plan. It was time to gather her courage and put her feelings out there for Lucas. Once she did, she'd be able to move forward with more confidence.

After another sleepless half hour had passed, Maggie quietly unzipped her tent and stepped out, into the chilly night air. This was why she loved November tours. The night air was cool and bracing, and the days were warm enough to enjoy the water but never reached the scorching temperatures of summer. She pulled her hoodie closer around her. As quietly as she could, she filled a pan with water and lit a burner on the camp stove.

"Can't sleep?" Lucas whispered, but he might as well have shouted. Maggie nearly dropped the pan.

"What are you trying to do? Give me heart failure?" Maggie whispered back.

"Sorry. I heard someone out here and decided I'd better check it out."

"I was trying to be quiet. I didn't want to wake anyone."

"You didn't wake me. I've been reading."

"What are you reading?"

"*Great Expectations.* That's one of the books I was supposed to read in high school but didn't. I'm going back now and making an honest man of myself."

Maggie laughed softly. "I didn't really like that book. I thought it dragged on too long with people afraid to say what they mean." She smiled at the irony of her words. "Want some hot cocoa?"

"Sure." Lucas pulled out two cups and two envelopes of cocoa mix from the food boxes. When the water was hot, Maggie poured it over the powdered mix. Lucas took his to one of the camp chairs a few feet farther from the tents, and Maggie followed him. "No need to wake up anyone else, or we'll have to make cocoa for everyone."

They sipped their cocoa quietly. Lucas seemed to be enjoying the stars overhead.

Maggie was trying to figure out how to tell him she loved him.

"They're amazing out here, aren't they?" he said.

Maggie looked up. The cloudless sky was filled with brilliant, twinkling lights. "Yeah. They don't look like this in town. They're even better from Dan's ledge."

It wasn't really Dan's, but years earlier he'd found the spot and named it Dan's Ledge, a rock that jutted out about twelve feet above the trail. Just past the outcropping was a steep but climbable path that cut back to the ledge. From the wide slab of rock, there was an unobstructed view of the sky.

"I haven't been there for years," Lucas said. "I'm not even sure I'd remember how to find it."

"I can. I go there a couple of times every summer."

"Let's go tomorrow night," Lucas said. "When everyone goes to bed."

Maggie felt the kind of relief known to every procrastinator when they realize that they can put off a hard thing until sometime later. Tomorrow night. That's when she'd tell him. Out on the ledge, under the stars, just the two of them. It would be perfect.

"I'll bring a blanket," Lucas said.

"And I'll make a thermos of cocoa."

"It's a date."

Nine

The great thing about camping is that you can really see what someone looks like at their worst. Something about the night air and a sleeping bag gives even the loveliest of people circles under their eyes and wild hair. When Jane and Montana stepped out of their tents the next morning, Maggie bit the sides of her mouth to hide her amusement. If they could see themselves, they'd be horrified.

"Good morning, ladies," Lucas said.

"Is it?" Jane said, stretching her clasped hands high above her head, showing several inches of stomach.

"She needs coffee," Montana said. "And so do I."

Lucas poured two cups of coffee and handed them to the women. "I hope you're hungry. I'm cooking up some sausage, and Maggie's making French toast."

"I never eat breakfast," Montana said.

"I'd be willing to wager you change your mind when you smell that French toast cooking. She uses cinnamon bread."

"I'll eat hers if she doesn't want it," Dennis said, pouring himself a cup of coffee.

Lucas was right. Everyone ate breakfast, and Montana even slipped an extra sausage link onto her plate when she thought no one was looking.

"So tell us about today," Mike said. "I've heard Mooney Falls is spectacular but a tough hike."

"That depends," Maggie said, whipping the eggs with a fork. "It's an easy hike if you just want to go see the falls from the top, but hiking down to the water is pretty aggressive. We'll be climbing through a cave, then down the side of the mountain, and it's really steep. Some stairs are carved out and there are some chains to help you get down, but those are still pretty primitive, and it's hard work. At the bottom, there's a ladder that gets you down the last twelve or fifteen feet, but it's missing a few rungs."

"It requires a lot of focus and no horseplay," Lucas said. "The falls are called Mooney Falls after a miner named Mooney who fell to his death. We don't want any casualties today, so let's be very careful getting down."

"It's probably scarier going down, but it's harder coming back up," Maggie said.

"Is it even worth it?" Siena asked.

"If you're asking me, I'd say yes," Maggie said. "The water under the falls at Mooney is even better than the water under Havasupai. It's a gorgeous pool of water, and the setting is spectacular. But it really depends on you. If you're not comfortable with the hike down, you can come along to see the falls from the top, then come back to camp. You could also spend the rest of the day at Havasupai. Whatever you choose."

"I'm staying here," Barbara said. "So anyone who wants to keep me company is welcome." When no one responded, she added, "But don't worry about me. I plan to soak my feet and spend the day reading and napping in that hammock right there." She pointed at the hammock closest to the stream.

Later that morning, Dennis kissed Barbara goodbye after she'd assured him she'd be okay in camp by herself. They were several yards from camp when Barbara called after them. "Maggie, could you show me where the bread is before you go?"

Maggie hurried back to camp and opened one of the coolers. "We made you a lunch when we were packing the others," she said.

"I know, and I know where it is. I just wanted to encourage you to be brave today."

Maggie laughed. "Don't worry. I figured out a plan last night. But it won't be happening on the hike to Mooney Falls."

"Don't put it off too long."

"I promise it will happen before we leave on Saturday," Maggie said, and Barbara patted her arm. A knot formed in Maggie's stomach as she caught up with the rest of the group. She'd just made a promise. Would she be brave enough to keep it?

She had to.

Ten

They heard Mooney Falls long before they saw it. As they made their way through the tunnel to the steep, rocky descent, the roar grew louder and louder. The view at the end of the tunnel was breathtaking. Water crashed one hundred ninety feet to a blue pool beneath it. Travertine deposits on the face of the cliffs looked like red icing dripping down the sides of a cake.

Lucas descended first so he could offer advice and encouragement from the bottom while Maggie gave instructions from the top. Mike and Siena had been at the front of the group, but after Mike went, Siena stepped aside and let Braden go. Every time it was her turn, she stepped aside until she was the last one left at the top with Maggie. They looked down at the line of people slowly and carefully making their way to the bottom.

Siena sighed. "I'm sorry. I'm just so afraid of heights."

"Don't worry about it," Maggie said. "I've seen a lot of people who are scared. The important thing is to keep your concentration. Just think about the next step, the next foothold. I think it's easier if you go down facing the wall, too."

Siena turned around and took a tentative step down.

"Good," Maggie said. "Now hang onto the chain and just look at the next place to put your feet. Move your left foot to that step. Good. Now put your right foot on that next one. You're doing fine. Don't forget to breathe."

Siena had moved down about eight feet, and Maggie was about to join her on the chain when Siena stopped. "I can't do it." A few hikers were gathered behind Maggie, waiting their turn.

"Sure you can. Just move your right foot." Siena lifted her right foot, then put it back where it had been.

"You've got it, babe," Mike yelled from below, but Siena shook her head.

"Maggie, I really don't think I can do it. My hands are so sweaty, the chain's going to slip."

Maggie encouraged her and Siena tried a few more times, but fear had overcome rational thoughts, and Siena couldn't get her feet to move. "I'm going back to camp with Barbara. I'm sorry I'm such a wuss." Siena was near tears, and she clung to the chain without moving before Maggie got her calmed down enough to climb back up. "I just can't do it."

"Hey, it's fine. It's scary. We have a great view of the falls from here. Don't feel bad."

Siena smiled but looked a little shaken. "Tell Mike I'm sorry."

"He'll understand. We'll see you this afternoon," Maggie said. When Siena was gone, Maggie descended the trail.

"Too much for her?" Lucas was waiting by the ladder when Maggie reached the bottom.

She nodded. "It's not easy for anyone, but when you're afraid of heights, it's tough."

The hours at Mooney Falls flew by. In their meager swimsuits, Jane and Montana demonstrated real skill in their flirting abilities.

"Lucas, would you mind helping me with this?" Jane asked, handing Lucas a tube of sunblock. "This sun is toasting me."

"You should probably have Montana do that. I put sunscreen on Maggie's shoulders one time and missed giant patches of skin. She was striped for a week."

"And my skin peeled in stripes," Maggie said.

Jane sighed.

"I'll do it," Montana said, and Maggie was pretty sure she saw her smirk.

It was almost time to head back to camp. Maggie was sitting on a warm slab of rock, drying off, when Lucas came and sat beside her. "That Dennis is a tough old guy," he said. Dennis had been enjoying the water as much as the younger hikers and had even jumped off the rocks into the lower pools.

"Barbara said he's wanted to do this trip for thirty years. I'm glad he's enjoying it so much."

"You've seemed a little preoccupied. Is everything all right?"

Maggie pulled her knees up and rested her chin on them. If he knew what was on her mind, would he really want to know? "I just have a few things on my mind," she said.

"Hey." He rubbed his hand up and down her back a couple of times, and she turned her head toward him. "If something's wrong, you can tell me."

Maggie smiled at him and tried to keep her wits about her. His hand felt so nice. "I know. I just might do that."

"Good." Lucas moved his hand and leaned back on his elbows, his face toward the sun. "We still on for tonight?"

"I'm planning on it."

"Is something happening tonight?" Braden asked, dropping down on the rock with them.

"Salmon chowder and biscuits with butter and jam," Lucas said, and he and Maggie shared a smile.

"That sounds good."

"It will be. Maggie's the best."

The silly girl side of Maggie was glad he'd just called her the best. He was probably talking about cooking, but she could hope he meant more than that.

When they got back to camp, the hikers changed, and soon the camp was filled with clothes and suits drying on lines and bodies resting in hammocks, chairs and open tents. Maggie wished she could join them. Mooney Falls days were always tiring—hot sun, hiking and playing in the water were an exhausting combination. Lucas took a cooler and headed out for water. Montana and Jane were too tired to follow him.

Maggie peeled and cut up potatoes, then sautéed the onions and celery she'd chopped and bagged before the trip. When Lucas returned, he helped her mix up the biscuits. She cut them and placed the round pieces of dough into a large, greased cast-iron skillet. She put the lid on it and turned the burner down to low.

There were no leftovers after dinner, and it was good that Maggie had made the rice pudding. This was a hungry bunch.

Once dinner was cleaned up, the evening dragged by. Maggie's nerves made her both excited and terrified to go to Dan's Ledge. She replayed over and over in her mind the words she'd say to tell Lucas how she felt. Would he feel the same? It felt like her whole future hung in the balance.

"I'm going to make some hot cocoa if anyone would like some," she said when it was dark.

"I think we're going to turn in," Dennis said.

Most of the group departed for their tents. Soon only Lucas, Maggie, Jane, Montana, and Braden were left. Maggie poured hot cocoa into the thermos and set it aside, then put out cups of cocoa for the others.

"I think I'm going to check out, too," Maggie said. She and Lucas exchanged a look, and he gave a slight nod. When Maggie turned her head, Montana's eyes were on her. Montana glanced back and forth between Maggie and Lucas, her eyebrows raised.

"G'night all," Maggie said.

"Sweet dreams, Mags," Lucas said.

Maggie didn't change in her tent. She sat on top of her sleeping bag and pulled out her notebook and a flashlight. She wrote a few notes about the events of the day. Then she turned the page and wrote, "Be Brave. You can do this. Lucas isn't scary!"

Was she in junior high? She smiled to herself as she scribbled the words, then lay back to wait for the others to go to bed. She could hear their voices talking around the lanterns that served as a makeshift campfire since open fires weren't allowed.

Maggie hadn't been listening to the conversation, but suddenly Lucas said something that caught her attention.

"I guess I'm an old-fashioned guy. I prefer to be the one to ask a woman out. I still think men should open doors and pay. I just think it's more gentlemanly."

"I was the first one to ask out my last boyfriend." It was Montana. "We dated for more than a year, and he said we probably would never have gone out if I hadn't done the asking."

"I don't mind if a girl asks me out," Braden said, "if she's hot. But most of the time, I'd rather do the asking so I don't get stuck going out with someone I'm not interested in."

"That's such a guy thing to say," said Jane. "And why should women have to sit around and do nothing, waiting for guys to make a move?"

"I'm not saying they should do nothing. Women are usually up to something if they're interested," Lucas said.

"What do you mean?" Jane asked.

"Women have lots of control over whether or not a guy asks her out. They can flirt and drop hints. If a woman drops hints, and I'm interested, I'm much more likely to get up the courage to ask her out. She might even put the idea in my head if it hadn't been there before."

"Wouldn't you rather have a girl just tell you straight up that she's interested?" Montana asked.

"What kind of hints do you want a woman to drop?" Jane asked.

Maggie rolled her eyes but leaned closer to the door of her tent, not wanting to miss a word and glad she'd heard what had been said so far.

"Oh, come on, ladies. There are all kinds of ways to drop hints. Some subtle and some not so subtle."

"You're not going to give us examples?" Jane asked. She always sounded like she was pouting.

"Absolutely not. Women are clever, and they know how to let a guy know they're interested without coming right out and saying it. That's part of the fun of romance—figuring out each other's clues."

"This is too old-fashioned for me," Montana said. "I'd rather just say it like it is and be done with it."

"Not much romance in that," Lucas said.

"We're talking to a guy who's more interested in romance than we are," Jane said.

Maggie felt lost. All day she'd been building up her courage to let Lucas know how she felt, only to find out he didn't want a girl who was forward. If she couldn't tell him, how could she let him know? He'd said women needed to drop hints, but flirting and dropping hints weren't high on Maggie's list of talents. In fact, they probably weren't on the list at all.

Maggie listened as Lucas detached himself from the conversation to go to his tent. The others talked for a few more minutes, but once Lucas was gone, their enthusiasm died down, and soon they all went to bed. The only sounds she could hear were the breeze stirring the trees, the stream behind the tents, and barking dogs in the distance. Her mind puzzled over her dilemma. What could she do to let Lucas know how she felt? She'd spent the whole day rehearsing a speech that she couldn't share. She'd needed a new plan, but her mind was a blank.

"Mags, you there?"

Maggie quietly unzipped her tent to see Lucas standing there holding a blanket. She pulled on her hoodie and slipped out, closing the zipper as quietly as possible. She picked up the thermos of hot cocoa where she'd left it by the camp stove, and they quietly walked out of camp and headed south to Dan's Ledge. They didn't speak until they were about twenty yards from camp.

"You'll have to tell me where to go," Lucas said quietly, sweeping the flashlight back and forth in front of them to guide their way. "I'm not sure I could find this place in the daylight, let alone at night."

"We take that trail right up there," Maggie said. She glanced at the sky. "The stars are going to be brilliant."

They veered off the trail, and Maggie looked back toward camp. A flashlight bounced up and down far back on the trail. They weren't the only ones out tonight. She turned her attention back to the trail, which was harder to navigate in the dark. The trees were a little thicker here, and protruding rocks were harder to see.

"Ah, I recognize where we are," Lucas said. "That's the ledge right up there, isn't it?" The outcropping jutted out above the trail. The rock was red, but in the moonlight it looked almost copper with purple shadows.

"And there's the trail," Maggie said. About fifteen yards past the outcropping, a steep trail jutted back toward the ledge. She scrambled ahead first, loose rocks shifting with each step until the path opened up and they stood on the rock above the trail. Lucas turned off the flashlight. Now that they were above the trees, the moon and stars provided all the light they needed.

Lucas spread out the blanket, and they sat down. "It looks like we're not the only ones taking a midnight hike," he said softly, pointing toward camp. A flashlight, probably the same one Maggie had seen earlier, moved back and forth on the trail. Someone giggled, and Lucas grabbed Maggie's arm and pulled her back so they were lying flat on the ledge, out of sight. "Shh. I think it's the girls."

At first they couldn't make out what the voices were saying, but as they got closer, they could hear. "I'm sure they turned down this path." It sounded like Jane.

"I don't see their light anymore."

"Let's go a little farther." Now they both giggled. "I can't believe we're spying on them."

They listened as Jane and Montana continued up the trail. Lucas still held Maggie's arm, just above the wrist. She wanted to sit up and watch the girls, but she didn't want to move her arm and remind Lucas that he was touching her, so she held still. "If we were mean, we could give them the fright of their lives," Lucas said. Maggie turned to look at him; he was grinning mischievously.

"Too bad we have to behave professionally," she said.

"Yeah. Really too bad. Those two have been driving me nuts."

"I thought you enjoyed their constant attention."

Lucas snorted. "Just two more days. I can handle them for two more days."

"How long do we give them before we act like responsible guides and go get them?" Maggie asked.

Lucas let go of her arm and sat up, craning his neck to follow the trail. "If they're not back in ten minutes, we'll go after them. Until then, let's look at the stars." He lay back down, his fingers laced behind his head.

They were quiet for a long time, and Maggie hoped Lucas wasn't thinking about Jane and Montana. Lucas was the one to break the silence. "You're not thinking of leaving us, are you?"

Maggie caught her breath. Could he read minds? "Why would you say that?" Her voice felt small.

"I just heard you talking to Dan last week, about jobs you'd seen in Mesa and somewhere else. Then you said you had a lot on your mind. Are you thinking of taking a teaching job?"

Maggie sighed. "I'm not sure what I'm thinking."

"Do Dan and I get a vote?"

"It depends on what you'd vote for," Maggie said, and Lucas laughed.

"I'd vote for you to stay put. Why do you think I came back after graduate school?"

Maggie held her breath. Had he come back for her?

"Why did you come back?" she asked quietly. When he didn't answer immediately, Maggie wondered if he'd heard her question.

"For you and Dan, of course."

Maggie sat up, frustrated and disappointed. She suddenly felt like crying. She loved Dan, but she was tired of being lumped together with him. It was silly and immature, but she hadn't wanted Lucas to include Dan in his reason. She wanted him to be here because of her.

"How far do you think they've gone?" Maggie was horrified that her voice was trembling.

"Maggie?" Lucas put his hand on her back.

"We should go find them," she said, scrambling to her feet.

Lucas pointed. "Look, that's probably them."

Maggie looked up the trail, and sure enough, there was the bouncing flashlight. Lucas reached for her hand and pulled her back down. "We haven't even had our cocoa yet. Be quiet while they go by so we don't have to share."

Maggie let him pull her back down, and they waited as the light got closer. If the girls had looked up, they could have seen them, but their eyes didn't leave the path.

"Do you think they're a couple?" Montana asked when they were beneath the ledge.

"No way. She's not his type."

"I don't know. You didn't see them looking at each other. Like they had a secret and . . ." Their voices faded off as they went back to camp.

Lucas reached across Maggie for the thermos. "Like they know my type," he said.

Maggie felt tongue-tied and awkward. Lucas poured cocoa into the cup and handed it to her before he drank directly from the thermos. She took a sip, then set it beside her and hugged her knees. The sky was beautiful. How could such a magical night have let her down so completely? Nothing had gone according to plan, and with all that she'd heard, she doubted she'd ever be able to let Lucas know how she felt.

Eleven

All through breakfast, Maggie felt eyes on her. She ignored Barbara's raised eyebrows. There was nothing to tell her. Jane and Montana were scrutinizing her, curious about the woman who had walked into camp with Lucas late the night before. They'd been sitting in camp chairs when Maggie and Lucas had come back to camp, and the girls had worn smug looks on their faces. And now Lucas was looking at her with concern. It was all too much. She wanted to leave the eggs to burn and go back to her tent to sleep for a few more hours.

But it was their last day to play. Tomorrow, they'd pack up and leave their supplies for the mules and begin the arduous hike out of the canyon. Today they'd spend the day doing whatever they wanted. Barbara had sworn off shoes, so she was staying in camp to read and nap. Dennis was joining Mike and Siena on a little trip back into Supai Village to arrange for some pottery Siena liked to be shipped home. Dennis was also planning to check on the cost of flying Barbara out by helicopter, but he'd only mentioned that to Lucas and Maggie. No sense getting Barbara's hopes up if he couldn't afford the fare. The rest planned to spend the day at Havasupai Falls.

Maggie disappeared inside her tent to wait until everyone had gathered their things and left. She'd have been happy to stay there all day, but the sun made the tent feel like a greenhouse—hot and stifling—and soon she was forced out into the cooler air. She grabbed a book out of her backpack and headed to a camp chair.

"How did it go last night?" Barbara asked. Maggie looked at her questioningly. "I heard the girls talking. They said you two left camp together last night. I figured you might have some news."

Maggie shook her head. "No news. Did you hear any of their conversation last night after you went to bed? Lucas doesn't want an aggressive woman."

Barbara laughed. "That's not what I got out of that."

"So you heard?"

"They weren't exactly quiet." Maggie smiled. "I heard a man who's a romantic at heart say he wanted a woman to drop hints."

"I don't have the first idea how to do that." Maggie closed her book. "All day yesterday, I planned and practiced what I was going to say, and then I heard them talking and knew I couldn't say any of it."

"So don't say it with words. Say it with your actions. Give him his hints."

"If only it were that easy."

Barbara hesitated, then continued. "Actions speak louder than words." She paused. "Seize the day." Another pause. "There is nothing impossible to him who will try." Maggie looked at Barbara. She was smiling. "Nothing ventured, nothing gained."

Maggie smiled. "Okay, okay, I get it."

"Don't stop me now, dear. I'm on a roll. A stitch in time saves nine. Look before you leap. A bird in the hand is worth two in the bush."

"You're ridiculous."

"Come on, Maggie. Join me. This is fun. Birds of a feather flock together."

"Carpe diem," Maggie said.

"Be original, Maggie. That means the same thing as seize the day."

Maggie laughed. "Give a man a fish, he'll eat for a day. Teach him to fish, he'll eat for a lifetime."

"Nice one. There's a pot of gold at the end of the rainbow."

"You can't teach an old dog new tricks," Maggie said.

"Hey, don't call me old. How about, youth is wasted on the young?"

"No pain, no gain. A picture is worth a thousand words." Maggie stopped. An idea was forming.

"Cat got your tongue?" Barbara asked, then collapsed into laughter.

Maggie couldn't help but laugh with her. "No, I think I have an idea."

"Give me another one," Barbara said.

"Not yet. I need to think about this."

"Then go think about it, and let me get back to my book," Barbara said. She opened her book and started reading.

Maggie went to her tent, got her notebook, and headed for a spot by the stream where she could be alone.

"Dropping hints doesn't have to be hard," Barbara said, lowering her book and calling after Maggie. "Don't overthink it."

Twelve

Friday night with Lucas on the trail meant pizza and music.

Maggie returned to camp to find him making preparations for dinner.

"Good, you're back," Lucas said.

"I told you not to worry about her," Barbara said.

"I just had some thinking to do," said Maggie.

"Do you need any help?" Barbara asked.

"You're on vacation," Lucas said. "I do the cooking on pizza night."

By the time everyone had gathered back to camp, Lucas had twelve balls of pizza crust ready to go. "I haven't figured out how to bake twelve pizzas at once on a camp stove, so we eat in shifts on pizza night." Two at a time, they came to the table. Lucas rolled out their crusts and put them in the bottom of a cast-iron skillet. He covered them with pizza sauce, then each of them topped their own crust. He had bags of pepperoni, onions, mushrooms, cooked sausage, Canadian bacon, and pineapple. Once they'd topped their pizzas, he covered them with a vented lid and let them cook for about twelve minutes.

Dinner took almost two hours from beginning to end, but the pizzas were delicious, and the campers loved them.

Maggie was tense and quiet. She had a plan, but she wasn't sure when to put it into action. She'd prefer to do it when everyone had gone to bed, but after last night, she was pretty sure Jane and Montana would be waiting and watching. Maybe she should just forget about them. So what if they saw? She'd never see them again after tomorrow, right? Her face burned at the thought of doing something so private so publicly. Barbara smiled at her across camp, and something about her smile and optimism gave Maggie courage. She'd do it as soon as Lucas finished with dinner. It was time.

"You bringing out your guitar?" Maggie asked him as they finished up their pizzas.

"In a while."

"Go now. I'll clean up while you play," she said.

"You sure?"

"Positive."

Maggie cleaned and packed up most of the kitchen while Lucas circled the chairs around a couple of lanterns and pulled out his guitar. Jane and Montana quickly snagged the chairs on either side of him. Lucas sang a couple of songs and then asked for requests. Dennis asked if he knew any Elvis, and Lucas played "Can't Help Falling in Love with You." Dennis joined in on the chorus, singing to Barbara. Their married children smiled, but the rest of the group groaned and rolled their eyes in a good-humored way.

When Maggie finished cleaning, she went to her tent and retrieved the stack of folded notes she'd prepared that afternoon. Already she was having second thoughts. Maybe this was a mistake. Did she really want to embarrass herself in front of all these people? She pulled up a chair next to Barbara and listened to Lucas sing an old Johnny Cash song. His voice was mellow and pleasant. His accent almost disappeared when he sang, but every once in a while, a word came through with a sound that was pure Lucas.

"Maggie, what do you want me to play?" Lucas asked, and she realized he was watching her. Could this be her sign?

"'Annie's Song,'" Maggie said. Lucas and Dan had teased her as teenagers because she was the only girl her age who listened to John Denver. She'd begged Lucas to learn "Annie's Song" when he'd taken guitar lessons, and she'd requested it so many times that several years ago, he'd sworn it off entirely, saying he'd never play it again. If he teased her and said no, she would leave the papers in her pocket and abandon her plan. If he relented and played the song, she would follow through. Bargaining with herself like this was silly, but she didn't care.

Lucas looked at her, and she held his eyes. *Please play the song.* Lucas's mouth turned up into a little smile. "We'll call this 'Maggie's Song' instead of 'Annie's Song.' I'm pretty sure she's listened to it more than anyone named Annie."

Maggie did her best to keep her expression neutral, but she could feel eyes on her from all around the circle of hikers. Lucas started playing the introduction on his guitar, and Maggie kept her eyes on him. Barbara reached over and patted her hand, and she realized she was white-knuckling the arm of the chair. She took a breath and tried to relax as Lucas started singing about filling up senses like a storm in the desert. She'd always loved this song, and now it was reaching her in a place she'd never thought possible. Her heart was pounding so hard, she could feel it in her clenched hands and hear it in her ears. Lucas glanced at his hands a few times, but most of the song, he watched Maggie.

Strangely, the words about love and laughter and dying in each other's arms calmed Maggie's nerves and gave her courage. As Lucas played the last chord, Maggie stood and walked across the circle to him. She reached in her pocket, pulled out the papers, and dropped them. Most landed in his lap, but one sat perched on top of the guitar, and a couple had fallen onto the ground.

Before Lucas could open any of the notes, Maggie sat back down in her chair, doing her best to look calm, even though breathing was difficult and her hands were shaking.

Maggie cringed when Montana picked up the two that had fallen on the ground, but when she handed them to Lucas without opening them, she felt a rush of gratitude.

Lucas picked up one of the notes and unfolded it. He looked at Maggie, a question in his eyes. He opened the second. Jane craned her neck to see what they said. When Lucas unfolded the third paper, a look of understanding crossed his face, and he smiled. No one spoke as he opened each of the papers, but eyes from around the circle darted back and forth between Lucas and Maggie. She knew she was blushing, but it was too late to do anything. She'd followed through with her plan, and now all she could do was wait to see what Lucas would do.

When the last paper had been unfolded, he leaned the guitar against the side of his chair and put the papers in his jacket pocket. "If you'll excuse us, Maggie and I are going to take a little walk." He crossed the circle and pulled Maggie from her chair. Her legs were wobbly, and she was afraid they wouldn't carry her. Lucas held her hand as they walked out of the circle. "We'll be okay. You don't have to come check on us," he said and winked at Jane and Montana.

They hadn't even made it to the trailhead when Jane spoke up. "*Hint.* The notes all said 'hint.' What does that even mean?"

"She's just dropping a few hints," Barbara said, and Maggie could hear the excitement in her voice.

Thirteen

The last sliver of sun fell below the walls of the canyon, silhouetting the jagged rocks against a gold backdrop. With every step, Maggie's heart slowed to a pace that didn't threaten a heart attack. In fact, every step brought a feeling of peace and calm. Lucas was still holding her hand. That had to be a good sign. She glanced at his face. He looked happy.

They turned onto another trail, and Maggie knew where they were going—Dan's Ledge. Finally Maggie spoke. "We're going to be stuck out here in the dark."

"I've got a flashlight."

When they reached the ledge, Lucas sat and pulled Maggie down beside him. Then his arm went around her waist and held her close against his side. "Oh Maggie, you're too much." He kissed the top of her head and rested his cheek against her hair.

What was he saying? Suddenly she felt nervous again. Was he trying to let her down gently?

"What do you mean?"

"I mean I can take a hint." He turned her face toward him, and his lips brushed hers. "It means I'm glad you're braver than I've been." He kissed her again. "I wasn't . . ." But Maggie didn't want to talk. At least not yet. She'd been waiting too long for this kiss to let words cut it short. She put her hand behind his neck and pulled him toward her, meeting his lips with her own.

She pulled away. "I was so afraid you were going to hate me and we wouldn't even be friends anymore."

"That's exactly why I haven't had the guts to see if there's more here than just friends. You've been my best friend for so long, I was afraid if I said too much, you'd dodge me." He leaned his forehead against hers. "You heard us talking last night?"

Maggie nodded.

"Good. I was trying to talk loudly enough for you to hear, although I thought maybe you'd grab my arm to feel my muscles or wink at me. I didn't know you'd actually drop hints."

"Too bad we don't have a campfire to put those in," Maggie said.

"Are you kidding? I'm hanging onto these forever. They may be the closest thing to a love letter I ever get."

"You mean my first day ever writing a love letter, I wrote a dozen of them?"

"You were a busy girl."

They kissed again and again as the stars replaced the setting sun.

Everyone was asleep when they returned to camp. Lucas held her face in his hands as he kissed her goodnight at the door of her tent before she zipped herself inside. On her sleeping bag was a note.

Did your bravery pay off? I'm so proud of you. –Barbara

The next morning, Maggie heard the sound of the zipper as someone opened the flap of her tent a few inches, dropped in a folded paper, and closed it again. She sat up and reached for the paper.

Dear Margaret,

I called you Margaret so you'll know I'm serious.

In my attempt to catch up to the dozen love letters you gave me, you can count this as my number one. I spent most of the night thinking about you. Staying in my tent was quite a challenge.

I'll do my best not to kiss you today on the trail. It will be difficult, but we should probably try to be professional. Just know that I'll be wishing I could.

I'm thinking we should go on a real date, so how about I pick you up at seven tonight? We'll go out for a nice dinner neither of us has to cook.

I love you, Maggie. I've loved you as a friend for ten years. I have a feeling this kind of love is going to be even more fun.

Happy trails!
Yours,
Lucas

Maggie tucked her first love letter into her notebook and packed it in her backpack. She tried to wrestle her smile into a less obvious expression before she unzipped the door. After a minute, she gave up and greeted the morning with the contented smile of a woman who'd just read a love letter she'd been waiting for all of her life.

ABOUT KAREY WHITE

Karey White is a *USA Today* bestselling author. Karey grew up in Utah, Idaho, Oregon and Missouri. She attended Ricks College and Brigham Young University. Her first novel, *Gifted*, was a Whitney Award Finalist.

She loves to travel, read, cook, and spend time with family and friends. She and her husband are the parents of four talented and wonderful children.

Find out more about Karey at www.kareywhite.com

Just Fly

by Krista Lynne Jensen

Other Works by Krista Lynne Jensen

Of Grace and Chocolate

The Orchard

Love Unexpected: With All My Heart

Falling for You

One

Wren Lario sat in her car outside her grandfather's house. Her mom would be inside, going over paperwork, making phone calls. Wren gazed at the small white house, the trimmed lawn and row of lilac bushes dormant in February. Simple. Just lawn and lilacs. But it had been lawn and lilacs for decades, and Wren couldn't help wondering what it would look like a year from now. Ten years from now.

On Saturday, William Tivegna, Gramps, Wren's seventy-four year-old grandfather, had shocked them all by lying down for a nap. The next shock had hit when he didn't wake up.

Wren looked at the appointment card in her hand. Her doctor had said they would have her test results back in a few days. But she'd asked them to hold onto the results until after the funeral. They would be too much to deal with, and her mom needed her now. As she'd left the office, the doctor had handed her this card with his cell number scrawled across it. "Wren, we don't know anything for certain until the test results are in. Call if you change your mind. Knowledge is a powerful thing."

Wren knew that. But endometrial cancer had taken Grandma Tivegna in her late thirties, soon after Wren was born. And she just couldn't deal with the possibilities. Not this week.

Wren shrugged against the knot in her chest. Gramps had raised her, taking care of her so her single mom could work her way up to managing the Walgreens. Wren was on her own now, in an apartment in their little town of Palisade, Colorado, with a good job. Gramps had been the only dad she'd ever known. She could've used one of his hugs right now.

She managed to call out as she entered the house, struck by the lingering scent of Gramps' aftershave. "Mom?"

"Come in here. I want you to look at something."

Wren found her mom at the kitchen table, sorting through piles of bills, notes, and mail. Sue Lario appeared older than she had three days ago. How much sleep had she gotten?

She looked up over her reading glasses. "Hey, sweetie." She handed her a paper. "Do you know anything about this?"

"What is it?"

"Read it."

Wren sat on a kitchen chair and focused on the slanted handwriting.

Billy,
Everything is all set. It took some finagling with the boy, but we're good to go. I hope you've gotten up the nerve to tell that daughter of yours, because there's no turning back. This is your baby, and I must say, one of your better ideas. It feels like Christmas Eve.

I'll pick you up at the airport on Wednesday. Tell Sue.
More as not, she'll be excited for us. Can't wait to see you.
    Yours,
    Dot

Wren frowned. "Who's Dot?"

"I was hoping you'd know."

Wren turned the paper over. "How old is this?"

"It came in the mail today. With these." She held out an envelope.

Wren peered at the contents and pulled out more paper. "Boarding passes. Seattle?"

"Mm-hmm."

"These are for Wednesday."

"As the letter says."

"But it's Monday. Does this person know that Gramps—" She stopped, unsure how to say aloud what she'd hardly begun to understand.

Her mom finished for her. "That he's passed away? I doubt it. I've barely finished letting extended family know."

The letter had come from Marysville, Washington, but there was no name above the return address.

"I wish Dad had used his cell phone more often." Mom shook her head. "There's no Dot on his contact list."

Gramps had never cared for cell phones. "There's a reason I leave my phone at home," he'd always said.

"What about the home phone?" Wren asked.

"I've already called the phone company. They found several calls to and from an unlisted number."

Wren read over the letter again. "It sounds like they knew each other pretty well." She tried to remember anything that would tie her grandfather to this woman, Dot. She fingered the plane ticket. "Do you think they were secretly dating?"

Mom ran her hands over her face. "I don't know." She looked up and directed her next statement loudly to the ceiling, as if Gramps were upstairs. "I wouldn't put it past him. *Flirt.*"

Wren almost smiled. Then sobered. "Mom, this is important. Like, lots-of-planning important."

"I agree."

"And this woman is going to be waiting at the airport, all excited. 'Like Christmas Eve.'"

Her mother sighed and removed her glasses. "What do you want me to do?" She took the letter back. "The fact that my father may have a kept woman in Seattle isn't sitting well with me." A slow smile came to her face, and she laughed for the first time in days. "Or maybe it is. I don't know."

Wren finally smiled too. "We have to let her know."

"Of course we do." She nodded and put her glasses back on. "But how?"

A search with Gramps' ancient PC for a Dot or Dorothy in Marysville, Washington, came up empty except for a seven-year old obituary for a Dorothy Fike. Wren guessed this was not the same woman. She looked again at the boarding passes. Maybe she could find out who had paid for the tickets. She picked up her phone and called the airport.

After the phone call, Wren returned to the kitchen. "Well, Gramps paid for the tickets. But it's possible to take his place on the flight if we have a death certificate. They can work it through the bereavement—"

Mom looked up, wiping a tear. "What?"

"Oh, Mom." Wren wrapped her arms around her mom's shoulders.

Mom shook her head. "I'm fine. Who knew that reading his electricity bill would trigger tears? What were you going to say?"

Wren hesitated. "Nothing. Just . . . trying to get ahold of this woman before Wednesday looks impossible. I let the airline know, so when he doesn't show and she goes to ask at the desk, they'll tell her."

Her mom winced.

Wren sat down. "The only other option is to take Gramps' flight, meet the woman, and tell her in person." She glanced at all the paper piles and shook her head. "But with all the funeral preparations and stuff . . ."

Her mom studied her thoughtfully. "It would be a friendly face, telling her gently what happened."

Mom had been the one to find Gramps cold and unresponsive on the couch in her den. He'd come over to help Mom with some winter yard work. Wren would never forget her mother's shock and immediate anguish.

"You could go," Mom said.

"I can't."

"Why not?"

Wren paused. "Because I can't leave you right now." The words tightened in her throat, her emotions swelling.

"Yes you can. Like you said, up one day, back the next. You meet this Dot, let her know what's happened, take her to dinner, and come home."

"But all the arrangements, all the legal stuff—I should be here for that, for you."

Her mom reached across the table and swept a lock of Wren's hair behind her ear. "I'm in good hands. But who will be there for her? Whoever she is, your grandpa made plans with her. What would he want us to do?"

Wren took a deep breath and let it out. "I'll think about it."

But she could already hear Gramps. *Get out. Go see what you're made of.*

Two

Wren watched Seattle slowly spin beneath her as the plane descended. With every drop in altitude, her heart beat faster. Though she'd rehearsed in her head how she would find and greet this woman, Wren had no idea what to expect. She'd imagined every possibility, including a scene in which the woman fainted. She hoped that didn't happen.

Wren exited the plane with the other passengers and followed the signs to baggage claim. As they approached waiting families and friends, Wren slowed. She searched the crowd, suddenly feeling that this was a crazy idea and an overnight letter would have been just fine.

The other passengers grabbed their bags off the carousel, and the crowd thinned. A woman caught her eye, just coming in the sliding glass doors from outside. Wren's heart pounded in her throat, but as another flight of passengers entered the baggage claim area, the woman smiled, waved, and approached a couple. Wren blew out a breath of frustration. This was ridiculous. What if Dot was waiting in her car in the pick-up lanes?

She glanced outside and remembered Gramps' cell phone in her purse. It had two new texts.

Can't wait to see you! Safe flight!

And the second:

Where the heck are ya?

Wren glanced around again. Her fingers shook as she typed in a message.

This is Billy's granddaughter. I'm at the airport in baggage claim. Where are you?

She took a somewhat uncomfortable picture of herself, hit send, and waited. *This is going to be a disaster.*

"Ahem."

Wren whipped around at the sound. A woman stood with her arms folded.

"You're Billy's granddaughter? You're Wren, then, right? Where's Billy?" She glanced around. "Is he using the men's room?" She looked back to Wren, appearing more amused than mad. "Did he drag you along? He didn't say a word." She stuck her hand out. "Dot. Pleased to meet you. Billy's told me a lot about you."

Wren shook her hand. Dot wasn't what she'd pictured in any of her scenarios. For one thing, she wasn't as old. Short red hair—likely dyed—jeans, scarf, and a leather bomber jacket. Her eyes had a spark Wren liked. Dang. She could totally see Gramps with this woman.

"I'm sorry—" Wren began. And then her words stuck. Dot watched her, waiting. Wren swallowed and tried again. "I came because . . ."

The woman's brow lifted as she waited for Wren to finish a sentence.

"Can we sit down somewhere, please?" Wren spotted some seating in a corner and gestured for Dot to follow her.

They both sat, and Dot watched her expectantly. Wren watched her fingers, interlocked tightly on her lap. The words she'd rehearsed all the way here were jumbled in her head, caged like the bingo balls at Palisade Methodist.

"He didn't come," Dot said. "He backed out. Why that cowardly son of a b—"

"No!" Wren's protest was louder than she'd intended, making several people look their way.

Dot had stopped her name calling and waited with eyes open wide.

"Last Saturday . . . Gramps lay down for a nap after working hard in the yard. He didn't wake up." She met Dot's gaze, and the woman's expression didn't change. Then she grew blurry. "He just . . ." Wren tried to pull in a breath, but her emotions didn't allow it. "He just . . . didn't wake up." Tears spilled over, and her dam of emotions broke in a gasping, wet display.

Great, Wren. *Way to be there for Dot.*

The woman reached over and patted her back as Wren pushed away tears and wiped her nose on the back of her hand.

"I'm sorry," she blubbered. "We didn't know how to reach you. All we had was your letter and a plane ticket. I couldn't find you on the Internet. I don't even know your last name. Gramps died and had plans with you, and you were meeting him here, and I pictured you waiting and waiting and we couldn't just . . . we couldn't just . . ."

But she'd said it. *Gramps died.*

"Well," was all Dot said.

She stood and took a few steps away. After a moment, she turned and put her hands on her hips. "Well . . . dammit."

Wren lifted her brow and sniffled.

Dot paced a couple times, her head bowed. Then she halted. "Okay. Here's what we're going to do." She looked at Wren. "Is that everything you've got?"

Wren looked at her carry-on. "Yes."

"Where were you staying tonight?"

"Holiday Inn Express."

Dot gave a nod toward the restrooms. "Go get yourself cleaned up. Then you're coming with me."

Three

Dot navigated the city onramps and freeways as Wren gripped the seatbelt across her chest. They'd said nothing for the first twenty minutes, and if silence helped Dot concentrate on the road, that was fine with Wren. Seattle traffic was nothing like Palisade or even Grand Junction, and with all of the overpasses, lane switching, and winding onramps, Wren became completely disoriented.

It suddenly occurred to her that she'd gotten into a car with a perfect stranger in a strange city. She clung to the fact that Gramps had bought the plane ticket and apparently knew this woman.

She pulled out her phone. "I need to call home."

"That would be wise."

When her mom answered, she sounded relieved. "Wren, honey, how's it going? Did you find her?"

"Yeah, sorry I didn't call earlier. I was distracted."

"That's okay, you're calling me now. Well?"

"Well . . ." Wren glanced at the woman next to her. "I found Dot."

"How did she take the news? What was she like?"

"Actually, she's right here. We're in her car."

"Going to dinner?"

"Uhh . . ." She put her hand over the mic and turned to Dot. "Where are we going?"

"My grandson's place, where I live. It's over in Marysville."

Wren turned back to the phone. "We're going to her house in Marysville."

Her mom dropped her voice to a whisper. "What's she like?"

"Whispering's not going to help, Mom. She seems . . . good. I took the news harder than she did."

Dot pressed her lips together and nodded.

"Rough, huh? But was going the right thing to do?"

"Yeah."

"Good. We can talk more later. Try to have a nice time. Be safe."

Wren got off the phone and scrambled to think of something to say. She'd never been a natural at conversation and, under the circumstances, would have been more comfortable curled in a ball under a blanket in her own room.

"Billy told me you're a dental assistant."

Wren nodded. "Yes."

"He says you sing."

Wren turned to Dot. "I sing?"

She nodded and took an exit. "He says you have a great voice."

Wren's mind raced to figure out when Gramps would have heard her sing. The shower? During homework when her ear buds were in? "I was never in choir or anything."

"Some things we aren't brave about, and some things we are. Sticking my hands into strange people's mouths has never appealed to me, but I bet it's a solid living."

Wren didn't know what to say to that. She'd wanted to be a dental assistant since her first teeth cleaning. She liked her job. But she'd never considered it brave.

"Do you hike?" Dot asked.

Wren paused, wondering if she'd heard the question right. "Uh . . . sure? In the summer?"

Dot nodded thoughtfully.

Wren stared out the window, gripping her phone, and reconsidered her decision to come here. *Never get into a car with a stranger.* Hadn't that been drilled into her head as a child?

"How do you know my grandfather?" Wren asked as they turned into a neighborhood.

"Here we are." Dot pulled into the driveway of an ordinary-looking home on an ordinary-looking street lined with similar homes all tucked in next to one another.

Dot sat back in her seat and looked at Wren. "My name is Dorothy Gallagher. I went to school with your grandpa in Madison, and we even dated for a bit before he left for Vietnam. We played tennis and poker, and in the summer after we got off work at the Woolworth's, we'd go jump off the train bridge into the river. He's one of my best friends. We lost touch, but that never changed. Weren't many men like him. Probably will never be many men like him." Her eyes glistened.

Wren smiled. "It's nice to meet you."

Dot nodded, sighed, and got out of the car. Wren grabbed her purse, opened the car door, and followed Dot into the house. Gramps had mentioned both his job at Woolworth's and the train bridge.

"Seth!" Dot removed her jacket and offered to take Wren's. "Seth!" she called again. "He's probably out back. He helped put together this whole thing. He's going to be so upset." At Wren's confused expression, Dot placed a hand on her arm. "Not at Billy. That's not what I meant. *Seth!*" She threw their jackets over the back of a sofa.

A door opened toward the back of the house. "Is that you, Grandma?"

A young man came around the corner into the front room. His wide grin wavered only a moment when he saw Wren. He stepped forward and kissed Dot's cheek. He stepped back, still smiling, and looked beyond Wren to the front door, then back to Wren.

"Who's this?"

He wasn't particularly striking, but nice to look at. Kind of bookish. His eyes were startlingly blue. Wren wished she had a smile that open. She brushed some of her dark hair behind her ear and looked at the ground.

"This . . ." Dot put her arm unexpectedly around Wren's shoulders. "Is Wren Lario, Billy Tivegna's granddaughter. Wren, this is my wonderful grandson, Seth. Seth, shake her hand."

He did, an amused gleam in his eye. Wren smiled.

"Wren came all this way to give us some very tough news."

Wren's smile faded. *Oh please*, she thought. *Please don't make me break the news to another stranger.*

But Dot motioned them all to a small dining table behind Seth. After they sat, he looked expectantly from Wren to Dot.

"Wren came in on Billy's flight." Dot took a deep breath. "Billy passed away on Saturday." She placed her hand over her mouth as her chin began to quiver.

"Oh, Grandma," Seth whispered. He got out of his chair and crouched next to her, wrapping her in his arms.

Wren worked past the lump in her throat and said, "We didn't have any way to get hold of her."

Seth looked at her. "I'm sorry. You came all the way here?"

Wren shrugged. "I couldn't let her find out from an airport employee."

Dot pulled out of Seth's embrace, grabbed a napkin out of the napkin holder in the center of the table, and blew her nose. "She did a very selfless thing." She shook her head and blew her nose again. "You've got a lot of your grandpa in you." She gave a definite nod to her head. "Seth? I have an idea. And it's a good one." She turned to Wren. "I bet you're hungry."

Wren hadn't had much of an appetite since Saturday. "I haven't eaten for a while."

Dot stood, and so did Seth. "Billy and I were going to Dixie's for dinner, so that's where we'll go. Seth, you're coming with us. Just as easy to seat a reservation for three as it is for two."

"I'll call the restaurant," Seth said and left for the kitchen.

Dot walked back to the coats and held Wren's jacket out for her. "When is your flight home tomorrow?"

"Eleven o'clock in the morning."

"Hm." She said no more.

When Seth returned, Dot looked at him. "We ready?"

He nodded.

"Let's go."

Seth opened the door for them and held out his hand. "I'll drive."

"Oh, all right," Dot said, a little disgruntled, and gave him her keys.

"Thank you."

Dot moved past him, and he smiled at Wren. He whispered, "You've experienced her driving skills firsthand. She's mad."

"I'm *bold*," Dot called from outside. "If you don't drive with purpose, you get run off the road." She kept walking.

Wren stared, looking after Dot. "Gramps used to say that."

Seth followed her gaze. "You're kidding."

She shook her head. "He taught me how to drive. Said it every time we got in the car. 'Remember, if you don't drive with purpose, you get run off the road.'"

"How was his driving?" Seth asked.

Wren smiled. "Bold."

He grinned.

The restaurant was crowded and noisy. Before Wren opened her menu, Dot asked a question. "Wren, do you know why your grandpa was coming here?"

"No. He didn't tell us about the trip. My mom thinks he'd planned to the day he . . ." She opened the menu to give her hands something to do. "He'd asked to come over to help with the yard on Saturday and said he had something to talk about."

Dot pressed her mouth in a line and nodded, reading her menu. "Did he ever say anything about me at all?"

"Grandma," Seth began.

"Let her answer."

Wren bit her lip. Her mind raced to find any mention, any reference to a woman named Dot, past or present. She took a guess. "Did he . . . teach you how to drive?"

Dot looked up from her menu, wide-eyed, and then broke into a smile. "You're darn right he did. In that beautiful blue Buick of his."

Relief flooded through Wren, so she smiled too. "Now that I think about it, he did seem extra cheerful the last few weeks. Like . . ." Wren remembered, trying to put words to Gramps' behavior until he'd gone in the house for a nap. "Like he had a really good secret. Like . . ." She paused, searching.

"Like it was Christmas Eve," Dot said, staring at her with glassy eyes.

Wren nodded, her heart breaking a little for this woman with the tough exterior.

"Well," Dot said, wiping at the corner of her eye and turning back to her menu. "What looks good?"

Wren peeked at Seth. He peeked back from behind his menu. *Thank you*, he mouthed.

Their food arrived, but Wren could only take a couple of bites. She kept her eyes on her plate. "So, why was Gramps coming here?"

Dot swallowed her bite and set her fork down. "Do you know what a bucket list is?"

Wren lifted her gaze. "The list of stuff you want to do before you—"

Dot nodded. "Kick the bucket." She shrugged. "Billy and I have a bucket list. When we got back in touch, both of us single and still kicking, we decided it would be a great thing to do, so we threw one together. We were supposed to start—" She couldn't finish; she looked at Seth for help.

He wiped his mouth with a napkin. After a moment he said, "I helped them arrange things on the list. This week they were going to have . . . well, they were going to have a blast."

"And we still are," Dot said with determination. She squared herself to Wren. "Because you're going to take your grandpa's place."

"I'm what?"

Dot narrowed her gaze. "You're going to take Billy's place. You're going to get his bucket list checked off. One by one. You're going to do it for him—" Her voice trembled a little. "You're going to do it for me." She lifted a finger and pointed across the table. "And you're going to do it for yourself, Wren. Because life is short. And meant to be lived." Her hands clenched into fists. "It's meant to be grabbed with both hands and spun around until you're dizzy with it."

It was as though Wren were made of glass and Dot could see right through her, right to the fear, her every hesitation, right to the invader in her body right now.

"Wh—when?"

"This week. We'll start right now. It's all arranged, right Seth?"

Seth nodded. "Good to go."

"But the funeral is next week. My mom needs me. She can't—"

"I'll talk to your mom," Dot said.

Wren's head swam. This wasn't the plan. She couldn't stay. She didn't know these people, and she needed to get home. There was so much to be done, and her mom was alone. Music, flowers, cemetery arrangements, pall bearers . . .

Dot interrupted her thoughts. "I hate to pull this card, Wren, but . . . your grandpa would be over the moon if you did this." She leaned forward, and Wren couldn't break her gaze. "Take his place. Right now. He was so excited about this. Do it because he can't."

Wren's throat closed up, and her eyes filled with tears.

Dot reached across the table and took Wren's hands in a firm grip. "Do this to say goodbye."

She was right. Wren knew it. She could hear him. *Go see what you're made of.* She blew out the breath she'd been holding. She picked up her napkin and wiped at her tears. "I'll need to call my mom. And change my flight."

Dot beamed. "There's my girl."

Seth laughed quietly.

"What are you laughing at?" Dot asked. "You'll be joining us."

"What? I'm just the travel guide. I'm good. See?" He smiled. "I'm at peace with all of this, and I pay my full respects to a man who lived a happy life." He put his hand over his heart. "Rest in Peace, William Tivegna. You seemed to be the kind of man who met an open door at full speed. May we all do the same."

"You're doing this with us," Dot said. She reached for an imaginary door knob in front of Seth and pulled. "Door. Opened."

A laugh escaped Wren as Seth looked as if somebody had pulled his chair out from under him. Dot didn't pay him any attention.

She turned back to Wren, raising her voice above an announcement coming from a mic in the corner of the restaurant. "Let's get this started. What song would you like to sing?" She pulled out a little pocket camera.

"I'm sorry?"

The restaurant patrons began clapping.

Seth cleared his throat. "First thing on the list."

Music started, loud and clear, and the blood drained from Wren's face.

Seth leaned forward, looking uneasy. "Karaoke."

Dot stood. "Let's go sign up." She turned and made her way between the tables.

Seth stood and pulled out Wren's chair for her. She looked up at him.

"Karaoke is on Gramps' bucket list?"

He nodded. "I'm afraid so."

Her gaze followed Dot over to the stage. "Well." Wren swallowed. "Dammit."

Dot chose her song. Seth frowned over the oldies list. The chaos of butterflies in Wren's stomach was enough to make her glad she'd only taken a few bites of food. But she'd chosen her song and was in the lineup. Dot's name was called, she gave them the thumbs-up, and waited next to the stage for her intro. Wren wasn't singing for a couple more numbers, so she returned to their table.

Seth joined her shortly. He put his head down on his fists and closed his eyes.

"Hey, are you okay?" Wren asked.

He shook his head. "I think I'm going to be sick."

"From the food?" He'd nearly cleaned his plate.

He shook his head.

"The singing?"

He nodded.

The mic hummed with feedback, and they winced. A man with bleached blond hair and a tattoo sleeve stood on stage and tapped the mic until it quieted.

"Welcome to Oldies Karaoke night at Dixie's. Nice to see all you folks here enjoying the food and drinks. Hope you enjoy the music, too. All are welcome, so if any of these brave patrons inspires you to give it a try, come sign up with our deejay, TJ, and show us what you got. First up, let's put our hands together for Ms. Dorothy Gallagher!"

Applause and whistles came from the crowd. Wren clapped. Seth took out his cell phone to record the performance.

"This is for Billy, who couldn't be here tonight." Dot kissed her finger and held it up toward the ceiling. And she started singing "Stand by Me."

Her voice was deep alto and a bit raw, but she knew the notes and sang them out, as if she were reassuring the audience of their truth.

"No, I won't shed a tear . . ."

"Well," Wren said. "That's about perfect."

"Yeah," Seth said.

"She's something else, isn't she?"

"Yes," Seth answered with pride in his voice. "She is."

They watched the rest of the performance in silence, then stood and applauded when Dot finished. Seth stuck his fingers in his mouth and whistled.

Dot made her way back to the table and dropped into her chair. "Well that about killed me."

"You did great!" Wren sat back down. "You didn't look scared at all."

"I'm a better actress then I am a singer."

Seth leaned over and kissed her cheek. "You were amazing, Grandma."

"Thank you, dear. I just kept picturing Billy stripped down to his nothings, yelling at me to jump off that train bridge the first time. No way was I going to let him see me scared."

Wren imagined a much younger Gramps in his skivvies, threatening a young Dorothy with a whooping if she didn't jump. Wren had heard the same empty threat herself. It didn't hold much weight when it came with a dashing grin. She smiled, and Dot did too.

Applause filled the room as the next song ended, clearing Wren's head of the memory.

"And now we'll hear from Miss Wren Lario. Wren!"

Wren's stomach dropped, and the blood drained away from her face again. She felt herself nudged up and forward, her feet carrying her toward the stage. The mic was adjusted to her height, and a spotlight burned her retinas. The room quieted, and she tried to speak. Her heart pattered like a rabbit's.

"Um, I'm being forced to do this."

The audience chuckled, all eyes on her.

She swallowed. "So . . . thanks a lot, Gramps. This is for you."

The deejay gave her a nod, and the lyrics screen came to life.

She glanced at the audience, then decided she'd be better off not looking at them.

James, forgive me. I'm about to sing your cheesy song in a karaoke bar. I've sung it a few times in the shower, so we should be good.

She shook her head, her heart pounding. She lifted the mic.

Wren started singing James Taylor's "How Sweet It Is," her voice frighteningly small in the microphone. This didn't sound like her in the shower at all. She filled her lungs and sang more clearly, peeking up at the audience. People were smiling. She found Dot, who waved, holding her camera. Wren smiled and headed into the chorus.

She was doing this. Having a little fun, even. Then, she

glanced at the next words on the screen, where she was supposed to sing about where she'd be without the other person in her life. A rock of emotion lodged in her throat, and all she could do was blink, her mouth opening and closing like a fish. The deejay got her attention and gave her a questioning look. She shook her head, but he didn't seem to know what that meant. All she felt was alone, left too soon. She closed her eyes and tried to breathe.

She opened her eyes at the sound of another voice with a mic.

Seth glanced at her nervously, then back to the monitor, picking up the lyrics she'd dropped. He threw her a look that said, *Help me? Please?* She was drawn back to the words on the monitor and joined him, finding her voice again. He was a pretty good tenor and looked relieved he wasn't doing a solo anymore. The stronger she sang, the wider his smile grew.

"I just want to stop—" She smiled at Seth.

He lowered his voice into the mic. "And thank you, baby."

She laughed, and they finished the song. When the music faded, they both practically threw their mics at the deejay, hurrying offstage as fast as they could, barely paying attention to the applause.

"Hey, where are you two going? You're Seth, right? You're next." TJ the deejay pointed to the clipboard.

"Oh, I think that counted." Seth turned to Wren. "That counted, right?"

"I think so." She nodded.

But the deejay shook his head with a laugh. "You're on the queue." He motioned toward the stage, set the clipboard down, and turned away, making it final.

Seth paled again.

"What are you singing?" Wren asked.

Seth picked up the clipboard and pointed.

Her brow lifted in surprise. She bit her lip and looked

back at the stage. She turned to Seth. "I'll sing with you."

Seth smiled.

Back up on the stage, they belted out "Born to Be Wild." Dot loved it.

That was all that mattered.

Four

Wren spoke to her mom, and then Dot took the phone and went into the kitchen. Of course Mom had been supportive and encouraging. She kept calling it a "wonderful opportunity." Wren still wasn't convinced that she should stay, but after hearing about the list and karaoke, Sue Lario wasn't going to let Wren come home to funeral planning. "Dot's right. Gramps would want this for you."

No argument could stand up to that.

Dot had made up the sofa into a bed, and Wren brought her bag in from the car. She'd packed for one night, not four days. She'd have to borrow the washing machine.

Seth came in with spare pillows. "Help yourself to anything in the fridge."

"Thanks, I'm good." Dinner had tasted better after the songs.

"Tonight was fun," he said. "I mean, after the nausea passed."

"It was. Thanks again for rescuing me up there."

He shook his head. "That was a moment of complete insanity."

"I appreciate your temporary madness."

He smiled. "It comes and goes, depending on the motivation." He leaned against the wall and shoved his hands in his pockets. "Things have been sane around here for a little too long."

That smile. He had a way of lifting the right corner of his mouth a little higher than the other, even when he spoke.

Wren lowered her gaze.

Dot came back into the room. "That's squared away. Your mother is lovely. I wish . . ." She sighed. "No matter. I'm beat. You need anything else? Toothbrush? You know where the towels are? Need a glass of water?"

Wren shook or nodded her head for each answer.

"Okay. I'm off to bed. What a night. One down, kiddos." She kissed her finger and pointed skyward, then walked down the hall.

Wren looked around as Seth lingered a moment. The house was newer, a cookie-cutter of its neighbors, but the furniture was a mix of old and new. "So Dot said this is your house?"

"Yeah. Boeing hired me after I graduated, and I moved here. Grandma came out to visit and made me an offer I couldn't refuse."

"Which was?"

"That if I rented her a room, she wouldn't move into the Wisconsin retirement community my parents were trying to talk her into."

"Oh." Wren glanced down the hall. "But some of those places are nice."

"Would Billy have wanted to live in one?"

"No, I guess not."

He shrugged. "She has diabetes. And mild hypertension. My parents are in California and were worried about her living by herself."

"So now she lives with you."

"Yes."

"And how is that . . . working out?" Living with his grandma had to be rough on his social life. Wren imagined Gramps moving in with her. Actually, that might have improved things . . .

He smiled. "She's my grandma. You've met her. She's great. But . . ." He scratched his jaw and lowered his voice. "It's not like having a puppy or something."

"A puppy?"

He moved closer and sat on the arm of the sofa. "Yeah, you know, to walk in the park. People come over and say, "Oh, how cute . . . What's her name?"

She smiled. "Is that how it works?"

He shrugged, grinning.

"And they don't do that with Dot?"

"No. When we go to the park, she's speed walking and yelling at me to keep up."

Wren covered her mouth as she laughed.

He shook his head. "Seriously, though, she loves it here. She has a group of friends she swims with at the Y. She still drives." He made crazy eyes, and Wren grinned. "She checks her insulin levels and beats me down in poker."

"So you're good for her."

He shrugged again. "I wouldn't have her where she doesn't want to be." He looked toward the kitchen. "I know she feels like she's cramping my style. And maybe she is." He looked back at Wren and shook his head. "But she's way cooler than I am."

Wren smiled. "Yeah. I know what you mean."

He watched her a moment. "Well . . ." He stood. "Good night." He turned to leave.

"Seth?"

He turned back. "Yeah?"

Wren peered down the hall. "What . . . was the relationship between Dot and Gramps? I mean, lately?"

He thought a moment. "My grandpa's been gone a long time. Eleven years. I never knew another man to grab her attention. But I think with your Gramps, she was considering it. She was . . . excited. She told me about when they were young, all the memories as they came back. Getting back in touch with Billy sort of brought back her youth. I think she was hoping for . . . more, you know?"

Wren frowned, nodding. "I'm so sorry."

"Hey," he said, "it's not your fault. In fact because of you, she didn't give up and throw it all in the trash. This bucket list thing is big. It's more than something to do. It's a tribute."

"For Gramps," she said.

He nodded. He reached and nudged her arm. "For you, too."

She looked up at him. Something in his gaze shifted, and it was a moment before she could look away. She leaned back against the couch. "So what else is on the list?"

"Hm. If you'd known we were going to do karaoke tonight, you would've never let Grandma bring you there."

"That's not true."

He raised his eyebrows.

"Okay maybe, but I've agreed to the list."

He studied her. "Really, I'm not sure I should tell you."

"He's *my* grandpa. I should know what's on his list."

"Actually, it's your grandpa's *and* my grandma's list. And it's not for the faint of heart."

She folded her arms. "Is it more karaoke-level stuff or will I . . . need a parachute . . . at some point?" She swallowed.

He laughed.

"I'm serious."

"I know. I'm sorry." He sobered. "You just surprise me, that's all. Listen, you won't need a parachute. Yet." Her eyes widened. He continued. "*I'm* nervous about this list, and I'm the one who arranged everything. You might turn tail and run, and then where would we be?"

"Tell me."

He took a deep breath and ran a hand over his head. "Okay, did you bring a swimsuit?"

"Of course not." It was February.

"Actually, that's probably fine," he murmured.

"What?"

"Nothing. I'm guessing you didn't bring anything more than jeans and t-shirts, huh?"

She nodded her head.

"I promise, tomorrow is really more of a sightseeing day. Just some things they decided would be fun and off the beaten path. Okay?"

She studied him. Was he right? If she knew what was on the list, would she worry and bail? Karaoke had been terrifying, but she hadn't had time to do anything about it. Like Gramps tossing her in the lake to learn how to swim. "Maybe you're right," she said. "Maybe it's better if I find out as we go. But I won't bail. I'm in this."

He smiled again. Why was he so dang happy all the time? "I believe you." He kept smiling.

"You know, when you smile like that all the time, it's kind of creepy. What's so great?"

He chuckled silently and sat across from her on the edge of the coffee table. "I just . . . we get to do this thing, you and I. We get to leap that chasm between believing you have all the time in the world and knowing your time is running out."

She sobered.

"It's kind of a jolt about what it means to live, that's all."

That's all. She nodded. She'd had that jolt. She'd entered that chasm at the doctor's office.

His grin softened. "So this week, we're living for Billy."

She nodded again, unable to speak.

He touched her shoulder. "Hey, I didn't mean to bring you down. Tomorrow will be fun, I promise."

Of course it would be; Gramps and Dot were in charge.

"Thanks, Seth." It came out in a whisper. She felt small and lost. His hand was warm on her shoulder, and at the moment, she really wanted to lean into him and have him wrap his arms around her. She missed being hugged like that. She imagined he was good at it.

He dropped his hand. "You're welcome. And I'll try not to smile so much." He attempted to look stern.

She had to smile again. He said good night once more and got up to go. He turned off the light and climbed the stairs, leaving her there in the dark.

Five

Oh boy. Ohhh boy. Wren pulled at the long white apron she wore and steadied herself.

"Ready?" Erik, a whiskered man wearing the same apron and black sweatshirt she did, gave her a you-can-do-this look, and heaved.

"Ohhhhh . . ." Wren held her hands out and caught the large salmon, gripping the leathery scaled skin and bringing it into her chest. She let out a breath of relief as applause rang out around her in the brisk, sea-smelling air.

"There's my girl!" Dot shouted from the other end of the counter as she wrapped up crab legs under Charlie's supervision.

Wren shivered and placed the salmon on a piece of paper. She lifted it to the scale, a smile etched into her face. Sam rang up the sale, and Wren handed the bundled fish to the happy customer.

"Well done," Sam said and called behind her. "Seth? You come around front with me and work the crowd."

"Yes, sir." Seth followed him around to the front of the seafood display as Sam turned back to Wren. "You catch. Just like that, okay?"

"Just like that," Wren said and laughed nervously.

Today, she, Seth, and Dot were employees of the famous Pike Place Fish Market, throwing fish with Erik, Charlie, and Sam. After a brief training and shouts of confidence in their new and temporary employees, the men had passed out uniforms and gone to work.

"Wren, catch!"

Seth sent a silvery fish her way as the customer snapped a picture. She reached out and caught it. It slipped, but she caught it again, and a cheer went up from the milling shoppers.

"Just like your Grandpa, eh?" Sam slapped Seth on the back. "Today we're doing this for Grandpa Billy!" Seth smiled at Wren, and another customer stepped up to ask about some lobster.

"I think I may be a fishmonger in my next life," Dot said as she hurried past with a basket full of shellfish. "Who knew?" Wren watched her as Dot, smiling, poured the shellfish into a pail to be weighed. This morning, Dot had met them at the breakfast table with bloodshot eyes and a headache. She'd been crying. When she'd suggested that they go without her, the two of them went to work with Excedrin and bacon and eggs. Then Wren had pulled out the big guns: *Is that what Billy would have wanted?*

Wren placed the fish she'd caught on the scale, and Charlie helped her ring it up.

Yes. This was fun. And Gramps would have loved it.

Later that afternoon, they left the fish market with bags of fresh halibut and king crab legs. They'd had their picture taken with the crew and were promised it would be framed and hung in Gramps' name. Wren was pretty sure Pike Place

Fish Market would always be one of her favorite places in the world after this.

The air was cool and wet as they made their way down a series of staircases, pausing at shops along the way. After their hard work, the world slowed down, even with all the bustle around them. The sights and smells of this boho-city culture drew her in.

They reached the large parking lot under the freeway and walked to the car. But Seth only put the fish in the trunk and locked it up again.

"Where are we going?" she asked as Dot followed him without question.

"To the Market Theater."

"Are we going to see a movie?"

"No, it's an improv theater."

Wren stopped in her tracks. Karaoke was one thing, but improv? *Uh, Gramps?*

Seth turned and smiled. "Don't worry; it's closed today."

"Oh." She continued to walk, relieved. "Then why are we going?"

Dot was digging in her purse. "There's something at the theater I've always wanted to see." She pulled out a small, brightly colored package. "Here, have some gum."

Wren hesitantly took the package of Hubba Bubba Max Mystery Flavor Bubble Gum. Dot was full of surprises, but this wasn't the kind of gum Wren expected a seventy-year-old woman to have in her purse. Still, they'd been working for hours in a fish market, and the garlicky pork steamed buns they'd bought from a vendor clear back at lunchtime probably hadn't helped her breath any. She took a small brick of the bubble gum, thanked Dot, and popped it in her mouth.

After Seth took a piece, Dot took two pieces and shoved them in her mouth. Seth didn't seem to find this unusual.

Just before they reached the theater, they turned down an alley and stopped.

"Wha—?" Wren scrunched up her face, not sure what she was looking at.

"Oh my," Dot said. "It's sort of beautiful, isn't it?"

Seth chuckled. He took out his piece of gum, surveyed the massive theater wall in front of them, chose a spot above him and stuck his gum between blue and green wads. He pulled at the sides a bit until it resembled a little sun. He stepped back and assessed his work.

"It's . . . it's bubble gum. Chewed-up bubble gum." Wren looked at Seth. "What is this?"

"You just said." He opened his arms wide. "A wall of chewed-up bubble gum in every color you can think of."

Wren stared at the rainbow of blobs covering every inch of the alley wall in some Willy Wonka version of graffiti. Dot was already getting to work on the piece she'd been chewing, rolling it into a snaky shape.

"How long has this been here?" Wren asked.

"I don't know. Years?" Seth said.

"And they let people do this?"

"Yep. I think they tried scraping it off a few times, but people kept sticking their gum here and started showing up to take pictures. So they just let it grow."

"That's . . . absolutely disgusting."

Seth laughed and nodded. "Agreed."

Dot was smashing her snaky pieces over some old wads in an intricate way. Seth and Wren walked over.

"There," she exclaimed in complete satisfaction. "What do you think?"

It read, in brilliant orange Hubba Bubba bubble-gumminess, *BILLY*.

Wren nodded and pulled out her gum. She worked at it a bit, then stuck an X and O just above his name. "There's a kiss and hug for you, Gramps."

"Perfect," Dot said.

"Gross," Wren said.

Seth laughed.

Dot passed around wet-naps from her purse.

As Seth took pictures, Wren felt the silliness of this wall, right next to the heavy fact that Gramps would have been here, *should* have been here, instead of her, plastering his own wad of bubble gum and smiling with his arm around Dot.

"What would your grandpa have thought of this?" Seth nodded toward the wall.

Wren faced the wall, and Dot linked her elbow with her own.

"He would have thought it was unsanitary and disgusting—"

Dot chuckled.

Wren finished. "—and incredibly human. He would have loved it."

Dot nodded her approval. "Let's go home. I'm exhausted."

Six

Friday's bucket item was a hike.

At least, Wren thought it was a hike.

"*This* is what you meant when you said I probably didn't need a *swimsuit*?" Wren glared at Seth. She had stopped in her tracks after Dot explained the actual destination for the day.

Seth grimaced.

Wren dropped her backpack and turned to Dot. "This can't be on Gramps' bucket list. I'm pretty sure my grandpa went skinny-dipping. He walked around the house in his boxers. Swimming naked was second nature to that man." She folded her arms, suddenly very cold after their four-and-a-half-mile walk through some of the most breathtaking rainforest she'd ever seen. The only rainforest she'd ever seen.

"Actually, Billy did skinny-dip a time or two," Dot said.

"But I never have. This is *my* addition to the list. The website calls it a 'wilderness experience.'"

"Well then, I don't have to do it!"

"You don't have to do any of it." Dot put her hand on her hip. "But Billy's twist on this particular activity was that he'd never been skinny-dipping *with me*."

Wren's jaw dropped. She covered her mouth and turned away. "Ew," she whimpered.

Seth chuckled; then it grew into a laugh.

Wren picked up her backpack and marched past him to the entrance of the Goldmyer Hot Springs "wilderness experience."

"At least I'm not skinny-dipping with my own *grandma*," she muttered as she passed.

Seth shut up.

"I'll have you know, young lady," Dot said, following her, "that I'm in pretty fair shape for someone my age. Better swimming naked with me than some unwashed, hairy backpacking stranger. We've got the resort to ourselves."

Wren turned. "Of course we do! It's *February*!" She continued marching, noting the mounds of snow off the trail. *I am* not *over-reacting*, she told herself.

"I don't know what you're so upset about," Dot said. "You've got a nice young body."

Wren spun again. She dropped her voice. "It so happens that I like to keep this nice young body *covered* when I'm in *mixed company*."

Dot, who had halted, pursed her lips. "Well . . . that's no fun."

Wren reached for something to say in response but couldn't think of one dang thing. Finally she let out a yell, turned again, and kept marching.

"Nobody's making you do anything," Dot called after her.

Sure, Wren thought. *Nobody but Gramps*. And time. Precious, elusive time.

Several minutes later, Wren followed the rough-hewn steps from the main building to the hot pools, the soles of her feet cold on the worn wood. She could see steam rising into the trees. The ethereal beauty of the place was not lost on her, but thoughts of what she was about to do, and the goose bumps on her skin, definitely distracted her. She bit her lip, shivering, and as she came up on the pool, glanced around cautiously.

Seth and Dot sat in opposite sides of a hot pool veiled with steam drifting off the water.

They both looked her way. She stood there wearing a gray Pike Place Fish Market t-shirt pulled down as far past her purple Fruit-of-the-Loom hipster panties as possible, clinging to a folded towel.

Seth's mouth opened and then shut as he met her warning gaze. He looked away quickly.

"Awfully pretty place you picked, Grandma," he said, studying some bushes topped with snow.

Dot splashed him, and he blinked. "It's a lot warmer in the water, Wren," she said.

Wren believed her, and it was the only reason she moved her feet to the edge of the pool. Without looking at either of them, she dropped her towel and lowered herself in, quietly sighing. Her feet burned like hot pokers at first but then acclimated along with the rest of her. Her goose bumps faded, and she nearly slipped all the way under but chose to sit on the underwater stone bench instead.

The t-shirt floated around her, so she pulled it down straight.

"There, now, isn't that better?" Dot asked. "I may never leave. You know, it's quite freeing."

Wren glanced up at Dot, who sat, shoulders just above the water, steam floating around her. Tiny drips clung to the ends of Dot's short hair, lit up by the sun filtering through the trees. She looked pleasantly rosy and hydrated.

"It's not exactly swimming though," Dot said. "I'll have

to go to the lake or something this summer. But for February, it's the best we could do."

"Grandma, you can't go taking off your swimsuit at the lake. They have rules."

"I know that. I'll just . . . have to be stealthy." Dot grinned and winked at Wren.

Wren fought a smile.

Seth ran a hand over his face and shook his head.

"What?" Dot challenged. "It's a privilege of growing old. To do what you need to do. I don't want to be dissatisfied with my life when I die. I want to be content."

"I imagine you will be," Seth answered.

She splashed him again, and he sputtered.

"What was that for?"

"Don't imagine me dead. It gives me the willies."

Wren laughed. It felt odd to laugh about dying.

Dot lifted her hands out of the water, holding them in front of her as they dripped. She looked at them, front and back. "You know, the human body is an incredible thing. So intricate. So wonderful, if you think about it. And so strong. And then, whether it's time or . . . or illness, things go south. Strength. Health. Sight." She looked up at the trees. "And when those things are gone, you realize you once had your chance. You once had strength. The guts. And you wonder . . ." She met Wren's gaze. "You wonder if you'll ever get it back. If you'll have another chance."

"You've still got tons of guts, Grandma," Seth said.

Dot looked at her grandson. "I know I do. I know. The ability to do something with all these guts, though . . . that's what I'm racing with, Seth. That's the race."

Wren stared at her hands just under the water. There wasn't anything her grandpa couldn't do. She'd always been able to ask him about anything, and he'd know; he'd experienced it, or something like it. But what did she know? Would she be able to answer somebody's every question? Was she satisfied with her life? Or would she just . . .

She took a deep breath and lowered herself under the silky water. She tugged and pulled and came up, blinking, her t-shirt in her hands. Dot was right. The hot water on her skin, the chilled air on her shoulders. It *was* freeing. She leaned against the stone wall and closed her eyes, letting her hair float around her, her t-shirt in a ball on the rock behind her.

She smiled, breathing in the winter air.

Seven

"I'm sorry I yelled," Wren said.

"That's okay. I told you the list wasn't for the faint of heart." Seth drove, and Dot slept soundly in the back. After a good long soak, they'd hiked five miles back to the car and were now headed back to Marysville. Seth had asked her to talk to him to keep him from nodding off.

"Yeah, you warned me. I was tired and . . . and caught off guard, I guess."

"Understandable."

She looked down at the sweatshirt Seth was letting her borrow for the trip home. Her t-shirt was still in a frozen ball in the trunk of the car. "Any wardrobe issues I need to know about for tomorrow?"

"You'll need something you can move around in."

"Move around like playing ping-pong? Or move around like swinging from a trapeze? Please say ping-pong. Or shuffle board. Am I buying cabana wear? Please?"

He grinned, reached over, and squeezed her hand. In that quick, unthinking moment, a thrill shot up her arm. They both glanced down, and he quickly let go. She turned to her passenger-side window to hide her blush of embarrassment. "So, when do things start in the morning?"

He cleared his throat. "Later. You can sleep in. And as far as clothes go, something nice would be good."

"How nice? I have jeans and t-shirts, remember?"

He looked at his sweatshirt on her. "Medium-nice?"

She rolled her eyes. "Can you please just tell me what we're doing and drop me off at a department store or something that's still open?"

A few minutes later, he parked the car in front of a Kohl's. Dot snorted from the back seat. He turned to face Wren, and she peeked at him.

"What?" she said quietly, so as not to wake Dot. "You have to tell me what I need."

His brow lifted. "What you need?" His very blue eyes studied her face.

"What I need . . ." she stammered a little and looked away. She checked the door of the glove box to make sure it was still secure. "What I need is to know what to wear." She folded her arms in her lap. "For tomorrow."

He sat back in his seat and rubbed his forehead. "Yes. Tomorrow . . . we'll be traveling. You need something rugged and warm. And then we'll be dancing."

"Dancing?"

"With lessons."

"Lessons?"

"Yes."

"What kin—"

"That's all you get."

She sat back and considered. "It's not square dancing, is it?"

He chuckled but said no more.

"Well, thanks. That helps a little." She picked up her purse and opened the door, but he rested one hand on her arm. She turned. "Yes?"

"I'm sorry you felt . . . pressured. Back there at the hot springs. It meant a lot to Dot that you joined us."

She shrugged. "Thanks. I'm over it." She turned to go, but he still touched her arm. "Yes?"

"I just wanted to let you know that it's . . ."

She frowned. "What?"

He swallowed. "It's not square dancing."

"Oh. Well, good. I won't buy a poofy skirt, then."

"Very wise." He removed his hand, and she got out of the car. She hurried into the department store, her arm still warm from his touch.

She found the women's clothing department and glanced around. "Oh, no."

All over, hanging from the ceilings, plastered on the signs and posters, were hearts. Big, red, pink, repeating hearts. She checked her phone and groaned.

Valentine's Day. Tomorrow was Valentine's Day. She'd completely spaced it. Not that she had any . . . *Valentine* to speak of. She glanced toward the car. But Dot . . . Dot and Gramps had picked this week. And she was here instead. Not what Dot had probably imagined. Ugh. And she'd been so awful today. And Seth . . .

Seth had been trying to clue her in without it being uncomfortable. She checked the time on her phone. The store closed in half an hour. She called her mom.

"Hello? Wren?"

"Hey, Mom, I need your help."

"What's wrong?"

"I have no idea what to wear for dancing lessons."

"Uhh . . ."

"Also, Valentine's Day is tomorrow. Am I the last person to know this?"

"You've been pretty distracted. I didn't think you were a big fan of Valentine's."

Distracted was an understatement. "Not the biggest fan, no, but this is about Gramps and Dot. They chose this week, and now . . . I feel pretty inadequate."

"Well, all Dot wants is for you to be part of their week. You don't need to show up with a tux and a dozen roses."

Wren considered that a moment. "Hmm . . ."

Eight

Wren slept hard and late. After an early lunch, she found herself forty-five miles away in the picturesque town of Issaquah, Washington, in a small shuttle bus, squashed between Seth and Dot, bouncing up a dirt road on the side of a mountain, wringing her hands.

Seth leaned toward her. "I told you we'd be traveling."

She looked at him. "I thought you meant by car. Or a real bus. Or foot. On the ground. Not *paragliding*."

"Yeah, well, remember the karaoke."

"Karaoke is on the ground."

"So is skinny-dipping." He hid a smile.

She ignored his charming display. "And how do they all know you?" She nodded toward the guides at the front of the vehicle.

He looked their way and then back at her; she couldn't help but like having him so near.

He leaned even closer. "I'm certified."

"Yeah, I'm starting to get that."

He nudged into her. "Not *certifiable*. Certified."

"Oooh. My mistake. And what is it you're certified *in*?"

"Jumping off cliffs and such while dangling from a kite."

"Mm-hmm." She turned to Dot as he chuckled. "And you've done this before?"

"You bet. With Seth. I mentioned it to Billy, and he added it to the list."

Wren faced forward, still wringing her hands.

Dot patted her knee. "You'll be okay. You just run and then *poof*, you're floating."

Run off the face of a mountain. Poof. *Easy.*

"You get an incredible view. Mount Rainier, Mount Baker, Lake Sammamish . . ."

"All of those things are on the ground. I like things on the ground. I like to be on the ground with them."

Dot smiled. "You flew here."

"Yes. And I had a very good reason."

Dot nodded. "Agreed. But you have a very good reason to do this, too. Every time you do something on this list, you get to know your grandpa in a whole new way."

Wren peeked at the mountainside as they continued to climb. "I guess."

Dot patted her knee once more. "Don't worry. Seth will be right there with you."

"He will?"

"Yup. He's your tandem guide. You two'll be peas in a pod."

Wren looked at Seth. He watched her for a second, then broke into a laugh. He lifted his arm and placed it around her shoulders, giving her a squeeze.

"Your unwavering confidence in me is evident on your face. Except maybe . . ." He reached over with his other hand and gently lifted her jaw so her mouth closed. "Hm." He studied her, then gently pushed one side of her mouth upward in a fake smile. "There. You trust me completely."

Wren swallowed, unable to move.

"Are you okay?" His joking demeanor faded, and he pulled his arm from around her. "You're flushed."

"Um." She struggled to find her voice. She nodded. "Nervous."

The shuttle rolled to a stop, and the side door slid open. Seth watched her a moment longer. His grin returned. "'Get your motor runnin' . . .'"

She couldn't fight it. Her smile returned. "'Head out on the highway . . .'"

"Peas in a pod," Dot murmured.

Wren suppressed any pleasure at hearing Dot's words. Seth was great. That was all.

Minutes later they were harnessed, their *wing* caught the breeze, and she and Seth ran to the edge, Wren in front and the horizon of the Pacific Northwest coming at them fast and broad.

"Keep going," he called. "Run. Lean into the takeoff. Now bring your feet out in front of you. Lean!"

Her heart pounded with every step, her breathing harder and faster than it should have been, and as she reached the edge, she lifted her feet as he'd told her to do. Although her heartbeat still echoed loudly in her helmet and the wind swept past them, the world became very quiet.

She could see Dot's *wing*, as the sails were called, not far below them, and then she looked down. Way down. She let out a cry and gripped her harness straps. Her legs dangled 3,000 feet above the ground.

"This is wrong!" she shouted.

"What's wrong?" Seth shouted back. "Sit back!"

"My feet should be on the ground!"

He laughed. "Wren?"

"Yeah?"

"You're flying."

She let that sink in. She looked over the landscape to the

horizon in front of them. Green hills, rising snow-covered mountains skirted by clouds. A large blue lake came into view. The weather was clear enough to see Seattle vaguely in the distance.

She unwound and sat back in her harness. "We're flying." She breathed in the cold, clean air.

"You're flying with Gramps. Enjoy the ride, Wren-bird."

She looked at Seth. He opened his arms out like wings. She smiled. When she turned back around, she did the same. They'd leveled out with Dot, who gave her two thumbs up.

They soared. Wren kissed her finger and raised it to the sky.

Nine

Watching her skirt, Wren turned a bit as she waited on the front porch. The black dress she'd found had a deep u-shaped neckline with a white faux blouse attached, a thin red belt at the waist, and a short swingy skirt. She'd been told her stacked patent heels would be great for dancing. She wasn't sure.

She'd put her hair up in a messy bun, because that's the fanciest way she knew how to do it, and put on the silver necklace she'd picked out. A small heart within a larger heart hung at her open collar, which was unbuttoned one more button than usual. She felt daring.

Wren rang the doorbell. She'd only just stepped outside the house, but Dot was still back in her room.

After a second ring—she'd told Seth not to answer—she heard Dot coming to the door. She smiled to herself in anticipation, bouncing a little in the cold.

The door opened.

Dot's eyes grew wide. "Well, what are you—?"

From behind her back, Wren produced a bouquet of a dozen red roses and a canister of Almond Roca, which Seth had said was Dot's favorite. "Happy Valentine's Day, Dorothy June Gallagher."

Dot had worked the short waves of her red hair to frame her face and sparkling eyes. She wore a coral blouse and her own pair of pointy heels peeking out from the hem of her gray slacks. Her hand covered her mouth.

"Billy isn't here," Wren went on. "I know he wanted to be. But I'm here, and I'd like you to be my Valentine."

Dot finally took the flowers and candy, then put her arm around Wren in an embrace. "Bless you, Wren. Bless you," was all she said.

She pulled away and motioned for her to come inside, blinking rapidly. After dabbing at her eyes a little, she said something about water and hurried off to the kitchen with the flowers and candy.

Seth stood at the bottom of the stairs in slacks, shiny shoes, and a black dress shirt, leaning against the wall, his hands shoved into his pockets.

She looked at the ground. "That went okay, I think."

"Mm-hmm." He pushed off the wall and approached her, picking her jacket up off the sofa as he passed it.

"So, good idea," she said.

He held her jacket open. "Good idea."

She slid her arms into her sleeves, and he settled the jacket around her. She turned to face him, glancing up. He watched her intently, a question in his eyes.

"What?" she asked.

He gave his head a small shake. "What were you like as a kid?"

"Why do you ask?"

"I don't know, I'm just . . ." He reached for his own coat on the hook and put it on. "I'm trying to get a picture here, and . . ." He stepped closer and brushed a wisp of her hair from her collar, sending chills down that side of her neck. He dropped his hand and shrugged. "One more day for the list. Just one."

"I know. It's been incredible so far."

He nodded and continued to search her eyes. She turned and pulled Dot's coat off a hook.

"Wren."

"Yes?" She smoothed the wool coat over her arm and pretended to check the time again.

"Look at me, please."

She did, feeling heat rise in her cheeks.

He swallowed. "You look prettier than a Boeing 787 VIP."

She lifted her brow. "Is . . . is that a *plane*?"

He looked away, rolling his eyes at himself. "Yup. I just compared you to a plane. Good, Seth. Good one." He turned toward the door.

Dot came in carrying a vase of her roses. "They're beautiful," she said. "I can't remember the last time someone gave me red roses. Thank you, Wren." She set them on the coffee table.

"You're welcome." Wren was still recovering from Seth's compliment. "I had some help picking out the candy."

Dot smiled at Seth and patted his face. "Thank you, Seth. You're much better at picking out candy than you are at giving compliments."

Wren suppressed a laugh. Dot slipped her arms into the coat Wren held out for her and continued outside. Seth held the door open for both of them, silent. He hurried past and got the car door for his grandma, and after she was in, he stepped to get the door for Wren. But he paused as she stepped forward.

"I meant it."

She looked up, surprised to see him worried. She blinked. "Brave."

His brow furrowed. "What?"

"You asked what I was like when I was a kid. My dad left us when I was three. So I was brave."

His expression softened and turned into a small smile. "I can see that. And I'm sorry."

She opened her mouth to tell him he didn't need to be, but Dot banged on the window. "Unless you're kissin' her, let's go. It's been a long day, and I wanna shake my bootie."

He closed his eyes and groaned, and Wren slipped into the back seat as quickly as she could.

Dot turned around before Seth got in the car. She whispered hastily. "*Was* he kissing you?"

"No," Wren whispered vehemently back. "Of course not."

"Well . . ." Dot turned back around. "Dammit."

Ten

Oh, Gramps, how could you? Of all the—

"One-swivel-hips, and two-swivel-hips. That's right. Dig the balls of your feet into the floor. Latin dancing is all about pressing your center of gravity toward the earth. One-swivel-hips. You've done this before."

Wren let the instructor's observation go as she stared straight ahead.

What on Earth were you thinking? Salsa dancing? Graaaamps.

"Slight bend to the knees. That's it. I'm just going to work with you, Dot. These two don't need me."

It was true. The class was small, but there were enough beginners to tell who'd done this before. In the wall-length mirror, Wren could tell that Seth also seemed to know what he was doing.

And so did Gramps. He'd known she could salsa. That

she loved it. That she secretly danced around her apartment to Oscar D'Leon and Celia Cruz. Tito Puente woke her up every morning in the shower. She worried about the neighbors finding out, so she kept the music down, but now it blasted in the dance studio, and she couldn't not dance. She couldn't not dance well. She couldn't not love it and not be mortified at the same time.

This was her secret joy. And Gramps was making her do it.

In front of people.

She bit her lip and caught Seth watching her. She threw her hand up over her face, and he laughed. She slowed.

"No need to be shy, *linda*. C'mon, let's see what you can do." Rosa, their Dominican instructor, pulled her to the front and stood opposite her as a partner. She took Wren's hands and led her through some basic steps, a few turns, some walks, and then some spins. Wren couldn't help smiling, though she wanted to hide. The teacher let her go as the song finished and the class applauded and whooped.

"From where did you learn this?"

Oh, not that question. "Watching. Practice." Watching YouTube videos, Zumba DVDs, and practicing by herself with the blinds closed.

And she had to admit, it was wonderful dancing with somebody real.

I am so pathetic.

"Not bad at all. No need to blush like that." Rosa beamed at her. "You and your partner are going to kick it tonight." She motioned to Seth.

"Partner? Tonight?" Wren looked at Dot, who nodded, grinning.

"At my salsa club, after class. Free admission with the first lesson. All of you, come. What better way to spend Valentine's Day than speaking to your partner through dance?" She clapped her hands and picked up with the class as the next song began.

Wren made her way to her place near the back of the room, a flutter of anticipation in her stomach.

After class, Dot found her. "I'm so excited to watch you kids."

Seth shook his head. "You pulled us into this, Grandma. You'll do more than watch."

"Well." A mischievous smile lit her face. "I think I just might."

Wren pressed her hand to her stomach. "I feel queasy."

"What?" Dot asked. "No. It's just nerves."

Wren sat on a bench and closed her eyes. "Gramps is laughing his fluffy white wings off, I'm sure."

Dot sat next to her. "You may be right. You know, this one was all his idea. He chose it because of you."

Wren opened her eyes and looked at Dot.

Dot nodded. "He said he'd seen you a few times, caught you with your headphones in or whatever they are now. Head buds. He said you looked like you were having the time of your life with nobody watching, and he wanted to give that a shot. He wanted to learn it."

"He knew how to do that."

She shrugged. "Maybe he did. Maybe he didn't. But he liked the way you did it."

Wren took a deep breath. She reached over and took Dot's hand. "And he wanted to do it with you."

Dot lifted her chin. "You bet he did."

Wren laughed.

They found a table in the crowded club and ordered drinks.

Seth stood. "Grandma, let's go out there and shake our booties. Wren, if you'll excuse us."

"Shake away," Wren said.

Seth guided Dot to the dance floor. They took it easy. Dot laughed and kept up pretty well. Wren allowed herself to imagine Gramps out there on the floor. She'd seen him dance a little. A spontaneous swing with Mom every once in a while. And Wren had danced on his toes around the kitchen. Always with a smile. Man, she'd love to see him smiling out there right now.

She sighed and refocused, and at that moment caught Seth's eye. His smile widened, and he turned Dot into a small dip. Dot beamed.

Wren clapped, got up from the table and met them on the dance floor. "I'm cutting in," she said.

Dot fanned herself. "Oh good." She turned for the table.

"Oh no you don't," Wren said. "I'm dancing with my Valentine on Valentine's Day."

Seth turned Dot around and excused himself.

Together, she and Dot danced and turned and swiveled their hips, laughing until they were nearly out of breath. As the song ended, Dot held her side.

"Whew. I'm sitting down. That was a hoot, Wren." She took her seat and a sip of her drink. "I'm all set to watch you two for the rest of the evening."

Wren stilled.

"Well." Seth became quiet. "You can sit, too, if you're tired."

Wren took a half-step toward her chair.

"Of course she's not tired," Dot said. "What are you guys, Twenty-four? Twenty-five?" She rolled her eyes and made a shooing motion. "Get on out there, pups, and show 'em how it's done."

Seth held out a hand. Slowly, Wren took it.

"Promise you won't leave me in the dust out there?" he asked with that lopsided smile.

She glanced at him out of the corner of her eye as they turned. "I'll do my best to keep you dust free."

"I appreciate it." He led her toward the crowd.

"Tell me something," she said. "How did you learn to salsa?"

He chuckled. "College. I was in engineering school,

116

going into aeronautics. My roommate was Puerto Rican. I needed to find something to make me less nerdy. He agreed."

She smiled. "Did it work?"

"If you have to ask, then no."

They reached the dance floor but stayed in the outer ring, which she appreciated. The dancers in the center took salsa to a whole new level.

They stood looking at each other a moment, and then he took both her hands. "Here we go." He swung their hands and they walked a bit; him pushing, then her pulling. Their smiles grew as the rhythm took over, and then, he surprised her.

He totally knew what he was doing. And she'd rarely danced with someone else.

He spun her close.

"Puerto Rican, huh?" she asked as he caught her.

"*Si*," he said, and spun her out again, grinning like he had a really good secret.

They danced two songs. Then three. Then five.

He frowned at his watch, not letting her hand go. And she didn't want him to.

She saw the time, though. "We need to get Dot home." She was breathing hard, but it felt good. She felt alive and wonderful.

He nodded. Dot sipped her drink, seemingly content to watch the dancers, leaning her head drowsily on her wrist.

The next song began. Seth met Wren's gaze. "One more?"

She nodded, and he stepped closer. This was a much slower kind of dance. The couples swayed and spun and held each other close. Seth pulled her in.

She was right; he was good at this.

He didn't do anything fancy, just kept it simple, swaying, every so often pulling her out to spin her slowly and then bring her back in. She wanted to be pulled back in, pressed to him. She felt his lips brush her forehead, and then he slowly spun her away again, and the song ended. He kept her fingers, watching her.

And a battle erupted inside her. *Oh, Wren, why did he have to know salsa?*

Eleven

Back at his house, they helped Dot to her room and made sure she was awake enough to dress and get to bed. Wren kissed her cheek. "Thank you, Valentine."

Then Wren and Seth stood at the base of the stairs. He took her hand again, and she watched his shoes.

"Tonight was fun," he said softly.

She closed her eyes and smiled. "It was the best time I've had in a while. This whole horrible, awful, wonderful week has been the best I've had in a long while. What does that say about me? That my grandpa has to die for me to—"

"Shh." He lifted her chin. "Don't say that."

She opened her eyes, and a tear fell. He furrowed his brow but continued to draw her closer. "Don't cry, Wren." He lowered his head to hers, watching her mouth. She felt a pull, like a magnet, his mouth toward hers. Just before he reached her lips, she placed her hands on his wrists and pulled away.

It took him a moment to blink and pull up. He ran a hand over his face. "I'm sorry."

"No. I . . ." But she didn't know what to say. "I . . ."

He brushed a tendril of her hair off her face. "It's all right. I misread. And you . . . you've been brave all week."

He hadn't misread anything. But she was exhausted. "I'm tired of being brave," she whispered.

He smiled. "I can help you there. Tomorrow is easy. Recovery day. Brunch at the Space Needle and then the Seattle Symphony." He gave her an encouraging look. "Easy."

"Then I go home."

He nodded. "Then you go home." He touched her face again, gently. "Wren, I'd like to see you again."

She swallowed, thinking that too. But she shook her head. "You can't. It's not—"

"It's not that far. I get flyer miles. Job perk."

She shook her head again and pulled away. "No, you can't. I mean, *I* can't."

"Wren, this whole week was about living life before it's too late—"

She turned away. "I know what it's about."

"And I know what I want to do—"

"How can you possibly know? You don't even know me."

"I have a good idea. I'd like to know you better." He reached for her hand.

"You can't."

"Why not?" His fingers found hers.

She spun, throwing off his hand like it was scalding water. He looked like she'd slapped him. She *felt* like she'd slapped him.

"Because I'm *tired* of being *brave*." She breathed heavily with emotion. Tears fell. He watched her, stunned.

Dot appeared in her doorway, clearly concerned. Wren

looked at them both. "I don't know . . . what to give you. I don't know what to promise or even *dream* about . . ." She closed her eyes and swallowed. When she opened them again, Dot had stepped out of her room.

Wren spoke to her. "Just before Gramps died, I wasn't feeling right." She shook her head. "I went to the doctor. They ran blood tests, all kinds of tests."

Dot stepped forward. "What did they find, honey?"

"C—cancer."

Seth ran his hand through his hair.

"They ran the imaging. My uterus. Just like—"

"Billy's wife."

Wren nodded. "My grandma."

She saw understanding dawn in Dot's eyes. "Oh, merciful heavens. Do they know how far along? Can you start treatment?"

"I'm waiting on more test results."

Dot put her hands on her heart. "And you kept this from us this whole time?"

"You . . . you were strangers."

"*Were*," Seth said quietly.

Her stomach flipped with ache and confusion. "I haven't even told my mom."

"Dear, sweet, foolish child." Dot pulled her arms around Wren and hugged her tight. She was good at it too. "Why on earth not?"

Wren sniffled. "Because of Gramps. Because of the funeral. Because I couldn't . . . I couldn't give her the pain that *I* might be leaving her too." She cried. "I couldn't do that to her."

She lifted her eyes to Seth. His were rimmed with red, his fists clenched. He watched her, though; he wouldn't look away.

"I couldn't do that to anyone. Not now." Her chest constricted with emotion. "I'm tired of being brave." She lowered her head onto Dot's shoulder.

Later, when Dot had tucked Wren into the bed on the sofa and kissed her head good night, Seth stayed behind. He knelt down by her.

"Please, Seth."

"I just want you to know two things."

She looked at him.

"One, this week has been the best of my life, and it was all because of you. All of it. We were doing it for Gramps, but you were doing it . . . for you."

Watching him, she nodded.

He reached for her hand. She let him take it, but she wouldn't let him keep it long. "Two, it's too late. You're already leaving me, and it's already enough to hurt like hell. I think I understand. But I do know you. You're a fighter, Wren. So you fight. Be brave enough so that you're doing yard work and making plans for a week like this one on the day you die." He wiped a tear and pressed his lips to her palm. "You . . . you drive with purpose." He kissed her hand once more, then got up and left, hurrying up the stairs.

She blinked at the ceiling, letting her tears get her pillow all wet. She pressed her hand to her chest.

Twelve

Wren had been home in Palisade for three hours, and still her bag sat unpacked at the foot of her bed. Her last day with Dot and Seth had been subdued, but pleasant and friendly. Every smile and touch was weighted. The goodbyes were nearly unbearable.

"You changed my life this week," she'd told Dot. "Thank you."

"Oh, my dear. Your life wasn't changed. We simply lived it. Don't forget that."

Seth tried to catch her eye at the end. But she couldn't look at him. His embrace was quick. His escape was quicker.

She had three days until the funeral. Wren had assured her mother she'd come over later for dinner and that her quiet behavior was because she was tired, so she was urged to take a nap.

But Wren couldn't sleep. She sat at her desk, a pen in hand, staring vacantly over a sheet of paper.

Wren's Bucket List

The rest of the page was blank. It wasn't that she couldn't think of anything. It was just that everything she thought of . . . she couldn't see doing without—

Seth.

Finally she threw down the pen, wiping tears away, and picked up the phone. She pulled out the doctor's number.

Thirteen

The funeral was stiffer than Gramps would have liked, but it was done, and Wren could see the weight begin to lift from her mom's shoulders. They were holding a small reception afterward, and then it would all be over. She'd give her mom a couple more days, and then Wren would tell her everything.

Wren shook people's hands as they passed. She smiled and nodded and thanked them, keeping an eye on her mom, yet her thoughts wouldn't stay focused. She held her hand out to take a young man's, but he placed an envelope there instead. Several people had given her sympathy cards, which she'd taken to read later. She thanked him and turned to put it in her purse.

"He says to read it now."

She looked at the young man. "Who says?"

The kid shrugged and continued past her. She looked

down at the envelope. *Wren-bird.*

She excused herself, her heartbeat picking up a little. Her mother looked at her questioningly. Wren reassured her with a nod and, her gaze darting around the room, left the reception to find a quiet place off the foyer.

A few people stopped her and expressed their condolences. She thanked them, trying not to appear hurried, and then moved on, finally finding a darkened area next to the coat racks.

She opened the envelope and pulled out a folded sheet of paper.

Her fingers trembled as she unfolded the letter. She took a deep breath, then read.

Seth's Bucket List
Love Wren
Love Wren
Love Wren
Love Wren
Love Wren
Love Wren . . .

She pressed the paper to her chest, no longer able to see.

"I thought we should get started right away."

She turned at the sound of his voice.

He stood there, hands pushed into his pockets, looking for all the world like Christmas morning.

"What are you doing here?" she asked.

"I came to pay my respects to the man who raised you. I hope that's all right."

She nodded.

"And . . . well, it says there." He gestured to the letter crushed in her hands. He wrinkled his brow. "Although, I may have to make another copy."

She shook her head. "This one is good."

"Yeah?"

She stepped toward him. "Yeah." She didn't stop, and he opened his arms. She pressed into him, and he wrapped his arms around her. She gazed up at him.

He watched her. "You're not looking away."

"No."

"I'm starting that list now, Wren. There's nothing you can do about it. I'm in this."

Her heart pounded, and she couldn't protest. "I believe you."

He pulled her closer, and she lifted her chin. He smiled, then touched his lips to hers.

She closed her eyes and, with the kiss, drew her arms around his neck, the smell of him surprisingly familiar. He pulled her closer and then eased. Their lips parted.

"Yeah," he said, breathless. He searched her face. "I'm in this."

She let the words float around her heart a moment. Then a question tumbled out. "Would you be in this if I didn't have cancer?"

He frowned, and his hands clenched against her back. "Of course I would. Dang, Wren, I loved you the moment you took the mic."

The gentle flurry of his words settled softly. "That's good to know. I got the test results back. I don't have cancer, Seth." She watched him react: first with hesitation, making sure he understood her, and then his eyes lit up.

"It's benign. There's a chance I could still get it because of my family history, but I can do things to pre—"

"Ha!" He laughed, loud. She let out a squeal as he picked her up and swung her around right there next to the coats. His smile blazed.

And all of the suppression, all the secret ache and worry and fear flew out of her like a little flock of birds painfully caged, suddenly set free. Off they flew, down the hallway, and out the doors.

Wren paid them little attention. Seth was kissing her

again, his bucket list clutched in her hand as they pressed into the coats of people attending her grandpa's funeral. She didn't care at all.

She was living.

And she thought Gramps would be kinda proud.

ABOUT KRISTA LYNNE JENSEN

Nearly every one of Krista Lynne Jensen's elementary school teachers noted on her report card that she was a "daydreamer." It was not a compliment. So when Krista grew up, she put those daydreams down on paper for others to enjoy.

When she's not writing she enjoys reading, hiking, her family, and sunshine. But not laundry. She never daydreams about laundry.

Krista writes romance and fantasy. She is the author of *Of Grace and Chocolate* (a 2012 Whitney Award Finalist), *The Orchard* (2013), *Falling for You* (2014), and *With All My Heart* (2014), through Covenant Communications. She is a member of ANWA, Author's Incognito, and LDStorymakers.

Visit her blog at KristaLynneJensen.blogspot.com

How To Rewrite
A Love Letter

by Diane Darcy

Other Works by Diane Darcy

She Owns the Knight

The Princess Problem

Beauty & the Beach

She's Just Right

Steal His Heart

A Penny for Your Thoughts

Serendipity

Once in a Blue Moon

A Christmas Star

One

"Okay, kids, this next letter holds a secret no one has been able to uncover in over three hundred years." Julie Ashburn looked out at the kids in her classroom, gratified to see her seniors all paying attention for once. She lifted the letter from her desk and held it high in the air. "Most of you know Ludwig van Beethoven as a composer. Does anyone know anything else about him?"

Caleb raised his hand. "He was deaf as a dodo bird."

Julie lifted a brow. "The expression is *dead as a dodo,* and as dodos were not deaf, I'm going to ignore the second half of your statement but agree with the first. Yes, he was deaf. He started losing his hearing in his mid-twenties." She paced in front of her desk. "What else?"

"He was Swiss," called out Evan.

Julie shook her head. "No, he was German."

"Same difference," Evan said.

Julie sighed and, for effect, shook her head sadly. "As this is honors English, not geography, I'll only comment that the German and Swiss peoples would not agree with your assessment."

As the kids chuckled, Julie waved the sheet of paper again. "So Beethoven was a German composer who went deaf in his twenties. Anything more to add? Does anyone know anything about his love life?"

Julie was delighted to see all eyes turn front and center. She cleared her throat and started reading.

Good morning,

Though still in bed, my thoughts go out to you, my Immortal Beloved, now and then joyfully, then sadly, waiting to learn whether or not fate will hear us—I can only live wholly with you or not at all. Yes, I am resolved to wander so long away from you until I can fly to your arms and say that I am really at home with you and can send my soul enwrapped in you into the lands of spirits. Yes, unhappily, it must be so. You will be the more contained since you know my fidelity to you. No one else can ever possess my heart—never—never . . .

Julie paced and finished reading the letter aloud, then ended with the valediction.

ever thine
ever mine
ever ours

She finished, lowered the paper, and looked over at the kids. "This letter was found in Beethoven's possession upon his death. No one knows who this unknown, Immortal Beloved was. To this day, people continue to guess at the mystery woman's identity. Books, plays, and the movie *Immortal Beloved* all examine, in great detail, who she might have been."

"Maybe it was a man," said Hannah.

Julie laughed. "Maybe so, but that's not what we're here to talk about today. I want to discuss how this intensely passionate letter has captured the imagination of so many. And why, hundreds of years later, the world is still trying to determine who Beethoven's true love was." She raised the paper. "And all of that is based on this short note."

She paused. "Why do people even care? At this point, the world will probably never be able to match a face to this mystery woman. Not for certain. No one will know how their relationship worked out for them, as this is all that's left of the love that once burned as passionately as the music for which Beethoven is known."

There were a couple of snickers from the boys, but Julie continued as she leaned against her desk. "Can you imagine receiving a letter like this?"

More laughter, but everyone still paid attention.

"Can't you just feel the emotion? These are not just words on a page. These are heartfelt sentiments that have lasted the test of time. What he felt for her is right here." She shook the paper. "So, what does this have in common with the letter we read from Napoleon to his wife?"

Brittany raised her hand. "You can tell they really loved the women in their lives."

"Exactly. These letters eloquently express what the writers were feeling. Remember, they didn't have airplanes, cars, or even motorcycles. So distances were a lot greater back then. They didn't get to Skype, tweet, or call on their cell phones. They didn't receive email updates or texts about what was going on at home." She raised her brows. "These men were sometimes separated from their families for months, sometimes years. They missed their wives, and they missed seeing their children grow up."

She rifled through the letters on her desk, found the one she wanted, and raised it. "Remember the letters from the Civil War? At night, these men were cold, hungry, perhaps wet, muddy, or injured. They didn't have fancy tents and sleeping bags to keep out the chill. And what did they think about? What did they talk about? Home and family. Wives, girlfriends, children, parents, friends, and other loved ones."

Lindsay raised her hand. "It's so romantic. I still love the idea of doing love letters for our fundraiser. Do you think Principal Parker will okay it?"

Julie glanced around, and a twinge of anxiety tightened her stomach. When she and her students had talked about it before, Julie had encouraged the idea. But what if it bombed? "Is everyone on board? Do you really want to write and sell love letters for the fundraiser? Candy bars may be easier."

The kids looked around at one another and talked amongst themselves for a moment. There were a few grumbles, but in the end, when Lindsay faced forward, she smiled and said, "Yes, definitely. We want to kick butt and outsell any fundraiser that came before us."

Julie smiled. Competitive much? "Okay, then. I'll give it my best shot." She must really like these kids, because they didn't know what they were asking of her. Six months after the "event" as she liked to refer to her embarrassing behavior, she still could barely look Dane Parker in the face.

Not Dane, she reminded herself, but *Principal Parker.* She needed emotional distance. His laughter, then embarrassment, over her passionate declaration—it all still felt like it had happened yesterday. Especially when she saw him face to face. The only positive thing to have come out of the "event" was that he seemed to have kept his mouth solidly shut about it. Otherwise, she probably would have tried to transfer to a different high school by now.

She straightened her shoulders, determined to forget about the principal and focus on her students. "Okay, take out your pens. We're going to practice writing sonnets."

Two

ane walked into the faculty lounge. As always, his gaze scanned for Julie. She had her back to him, her long, golden hair curling about her shoulders, as she talked to the history teacher, Clive Hansen. As usual, her hands flew in the air as she spoke. Whatever she said was apparently fascinating, because the man couldn't take his gaze off her.

Dane understood, because he had the same problem. She made it too easy. She never looked in his direction anymore, which allowed him to look his fill.

Dane cleared his throat. "Okay, folks, let's call this meeting to order."

Karen McDonald, his super-efficient secretary, hurried forward to give him the agenda.

As everyone took a seat around the oval table, he laid the sheet of paper in front of him and scanned the list of items to discuss. One was the fundraiser Julie was in charge of. Once he brought it up, she'd have to talk to him directly. It immediately went to the top of the list.

"Okay, everyone. It's time to talk about the fundraiser. Julie, I believe you're in charge this year, so I'll turn the time over to you."

As usual, Julie's gaze slid away from his as she stood. She looked nervous, her beautiful, heart-shaped face serious as she looked around at the other teachers. She cleared her throat. "As many of you know, we've been doing the same tired old fundraisers for years—specifically, selling candy bars and wrapping paper. The kids have come up with some new ideas this year that I think you'll all be excited about. It's something that's never been done before, and the kids are ready and willing to step up to make it a success."

She cleared her throat again. "As you all know, I teach honors English. We've been reviewing great love letters in history."

Dane couldn't help it. He flinched as Julie looked his direction, her brown eyes wide and vulnerable. She straightened her shoulders, and her cheeks pinked before she looked away.

Dane tried to keep his expression blank. But *love letters? Really?* After what had happened between the two of them?

She took a deep breath. "Anyway, the kids came up with the great idea of writing and selling love letters at lunchtime in the commons. It will give them a chance to use their writing skills, and we think it could really take off with the student body."

"Wait," Dane said, holding up a hand.

She didn't so much as glance his direction. "We could sell generic love letters in bulk and personalized love letters for a higher price. We plan to call them all *love letters*, but they could also be personalized notes of appreciation for parents, friends, or teachers, too. Some will be in poetry."

Dane could see teachers around the table shaking their heads in disapproval.

"We realize that the possibility exists that some letters could be given in jest," Julie spoke faster. "But I trust my students not to cross any lines, and I think this will be a good experience—"

Dane stood. "No."

Julie straightened. "But the kids are really excited about it."

"While I appreciate the fact that you've put a lot of thought into this—"

"Not me! The kids. Believe it or not, this wasn't my idea at all."

He sat back down. He didn't believe it. Not for a second. What he believed was that she came here to beleaguer, harass, and otherwise torture him. If that was her agenda, she was succeeding. "Be that as it may, I see too many problems associated with the idea."

Her eyes narrowed. "For instance?"

He tapped his index finger on the table. He really wished he could give her what she wanted. He wished she'd look at him with gratitude rather than with anger. "Hurt feelings. Bullying. Kids sending love letters to other kids in a mean-spirited way." He considered keeping his mouth closed, then changed his mind. "Or, someone who isn't ready for something as big as a heartfelt love letter coming his or her way and unintentionally hurting the sender's feelings."

Julie glared at him from across the table; hopefully she'd received the message. He'd never been able to smooth things over with her after he'd reacted so horribly, and taking the chance now, in a room full of people, ensured that she'd actually hear him.

She laid one clenched fist on the table. "I think the kids may surprise you if you'd give this a chance."

"They'll have to surprise me in other ways. Like in how much money they make. We're planning for the proceeds to buy a Wolverine sign to place on the outside wall of the gym. The seniors are really excited about it. If we use a tried-and-true formula, we can pretty much count on making the $3,000 needed for the sign. If we do an untried and untested fundraiser, it could end up being a flop, and we won't have the money when we need it."

"It won't flop."

"It could. You can't guarantee it. I say we go with chocolate bars."

Julie took a deep breath. "I say we take a vote. And keep in mind my honors English class will be completely disappointed if this isn't approved. So who's for the love letters?"

Most faculty members looked away, and only one, Julie's best friend, Kayla Stone, raised a hand in support.

As Julie's mouth tightened, Dane found himself feeling sorry for her and wanting to comfort her. Not that he would or could in the circumstances.

"Are you kidding me?" She lifted a hand into the air. "Come on. Do we really want to send these kids the message that creativity is not to be encouraged? How are they supposed to feel when I go back and tell them that it's going to be candy bars again? How can I face them?"

Dane shrugged. "By telling them that sometimes playing it safe will help them reach their goals?"

Julie placed her palms on the table and leaned toward him. "Fine, but there are two parts to this, and the second one involves you personally. Are you going to disappoint them twice?"

Dane sighed as he looked over at Julie, who was quivering with passion, and he really hoped he could give her the second part of what she was asking for. "Okay, let's have it. What is it?"

"You said yourself that the kids usually make about $3,000 on these fundraisers, right? Well, they came up with a plan to help sell the love letters—"

"Candy bars," he said.

"Fine, candy bars. If we sell $5,000's worth of candy bars—"

The math teacher snorted. Julie glared at the man, and Dane was glad her ire was raised at someone else for the moment. But he had to admit he agreed with Scott. No way could they raise that much in four weeks.

"Yes?" Dane prompted. "If your fundraiser makes $5,000 . . ."

"Then you'll shave your head at the Valentine's dance."

Dane's brows rose. He chuckled. "Shave my head? No way. It's January. I'd freeze."

"In Southern Utah? You'll be fine. Besides, it would give the students the motivation to sell more *candy bars*." She stressed the last two words.

He shook his head. "Forget it. Chalk the whole thing up to a bad idea."

"According to you, they won't possibly sell that many candy bars anyway. You implied that $3,000 is their limit. What do you have to lose?"

"My hair."

Laughter filled the room. He'd be tempted to agree if he didn't think the reason she wanted him to shave his head was because she wanted payback. He knew good and well what this was really about. When she'd written him that cursed flowery, eloquent letter six months ago he'd thought she was joking and laughed. Only when he'd looked up to see her watching him across the commons, her expression devastated, had he realized she'd been sincere.

"Fine," said Julie. "I'm sure the kids will be surprised at your lack of support." She finally sat down.

Dane took a breath. "Okay, next on the agenda." As the meeting continued, he tried his best not to look at Julie smoldering at the other end of the table.

When the room started clearing, she was the first to gather her things. He considered calling her back and trying to talk to her alone but knew it wouldn't do any good.

She was as unforgiving as she was beautiful. And he needed to come up with something better than a short talk in his office if he was ever going to win her.

Three

Dane looked over at his friend Chad, realized he was almost done folding his parachute, and pressed his own against the picnic table to make sure all the air was out of his next fold. He looked up at the empty sky. "Where's the plane?"

Chad shrugged. "I talked to Jerry this morning. He should be here anytime. Did you bring your gloves?"

"I did." The weather wasn't too bad. A clear day, mid-forties, in January was certainly bearable. Having grown up in Minnesota, Dane found Southern Utah practically balmy. But when they made the jump out of a plane at 12,000 feet above ground level, it would be freezing. Fortunately the adrenaline rush would offset some of the cold.

"So what's new on the Julie front?"

"Don't ask."

Chad lifted his head, blue eyes amused, brown hair

lifting slightly in the breeze. "Come on. I'm asking. I really want to know."

"She wants me to shave my head."

"What? And then she'll take your sorry butt back again?"

"We were never a couple, so she can't exactly take me back, can she? Not that getting together was ever on the table. If it were, I'd shave my head today, tattoo it with her name, and walk in a Speedo down Main. Bluff Street too, if she wanted. But, no. I think the humiliation factor is all Julie is thinking about here. She wrapped it up in a fundraiser. *If we make so much money will you shave your head?* She thinks it'll inspire the kids or some such crap."

Chad was laughing by this point. "Oh, man. That sucks. She's never going to forgive you, is she? Hearing stuff like that makes it scary to date these days. You never know if you're going to end up with a psycho or not, you know?"

"Julie is not a psycho. She's the furthest thing from it. She's passionate, that's all."

"Yeah," Chad said doubtfully. "I guess. But still. Her writing you that love letter and all . . . then not talking to you when you didn't give her back your heart on a platter or something. I'm just sayin'."

Dane finished packing his parachute and looked up so he could glare. "Sayin' what?"

"I'm just sayin' get online, find a date, and forget about Julie. Or better yet, let me set you up on a blind date. It'll be fun."

"I'm still holding out hope that she'll change her mind and decide I'm one of the good guys."

"Dude. Wake up. She already did change her mind about you. She liked you, and now she doesn't. Anyway, you weren't even that into her when she wrote that letter."

He checked his gear again. "I wasn't sure how I felt back then. I was confused. It's not easy to admit that there may be only one girl in the world for you when the world is full of them."

"And now you know?"

"Now I know."

"Because of her letter?"

"Among other things."

"Like what?"

Dane shrugged. Her hair, her face, her curvy figure, the passionate way she attacked life. Everything about her appealed to him. He thought about the cat currently taking up space in his house. Five months ago, as a kitten, it was supposed to have gone to Julie. It was meant to soften her heart. When she'd refused to accept it, or anything from him, he should have gotten rid of the thing. But in his mind, it was still Julie's cat, and as soon as she forgave him, he'd try giving it to her again.

A soft buzzing turned out to be the airplane they'd been waiting for, and they turned to watch as it descended, finally landing on the short tarmac near the Hurricane, Utah, sign.

"Let's go," Chad said.

Dane finished strapping on his gear and zipped his jumpsuit. He checked his shoelaces, popped in a breath mint to avoid cotton mouth, and picked up his pack and helmet. He grinned. "Let's do this."

As they walked out, Jerry hopped out of the small airplane and greeted them with a firm handshake. "You boys ready?"

"Ready," they both agreed.

Jerry helped stow their gear. Chad climbed into the plane, and Dane followed.

Once they were settled, Chad asked, "Do you still have it? Her letter?"

"Yes," he said, as Jerry climbed back inside, did a check, and guided the plane toward the far side of the runway.

"You ever going to let me read it?"

Dane shook his head. "Not on your life."

"Must have been some letter. Have you ever considered the fact that pining for Julie is your way of staying out of the dating game? Playing it safe? I mean, I get it. It can be a total drag doing that first meet and greet and trying to come up with something to say."

Dane turned to look at his friend. "Are you saying I'm playing it safe? You do realize I'm about to jump out of an airplane, right?"

Chad grinned and slapped Dane on the back. "Dude, seriously. Even I know that risking your life is way easier than risking your heart."

As the airplane rose into the air, Dane looked out the window. Was that what he was doing, staying safely in bachelor mode by pinning his hopes on a girl who wouldn't have him?

He shook his head to clear it. Maybe it was time for him to take this game he was playing with Julie to the next level. Find out if there really was anything there and, if there wasn't, admit it was time to move on.

Four

Julie was running a bit late. In fact, she was a little reluctant about facing her class today. To make things worse, when she finally walked into honors English, the kids, half of them sitting on top of their desks, were already in a heated discussion.

She moved to stand in front of her own desk. "What's up?"

Evan straightened from a slouch. "We heard that Principal Parker says we can't write love notes. It's not like we were dying to anyway. It's just that we want to make some real money."

Julie slowly set her book bag beside her chair, giving herself time to think. She straightened. "Kids, I can't tell you how sorry I am. I went to bat for you, but he refused."

"Is he still going to shave his head if we sell a lot of candy bars?" Hannah asked.

Julie shook her head. "No. He's not going to do that. Again, I'm sorry." She looked at their disappointed faces and wished there was something she could do.

"What exactly did he say?" Caleb asked.

Julie shrugged. "He just said no. He didn't give a reason." She tried to keep her face carefully neutral, because she was afraid she might look guilty. She *felt* guilty. While she couldn't know for sure, she suspected that *she* might be part of the reason he'd refused. No doubt after she'd humiliated herself in front of him six months ago, he considered her some kind of crazy person. He probably wouldn't do anything she wanted for fear she'd fall for him again.

Which I won't.

But for him to take her sins out on the students? She really hoped she was wrong. Maybe he just had a bad case of vanity.

"But if all we get to do is sell candy bars, we still want to motivate kids to buy them." Jae, who rarely spoke, shook his head in disgust. "We want this fundraiser to go on record as being the best. The one that classes coming after us try to beat."

The others murmured in agreement.

"Oh." She smiled at their competitiveness. All of them were straight-A students with several honors classes. Rivalry was apparently part of their makeup. "That's an admirable goal. Since the love letter idea has been nixed, why don't we try to set a record with the candy bars? I like it. I'll do anything I can to help."

"Ms. Ashburn," Jae spoke up again. "That's fine and whatever, but in my last school, the principal shaved his head at the end of the fundraiser, and we earned a ton of money. Why won't Principal Parker do the same? Believe me, it'll get more kids buying. Can't you talk to him again?"

Julie looked over the expectant faces and wished she could do something. Finally, she bit her lip and shook her head. "I really am sorry, but the principal was pretty adamant."

The kids looked angry and disgusted. Julie drew in a breath, then slowly released it. She picked up her book. "Okay, let's get some work done. Please open your books to the section on Elizabeth Barrett Browning."

A series of groans went around the room, and the kids were slow about doing it, but eventually everyone took their seats and opened their books.

It was a shame about the fundraiser. These really were good kids. Was it possible that now that Dane had a chance to think about it, to get used to the idea, he'd change his mind? Even she had to admit that he was basically a good guy.

Maybe if she went to his house, rather than putting him on the spot in the faculty room, she could get a better response. It might be worth a shot. And if he refused again, at least she'd know that she'd tried her best.

If she didn't tell the students her plans, they wouldn't have to be disappointed twice if he refused. Decision made, she opened her book.

Five

As Julie approached Dane's house, her heart pounded in her chest. *She shouldn't be doing this.* She stopped on his front porch, arms crossed as she stared at the stark white door, and forced herself to even out her breathing. *What if she said something stupid? What if he said something horrible? What if her coming here made everything worse?* She quickly raised her fist before she could change her mind and knocked sharply.

Within seconds, Dane answered, and his brows rose. He looked so handsome standing there, his light-brown hair slightly rumpled as if he'd been lying down, his body fit and looking good in casual clothes, his expression so happy her stomach tightened in reaction. She felt a strong tug of attraction but, clenching her fingers together, tried to ignore any and all sensations. When would these feelings for him shut off? When would they fade away? When could she get on with an emotional life that didn't include this man standing before her?

Julie suddenly had a really bad feeling about this—sort of like the feeling she'd had when she'd sent one of her students to give Dane the heartfelt love letter at the end of the school year last summer. Too late now. At this point, she had to say something. "Principal Parker, I really need to talk to you."

"Julie, please call me Dane." He stepped back to allow her more room. "Do you want to come in?"

She hesitated but, not wanting him to think she was afraid of him, went inside to see a tastefully decorated living room with masculine, plush furniture, all done in beige.

It was so completely different from the colorful splashes she had in her own place, which reminded her that she'd never been here before, which made what she'd done six months earlier seem even crazier. Her cheeks heated.

"I'm here to try to talk you into agreeing to shave your head for the fundraiser." When he opened his mouth to say something, she held up a hand. "You've already gotten everything else your own way. You'll be happy to know we're not writing the—love letters." She swallowed, almost choking on the last two words. She couldn't help it. She still cringed every time she thought about the way her letter had exposed her feelings to a man who wasn't the slightest bit interested in her.

"I'm just trying to find a way to motivate the kids," she went on. "They're very disappointed that you won't go along with this. I don't understand what the problem is. You're a guy, and it's just hair, and it'll grow back fast. Lots of guys are bald, anyway."

"Do you want to sit down?

She didn't, but if he was going to be hospitable, maybe that boded well for the negotiation. At least he wasn't kicking her out.

An off-white cat with brilliant blue eyes strolled into the

room, jumped up on the beige couch, and curled up on one side. It matched the furniture almost exactly. But it answered that question. Julie had often wondered what had happened to the kitten he'd tried to give her.

She sank onto the loveseat, leaned back, and crossed her arms and legs.

He sat in the armchair across from her and leaned forward, resting his elbows on his knees. "Julie, if I really thought this was about a fundraiser and motivating the kids, I might be tempted to say yes. But I suspect this is more about what happened between us six months ago. I've already apologized, but I'd like to say again that I'm sorry."

Julie swiped a hand in the air. "This is nothing to do with that. This is about the students and what they want."

He let out a breath and leaned back into the couch. "I'm not convinced, so the answer is still no."

Julie jumped up, paced to the window, and looked out. "How do I convince you that one thing has nothing to do with the other?"

He sighed. "Sorry, I'm not buying it."

She turned to look at him. "What do I need to do to convince you?"

"If you truly have no hard feelings, how about dinner on Saturday night?"

Fear spiked down her spine. She headed for the door. "We have nothing else to talk about."

He stood. "Julie, please, sit down. We've needed to talk for a long time now, and I, for one, am glad you're here."

Julie stopped and looked at the sleeping cat. "I want my cat back."

Dane followed her gaze and shook his head. "No way. You didn't want the cat. You gave it back to me, and now it's mine."

"Then I want my letter back." At that statement, she could feel a rush of heat to her face. But while she was here, while she was in the same vicinity as the letter, she might as well try to retrieve it. The thought of him over here reading it, rereading it, showing it to friends and family, laughing, had eaten at her for the last six months. "It's mine."

"What's really going on here?" he asked.

"What's going on is that I want my letter back."

"I don't have any letter that belongs to you."

"How can you say that? I can't stand knowing that you have it, and I want it back."

"It's mine."

"Then give me the cat."

"The cat's mine too." He sighed. "Look. Please sit down. I'm glad we're having this chance to talk."

"I bet you are." She could not believe she'd asked him for the letter. All these months, she hadn't said a word about it, and neither had he. Now it was out in the open, the elephant in the room, and her bringing it up only highlighted how much it meant to her. Maybe even how much his rejection had hurt. Certainly, how much it had embarrassed her. Why had she said anything?

Again, she headed toward the door.

"Hold on. Where are you going?"

But she didn't stop. She wrenched the door open and hurried down the walk and out to her car, which was parked against the curb. She didn't realize he'd followed her until she unlocked the door. She got inside and, with a press of a button, locked all the doors.

His expression impatient, Dane tapped on the glass. "Julie." His voice was muffled.

Her hands gripped the steering wheel. Why did she have to keep messing up with this guy? What was it about him that made her turn into an idiot every time she was around him? She started up the car and pulled away. Maybe it was time to find a new job.

Six

"Wait up!"

Julie turned around to see Kayla Stone hurrying after her, curly red hair teased high, moving this way and that as she dodged kids in the hallway then closed in on Julie.

"Hey," Julie said. "How's it going?"

Kayla grinned. "Oh, you know, it's great, if you don't mind drool on all the desks. We're watching movies today in video productions, and at least half the kids fall asleep every period, dripping puddles onto their desks. It's disgusting. We have to clean up with Windex and paper towels before the bell rings. Yuck and double yuck."

Julie laughed and started walking again. "We're still studying love letters in honors English, and so far, no one is falling asleep."

"Ooh." Kayla's eyebrows waggled. "Anything risqué?"

"Oh, sure. I found plenty of naughty letters." Julie winked at her friend. "But those aren't the ones we read in class."

"Too bad. Set them aside for me. Anything new with you?"

Julie looked around at the students crowding the hallway and, when she didn't see Dane, turned back to Kayla. "I went by Principal Parker's house yesterday," she said, her tone low.

Kayla's mouth fell open as she moved around a crowd of girls, then came close once more. "Oh my gosh. Oh my gosh. What happened? Tell me everything. Don't leave anything out."

Julie laughed but looked around again. "I asked him for my letter back."

Kayla's eyes went wide. Her mouth gaped. "*No.* You did not do that. You just did not! What did he say?"

Julie shrugged. "He said no. He says that to me a lot lately."

Kayla grabbed hold of her shoulder, stopped her, and forced her to turn around. A kid jostled them, but Kayla maintained eye contact. "Are you telling me you went to his house, asked him for the letter—"

"And for the cat."

Kayla's eyebrows pulled together. "The one he tried to give you? And he said no?"

Julie nodded once. "That's what I'm saying."

Kayla let go of Julie's shoulder and twirled in a circle, earning her a few looks from the kids trying to get to class. She stopped, a wide grin on her face. "I can't believe this, Jules. This is unbelievable. You go to his house, you humiliate yourself, and he says no?"

Julie shot her friend a glance. "I didn't exactly humiliate myself."

"Close enough. And he wouldn't even give you the cat? You know what this means, don't you?"

"Yes. I don't have a letter or a cat."

"No. It means he *likes you*."

Julie made a scoffing sound. "Six months ago, he made it pretty clear how he feels about me."

"I don't know. What if we got it all wrong? He did try to give you an expensive cat."

"We didn't get it wrong. *I* didn't." Julie shook her head and started walking down the hall again. Kayla quickly followed.

"Ms. Ashburn," a breathless voice said behind her. "It's working."

Julie and Kayla stopped and turned to see Angela Hart a few feet away and closing fast. She held up a five-dollar bill.

"What's working?" Julie asked.

"We're selling candy bars for a dollar apiece. But if someone wants us to add a love letter, we charge another four dollars. And people are paying it!"

"Wait. You're selling love letters?"

Kayla laughed and clapped her hands.

Julie shot Kayla a narrow-eyed glare. "You're not helping." She turned back to Angela. "I thought I'd made it clear that Principal Parker nixed the idea of writing love letters. He said we couldn't do it."

Angela's chin rose. "All the money is going into the fundraiser, so what does it matter?" She took off running.

"Angela, wait!"

The young girl was quickly lost in the lunch crowd.

Julie turned to Kayla. "What am I going to do about this? Dane is going to kill me."

Kayla arched a brow. "*Dane* now, is it?"

Julie blushed. "Principal Parker."

"I say just go with it. You told the kids not to do it. If they're selling love letters under the table, it has nothing to do with you."

"He'll never believe that. I wish I didn't know about it."

"So pretend you don't. Just tell the kids that if they're doing it, to keep it to themselves. Wink, wink."

Julie shook her head. Somehow, this would come back to bite her on the backside.

Seven

The next day, Julie stood in front of her honors class, brows raised. "Does anyone want to explain what's going on with the love letters? I thought we agreed not to write and sell them."

"We don't know anything about that, Miss Ashburn," the suddenly quiet Jae said from the front row. His lips tilted in a barely there smile.

"Uh huh." She looked out at the classroom. "Just so you know, I can't condone going behind Principal Parker's back. So no more love letters, please."

"Yes, Ms. Ashburn," the class said as a whole.

She pursed her lips. "All right. So long as we understand each other. Open your books to page 64. Jae, start reading the second paragraph aloud, please."

With her book open, Julie read along as she walked back and forth at the front of the classroom, throwing out an occasional comment. When Jae finished, she gave out a writing assignment that would take up the rest of class time.

As the kids started it, Julie sat at her desk and noticed an envelope lying off to the side. She picked it up, pulled out two folded pieces of paper, and started to read.

A few paragraphs in, her eyes narrowed, and she glanced up at the class. No one was looking at her. No one paid her any attention at all as they wrote their assignments.

She flipped to the second page and glanced at the signature. Dane Parker? Her breath caught as her heart started to pound. The signature was bold, like the man himself. She flipped the page over and started to read again.

I'm sorry for the conflict between us. I can't get you out of my mind. I hope you can forgive me for being such a hard case. My attraction to you makes me nervous, and I'm not myself around you. Your eyes are like starlight; your face, your voice, the very thought of you keeps me awake at night. I've dreamed of sliding my fingers into your hair, of holding you close, and . . .

Breathless, she flipped the page.

to prove myself, if your students earn $5,000, I'll shave my head.
Love, forever and eternally,
Dane Parker

Julie quickly glanced up at her students, certain she'd catch some of them watching her, but no one paid her the slightest bit of attention as, heads bent, they worked on their assignments.

She read the signature again, read the entire letter again. When the bell rang, the students stood, gathered their things, and hurried toward the door. Not one of them acted out of the ordinary.

"Are you coming to the assembly, Miss Ashburn?" Hannah, the last one out, asked at the door.

"Oh. Yes. I'm coming right now." Julie placed the letter in her purse, slung it over her shoulder, and headed down the crowded hall to the assembly.

As it was her job to introduce the fundraiser at the assembly, she headed to the front row, where Dane and several teachers sat. Normally she would have taken the empty chair on the end, as far from Dane as possible. Today, she took the seat beside him and smiled shyly.

He shot her a questioning glance, then smiled back. She looked down, pleased and embarrassed at the same time.

Announcements were made, and the juniors put on a couple of skits, and then it was her turn to talk about the fundraiser.

She removed the second page of the letter, stuffed the envelope back in her purse, and slowly walked up the stairs to the podium. She glanced at Dane and smiled again before starting. "As everyone knows, we are doing the candy bar fundraiser again this year."

Groans rippled through the audience, followed by a couple of loud boos. She chuckled; nothing could break her good mood.

"We usually have a goal of earning $3,000, but this year the plan is to go higher. And to help motivate us to reach our goal, Principal Parker has agreed that if we raise $5,000, he will shave his head." She held up the letter as proof.

The kids erupted into cheers. She looked down to the front row to smile at Dane, but he shot her an incredulous, angry look, surprising her.

Shaken, she lifted her chin and looked over the audience. "Let's give it our best shot!"

As everyone cheered, she returned to her seat, passing Dane as he headed toward the stairs. He snatched the letter out of her hand as he walked past her and climbed the stairs. He quickly scanned the page, then, setting the letter down and gripping the wood of the podium, he sighed loudly and began to speak.

"Well, it looks like I'm good and caught. On the positive side, we've never made more than $3,000 on this fundraiser. While I was hoping to make more this year, I'm now hoping we don't earn more than $4,999. So don't feel like you need to sell *too* many candy bars."

As the kids laughed and yelled encouragement to each other, Julie sat stunned. She fingered the necklace at her throat, crossed her legs, and bounced her foot. What had just happened? She glanced over her shoulder and saw two of her students, Angela and Jae, looking very pleased with themselves as they whispered to each other. Jae spotted her and froze.

She sank back into her seat. They had written this letter. Her chin trembled as humiliation washed over her. They'd used her to trap Dane and force his hand. How could they have guessed that such a letter would lure her into action rather than embarrass her? Had Dane told someone at the school about the letter she'd written? She didn't think he'd do something like that, but . . .

She pressed her hands to her hot face. As she thought about how gooey she'd gone inside at the slightest bit of attention from him, shame enveloped her. She was so pathetic. She was so glad he didn't have the first page in his possession, only the second.

As soon as the assembly ended, she jumped up and hurried away.

"Julie. Wait up." From Dane's tone, she could tell that wasn't a request, but a command. She stopped and slowly turned.

He walked over and held up the letter. "What do you think you're playing at? I never wrote this."

"Yeah, I kind of just realized that. It was on my desk this afternoon. "

"You thought I'd written it?"

Lips compressed, she nodded once. "Your signature was on it." Again, she was so glad she had the first page, with all its talk of love and sensuality, in her purse.

"Was there more to the letter? This looks incomplete, and it's signed 'Love, Forever and Eternally.'"

Her cheeks were on fire. "I threw the first part away."

His head lowered, and his lips pressed flat as he studied her face. She could tell he didn't believe her, but he didn't press the issue, for which she was grateful.

"I'm really sorry about this, Principal Parker. Maybe we won't earn the money, and you won't have to go through with it."

"We can only hope."

She nodded. "I really am sorry." She looked around for Jae and Angela, but they were long gone. She rubbed her forehead. "Look, I have to ask. Did you show anyone the letter I wrote you? Someone here at the school?"

"No. I haven't shown it to anyone."

She couldn't even look at him. "I'm just wondering how the kids thought to send me this letter today."

"I have no idea, but not from anyone seeing your letter, I can guarantee you that."

She nodded once. "Okay."

"So you know who wrote it?"

"I have my suspicions. I think some of my honors students need to spend a little time in detention after school."

He sighed. "Look, it's okay. If they make the money, it's not a big deal. I'll do it."

"Thanks," she said weakly. She just wanted to disappear. "That's great. I'll let the kids know." She snatched the fake letter out of his hand and walked away.

"Julie, wait."

But she didn't. Once again, all she wanted to do was get away from him.

Eight

Dane placed his hands behind his back and gripped his wrist as he watched Julie hurry through the crowd, her eagerness to ditch him apparent. He stood there, his muscles rigid, his jaw clenched.

Their every interaction, no matter how big or small, never seemed to turn out right anymore. He remembered how she'd acted toward him when she'd sat down today in the auditorium. She'd been softer and had actually smiled at him. Sort of like the old days before she'd written him that love note.

Last night after she'd left, he'd taken the letter out of his dresser drawer and reread it. He'd cursed his old self for being such a schmuck. What he wouldn't give to relive that moment, find Julie in the crowd and smile back instead of laughing at the flowery language. What an idiot he'd been. She'd laid her heart bare, and he'd laughed. He probably didn't deserve her.

In retrospect, he wished he hadn't called her on the forged letter today. He should have just gone along and acted like he'd written it. Pretended that shaving his head had been his idea. He'd ended up agreeing to it anyway, so he might as well have earned her gratitude for it.

What could have been written on the first page, anyway? Whatever it was, it had definitely mellowed her attitude toward him. He'd pay good money to know what the key to softening Julie's heart was.

He considered asking her honors English students, but he'd probably end up looking like the love-struck idiot he was. How had they known to write her that letter, anyway? He chuckled without humor. They were smart kids. The way he looked at her, his heart on his sleeve, probably gave them the idea.

The vice principal headed his way, and Dane willed his features to go blank as he walked toward his coworker. Now wasn't the time or the place, but eventually he'd have to have it out with Julie, and soon, before she drove him absolutely crazy.

Nine

The next afternoon, Julie faced her honors English class. She didn't say anything for a long moment, just looked at each student in turn. There was a lot of squirming and uncomfortable glances upward, then down again, plus a little bit of outright alarm. When the silence was practically screaming, Julie finally spoke.

"Here's the deal. I'm not going to name any names, even though I think I know who the culprits are. I'm just going to say that when we came up with the idea of writing love letters, it was supposed to be fun. Maybe Principal Parker was right about bullying and hurt feelings resulting from a fundraiser idea like that." She paused a long moment. "Was he?"

Some heads stayed down; other kids looked confused as they looked at their classmates and tried to understand what they'd missed. A few mumbled no, and she heard a lot of foot shuffling.

Since no one seemed to be looking at her, Julie considered the possibility that they'd all been in on it. "I'm not saying that my feelings were hurt by the fake love letter someone left on my desk." She lifted the two pieces of paper in one hand. "All I'm saying is that I thought I'd been quite clear that these were to be *nonfiction* letters, not fictional ones."

She walked over to the board, where she tacked up the word FICTION, a piece of paper she'd prepared earlier, and attached the letter, minus Dane's forged signature, to the board. "I'm just going to consider this letter as fictional. Basically, whoever wrote it lied. Luckily, your principal is a good sport." She turned around again. "As am I. Here's what we're going to do. No more love letters. We're selling candy bars. Period."

The kids groaned—she finally got a reaction out of them. She raised an eyebrow. "Yes? Any comments?"

"Come on, Ms. Ashburn," Jae said. What had happened to the kid who never spoke up in class? "The letters are selling really well. We make three times the money when we attach a love letter to a candy bar."

Julie's brows rose. "Three times?"

Angela raised a hand. "They really are making us a lot of extra money. Don't you want to see Principal Parker shave his head?"

"Sure," Julie admitted. "I'd love nothing better. I just don't want you hooligans running around the school with poison pens, writing letters for people whose feelings could end up getting hurt."

"We swear we won't do that," Jae said. "It's just that you're such a good sport, we thought it'd be funny."

She eyed the boy, gratified that she'd been right about one of the culprits. "What you thought was that I'd announce Principal Parker's agreement to shave his head, and then he'd be forced to go along with it."

A pleased smile briefly lit the boy's face, and she narrowed her eyes at him until he looked down. The kid was too smart for his own good.

"You're really making three times the amount?" asked Julie.

They all nodded. She thought about how pathetic she must have looked to Dane when she'd been all smiles, standing at the podium earlier. Heat built in her face. "As much as I'd love to see Principal Parker shave his head—and believe me, I do, quite a bit—I can't condone selling love letters after the principal specifically said no."

"Come on, Ms. Ashburn. Have a heart," Evan said.

"Of course . . ." Julie sat in the chair behind her desk and picked up a piece of paper, then started scribbling nonsense. "The problem is, I'm obligated to shut you down when I know you're doing something wrong. This is your official shut-down notice. If I hadn't known about it, we wouldn't be having this conversation. But since I *do* know about it, it's back to the candy bars."

She glanced up to see the kids straightening in their seats and grinning at each other.

"We're clear, right? No love letters with the candy bars." She figured kids as bright as her honors students would get the message.

"Yes, Ms. Ashburn," they chorused.

"Okay, then. If you will all open your books to page 85 . . ."

She felt a little guilty. She shouldn't have encouraged the kids. But if they'd really learned their lesson, and if they really were making three times the money, what was the harm?

If Principal Parker asked her if she had anything to do with it, she could honestly say she'd told the kids not to do it. And if the kids made $5,000, it would serve that smug, self-righteous man right. Watching his glossy hair fall to the gym floor would go a long way toward assuaging her embarrassment.

Ten

Dane sat in his office, staring at his computer screen. Between interruptions and phone calls, he wasn't getting much done.

He kept seeing Julie's face in his mind. Kept reliving the way she'd met his gaze. Her shy smile and shining eyes.

What on earth could have been on the missing page that could have put that look on her face? And how could he recreate it?

He focused again, typing a few more words on the fourth draft of the letter. As soon as he finished, he'd write it out, but it turned out expressing feelings was harder than he'd expected. Maybe he'd been too quick to nix the love letter fundraising idea. If he'd allowed it, he could have hired one of her students to write this letter for him.

He gave a snort of exasperation. After laying her heart on the line the way she had, Julie deserved a real love letter.

One he wrote himself. Otherwise, it wouldn't count. Not in her eyes, anyway. Instinctively, he just knew.

He put his fingers on the keyboard again, bouncing one knee up and down. He should have done this a long time ago. Unfortunately he'd been too thick-headed to realize it. He started typing again as he tried to lay his heart on the line. But he ran out of words, rubbed his forehead, and sat back. He picked up a stress ball and threw it hand to hand. Trying to declare his feelings once and for all was exhausting. As soon as he got the words right, he'd write it out in longhand, attach it to a candy bar, and finally let her know how he felt.

If his letter could elicit the same reaction as the other letter, he'd be a happy man.

Eleven

Coming back from lunch with Kayla, Julie locked her car and headed toward the front doors of the high school. "Thanks for going to Cracker Barrel with me today. I needed to get away."

"You shouldn't let the little buggers get to you so much."

Fake letter aside, it wasn't so much the students getting to her as it was the principal. She didn't want to discuss the whole thing quite yet, and reaching that point would take longer than a lunch break. She shrugged. "It's just been a long week."

"When the kids get to me, I pull out a can of mace and a hammer, set them on my desk, and stare the class down."

Julie laughed. "You do not."

Kayla smiled, her wild red hair blowing in the breeze. "In my mind I do, so it's almost the same thing. It makes me feel better, and I think it puts a vibe out into the air. It says, 'I'm on edge. Don't cross the line, or you'll regret it,'" she said menacingly. She stuck her straw in her mouth, took a noisy sip of soda, then chucked the paper cup in a garbage can outside the doors. "It could just be my imagination, which I admit is a good one, but it makes me feel better anyway."

"I'll remember that," Julie said dryly. She opened one of the doors and let Kayla go first. "You're a kook, do you know that?"

Kayla grinned. "Yes. Yes, I do."

"Ms. Ashburn? *Hey, wait up.*"

Julie and Kayla turned as one to see Mason Wright, a sophomore from second period English, running toward them.

"I've been looking everywhere for you. I'm in the office during second lunch, and if I don't get back soon, they'll think I'm ditching." He handed her a small package. "This is for you. Gotta go." He turned around and took off running.

It was a candy bar with a note wrapped around it. Julie shook her head. She huffed out a breath and looked at Kayla. "Those kids are really pushing it." She held up the candy bar. "I told them I don't want to know about it if they're still selling love notes, so they send me one?"

"Maybe it's not from them. Or maybe it's a thank you for being such a cool teacher. I got one of those from a kid hoping I'd let him do extra credit." She grinned. "It worked."

Julie plucked the love note off the candy bar, opened it, and scanned the text. Her lips tightened. "Are you kidding me? Seriously, those kids are so dead."

"Mace dead or hammer dead?"

Julie laughed and handed the note over. "That imagination of yours is going to get you in trouble one of these days. I think I'll stick with detention, or at least the threat of it."

As they walked toward the stairs, Kayla read the note.

"Another one from Principal Parker? They're not very original, are they?"

"Ooh. Good one. I'll use that. When I tell my honor students they lack originality, it will tweak them worse than mace or a hammer would."

Kayla handed the paper back. "It's sweet. Don't give them too hard a time. They probably can tell you still have the hots for our good principal and are trying their hand at matchmaking."

Julie stopped in her tracks. "I do not have the hots."

"Never, never underestimate the cunning or intuitiveness of a seventeen-year-old. I don't. I'm always on guard. A fleeting expression probably gave you away."

Julie sighed and started walking again. "I repeat, I do not have the hots for that man."

"Whatever. Come on, let's get to class before the little buggers run riot. At this age, they can flash to mob mentality in seconds. It's the hormones."

"Why do you teach high school if you're so distrustful of teenagers?"

"Are you kidding? That's what makes them interesting. It's almost like I have a job taming lions or tigers or bears."

"Oh, my." Julie laughed again. "You really are a loon."

Kayla grinned. "It's why you like me so much."

They parted ways at the top of the stairs, and Julie headed to her classroom. If her students were matchmaking, she would put a stop to it before they embarrassed her again.

Twelve

When Julie entered the classroom, her gaze immediately shot to Jae Boswell, then to Angela Hart. Neither looked particularly guilty of anything, but you never knew for sure. Julie chuckled. Kayla's distrustful attitude was rubbing off on her.

She stopped in the front of the room and cleared her throat. When all eyes centered on her, she walked to the corkboard.

"Okay, kids." She took the new love letter and tacked it under the FICTION label with the other bogus letter the kids had written. "While I'll admit this one is well thought out, and rather quite sweet, I must inform you that pulling the same stunt twice in the form of sending me another love letter from Principal Parker, is . . ." She turned so she could look out at the faces to see if anyone flinched. "Completely unoriginal."

No one moved. Not a cringe, a grimace, or a double-blink in sight. The little fakers. She rounded her desk so she could sit on the edge and cross her legs in front of her. "I thought we'd talked about this already, but if you feel the need to have another lecture on the subject, I'm game. The candy bar fundraiser is just that. We are *not* doing love letters, but if we were, the notes would be touching, funny, or complimentary. Above all, they would be non-fiction, like the ones we've been studying. Writing pretend love letters from one person to another leaves both parties feeling foolish. So *stop it.*"

The kids looked at one another as if searching for the culprit, innocence and confusion on their faces. Oh, yeah. They were good. "Are we clear?"

"Yes, Ms. Ashburn."

"Are we wanting extra homework assignments for the weekend?"

"No, Ms. Ashburn."

"Okay, then." She glanced over her shoulder at the love letter and felt a pang of regret. If Dane had really written any of those things, she'd have melted into a puddle, just like she'd done when she'd read the first one. She turned away to see a few students still watching her and remembered Kayla's warning that a fleeting expression could give her feelings away.

To Dane as well? The horror of that thought made her really want to put some distance between the two of them. Maybe it would be a good idea to start lining up something new for next year. If she transferred schools, she could better protect her heart.

So why did the idea of never seeing Dane again make her chest ache?

Thirteen

Dane drummed his fingers on his desk, sank back into his chair, and stared out the window. He was eager to see Julie's reaction to his letter. He glanced at the clock on the wall. She was teaching a class, so it wasn't like she could come see him. She wouldn't be free for a couple of hours, but he wasn't sure he could wait.

Pushing himself up, he headed for the door. He could easily call her into the hall for a moment. He wasn't getting any work done anyway. He grabbed his cell phone, stuffed it in his pocket, and headed out the door.

Karen straightened as he passed her desk. "Where are you going?"

He shrugged. "Just catching up on a few things."

She picked up her iPad and stood. "Do you want me to go with you to take notes?"

Dane managed to keep a straight face. As there might be

groveling involved on his part, Julie might appreciate notes so she could remember the conversation word for word. But *he* didn't need an audience. "No, thank you. You stay here."

Hurt flashed across her features.

He smiled gently. "You know how I depend on you to take care of things when I'm not around."

With a pleased expression, she sank down.

He nodded. "And I have my cell phone if I'm needed."

"Yes, sir."

He headed down the hallway. When Julie read the letter, had she been surprised? Probably. But what else? Happy? Charmed? Forgiving? A man could hope. He'd laid it on sort of thick, and perhaps a bit wordy, but she deserved it. She'd laid her heart on the line, and he could do no less.

He headed up the stairs to her classroom, taking his time, enjoying the sense of rising anticipation. How would she look? What expression would she have on her face when he showed up at her classroom? Julie could never hide her emotions. Everything she thought or felt flickered in her expressive brown eyes.

He reached the landing and headed down the left hallway, trying to think of an excuse for interrupting her class. No doubt she'd see right through him, but he needed something to distract the students.

He could ask if she needed anything . . . but . . . that would be weird.

He could check to see if she remembered the faculty meeting next week . . . but that was too far away to be convincing.

The fundraiser. Of course. He could check to see how the fundraiser was going.

Excuse at the ready, he reached her classroom, saw her sitting at her desk and heard her talking about composition. He lightly knocked on the open door. When she looked up, he entered. "Ms. Ashburn, sorry to interrupt, but I thought I'd stop by to ask how the fundraiser is going."

She glanced at him once, then away, her hair hiding her face so he couldn't see her expression. "Oh. Well, according to the kids, it's going great. But as the money won't be turned in until just before the dance, I can't give real numbers."

"You'll be impressed, Principal Parker," one of the boys said.

"Get ready to shave your head," a smiling girl added.

Dane raised a brow. "You really think you can earn the $5,000?"

"Piece of cake," said a cocky-looking boy with a smirk.

Dane reached up to rub the top of his head. "So, I won't need gel anymore?"

"You may need a hat to protect against sunburn," a girl offered. "Even in the winter, St. George is sunny."

"And some wax to shine it up," a boy said.

Another boy laughed. "*We* might need sunglasses to avoid the glare."

Dane chuckled. "I can see you're pretty confident, but talk is cheap. I'm not trading in my gel for wax until I see the cash."

The kids were all smiling when Dane turned to Julie so she could share in the fun, but when he looked her way, she ducked her head. Frustrating. He wanted, no, *needed* some kind of reaction from her. What had she thought of his letter? Had she even read it yet? Did it make up for him laughing at hers? Did it soften her feelings toward him in the least?

He blew out a breath. It looked like his questions would have to wait until the two of them could be alone for a moment, and apparently now wasn't the time. He sort of wished he'd waited for her to come to him now. "Okay, everyone. Carry on. Sorry for the interruption."

He turned to leave, but when he did, he glanced at the corkboard and paused. Two letters were posted there, both under the large label of FICTION. Unable to help himself, and needing to ease his suspicions, he moved forward. His heart started to pound. No way. She wouldn't. She couldn't. She didn't have that sort of vindictiveness in her.

A foot away, he stopped to scan the page and recognized his handwriting before he read the words he'd pored over. Fists clenching, jaw thrust forward, he slowly turned to look at Julie.

She looked back, her brows raised in question, of all things. Her expression saying, *Yes? Can I help you with something?*

Anger, sharp and burning, rose through his pounding chest and seemed to lodge in his head, building heat and a sharp pain in his right temple. His lips tightened, and he nodded toward the note. "Nice, Julie. Real classy."

She looked from him to the letter, her brows pulling together.

He wanted to tear the letter down, wad it up, and throw it at her feet. He managed to control himself, sharply turning and leaving without another word. If she wanted the world to read his letter, let her have her moment of satisfaction. Her *revenge* was more like it. He'd obviously made a mistake and, in the process, made a fool of himself. No way would she ever reciprocate his feelings.

He'd been mooning after her for *six long, wasted months,* telling himself he'd missed his chance, *ruined* his chances with her. He'd finally worked up the nerve to make up for his behavior, only to find she wanted nothing to do with him.

And she'd posted it under fiction? What was she trying to say, that she didn't believe a word of it? Fine. He was done beating his head against the stone wall that was Julie Ashburn.

Fingers shaking, he dug his cell phone out of his pocket, found Chad's number, and dialed.

"Chad here. Speak."

Dane stopped at the top of the stairs and gripped the

iron rail. "Are you still interested in lining me up for that double date?"

"Of course. Name the time."

"How about tomorrow night?"

"You got it. You sound strange. Is something wrong?"

"Nope. Just taking your advice and moving on."

"I knew you'd see sense sooner or later. I'll set it up and text you."

"Sounds good." He hung up but didn't feel any better. He rubbed at the ache in his chest. He knew what *would* make him feel better. He ought to go home, get the love letter she'd written him, and post it in the commons. He savored the idea for a long moment but discarded it with a sigh.

He wasn't a child. He'd take the high road and give that spiteful, vengeful she-wolf her letter *and* her cat. She could choke on them both. He was through pining for Julie. He was through regretting anything that had happened between them. He'd throw himself into dating, and in a month, he'd barely recognize her.

He'd forget all about Julie Ashburn. And he'd do it fast.

Fourteen

A gasp caught Julie's throat as she sat frozen in her chair. Dane's angry, *hurt* expression had said it all. Dane had written the letter. And she'd posted it on the board for all to see. She couldn't move at all as she took that in.

What had she done? Well, she knew what she'd done. But how could she have done it? Why had she assumed the letter was from one of her students? Why hadn't she questioned the sophomore who'd brought it to her? How had this happened? She clenched her eyes shut. She could just imagine how he was feeling right now. She'd lain awake nights worrying that he'd show her letter to others, and then she'd turned around and done it to him? She couldn't believe this.

"Um, Ms. Ashburn?" Lindsay's voice penetrated Julie's haze. "I don't think that letter you posted was fiction."

Julie looked around at the kids, all of them watching her

in apparent fascination. She couldn't seem to think. "What have I done?"

Caleb grimaced. "The question isn't what have you done. It's what should you do right now. Did you see his face? Whoa, teach. You have some making up to do."

"You know," Angela said, "it's like one of those letters you've been reading to us. Sometimes what makes them so romantic is that the sender was desperate to have the recipient's love. The principal did seem sort of desperate before he took off."

"Yeah," Evan said. "Then he just looked mad."

"What does his letter say, anyway?" Brittany asked. "Can we read it?"

That finally got Julie moving. She jumped up and crossed to the wall. "No one is reading this letter but me." With shaking fingers, she carefully removed the tack, took it down, and started to read.

Of course, she'd already read it once. But that was before she'd known it really was from Dane. When she'd thought it was one of the kids writing it in his name.

Dear Julie,

I'm writing this letter to try to rewrite the history between us. You obviously don't know this, but to me, you are as brilliant as the stars in the sky. No. That is sparse praise indeed for one as lovely as yourself. You are the moon, the sun . . .

Reading it now, realizing he'd taken the time to write something as similar and heartfelt as what she'd written to him, touched her. And he thought she'd rejected his letter? No one knew better than she did what he felt right now.

Mason spoke up. "In the movies when something like this happens, they always go after them," he said. "So what are you doing standing here? Shouldn't you go after him?"

Good idea. Within seconds, she was out the door.

Fifteen

Julie ran after Dane, only to overhear him setting up a
date with another girl. When he disconnected from his
call, she asked, "What are you doing?"

He spun around, and his face immediately clenched, his
lips tightening, his eyes narrowing. "And that's your business
how?"

"Well, if I'm your stars, moon, and sun, I think I have
the right to know about you dating other girls, don't I?"

His brows slammed together. "Watch it. This isn't a
good time to quote what I wrote."

"I didn't *know* you wrote it. With the deluge of fake
letters roaming around the school, forgive me for being
suspicious a second time. And I think it's a great time to
quote you. Apparently you need reminding. Plus, I'm a little
concerned."

"What are you talking about?"

"This girl you just made a date with may end up feeling like a third wheel when I come along. It's hardly fair to her, is it?"

Dane hesitated a long while. "You'll be the third wheel, not her."

Hearing the softening in his tone, Julie smiled. "You think so?" She glanced at the letter again. "How could I possibly feel that way when I'm 'your everything,' and 'all that is wonderful and lovely in your eyes'?"

He looked cornered, trapped, but he didn't try to move away. "What do you want me to say?" His tone was calmer, milder, his handsome features less grim.

"How about you say that it's true?"

"What's true?" he asked. "That you love me 'with a perfect love beyond all expression'?"

She smiled. "You memorized my letter."

"I didn't mean to," he said. "But after reading it so many times, it sort of stuck."

"How many times did you read it?"

"Hundreds." He took a step closer. "Thousands."

She grinned. "Liar." This was looking better and better. She held his letter up and looked at it. "Apparently, you fell in love with me the first time you met me. Only you didn't realize it until it was too late. I think I'd like a little clarification on that point."

"I thought I'd blown it. That there'd be no going back."

"And now?"

"I'm starting to feel hopeful."

"Oh, really? Well, about this other girl. How long, exactly, are we going to be dating her?"

Dane laughed. He held out his arms. "Come here."

She stepped closer, and he locked her to him gently. "You're a nut, do you know that?"

"That's not what you called me in this letter. You said—"

Relaxing his hold, he framed her face between his

palms. "Forget the letter. Forget what I said." He leaned down and kissed her, his mouth moving slowly, thoroughly over hers. She couldn't help it. She kissed him back, kiss for kiss, as if they had all the time in the world. As if they weren't standing in the hallway of a high school.

A moment later, he pulled back to stroke a hand through her hair.

She grinned. "Best. Kiss. Ever." She shivered. "Now, about this other girl . . ."

He chuckled. "I'll cancel the date."

When she smiled, he leaned down again. Just before their lips touched, she said, "I was hoping you would."

Sixteen

Red and pink balloons decorated the gym. Tables set with heart-shaped cookies and pink punch lined the far wall. A cameraman worked out front in the hall with a backdrop of cupids, roses, and hearts, with the line of couples patiently waiting for their turn.

As Dane leaned against the wall and watched the students dance, he played with the top button on his shirt, rubbing the shiny circle repeatedly with his thumb. The day of reckoning was here, and there was nothing he could do about it.

Karen McDonald was on the stage with the vice principal, busily counting money and stacking it to take to the bank. They were almost done counting. He knew she'd already counted it out and was doing it now for show. The unholy gleeful look she'd cast him the last few days spoke volumes.

Julie came up beside him with Kayla Stone. "Ready?"

He blew out a breath. "Ready."

"You look nervous," Kayla observed. "Remember, never let them see you sweat. Once you lose control, it's almost impossible to get it back. And packed in like they are, it's a small step to mob mentality. Watch yourself."

Julie laughed, then turned to place a hand on Dane's shoulder. "Do you want to dance before your life changes forever?" She gently teased him.

He shook his head. "No, I'm good. At this point, I just want it over with."

Karen, looking self-important and pleased, headed for the podium. She tapped the microphone a few times and cleared her throat. The crowd quieted quickly.

"This is the moment you've all been waiting for. Principal Parker, can you come up here, please? And Ms. Ashburn, who has been in charge of the fundraiser this year, can you come up too?"

Shoulders back, Dane headed for the stage, climbed the steps, and tried to look nonchalant about the entire thing. Julie followed.

Dane stepped up to the microphone. Was it his imagination, or did the kids, breathless and eager, look more like a horde of animals smelling blood than like teens at a party? "Let's see if I remember this correctly. I agreed to shave my head if a certain amount of money was reached. $7,000? Was that right?"

The teens booed, hissed, and generally made a lot of noise.

Dane chuckled. "Okay, okay, $5,000 it is. I know you've all been busy making this fundraiser a success, so let's see what the damage is. Julie?"

She stepped forward. "I want to say how proud I am of all of you kids. I've never seen a more motivated group, and the money you've raised for our school will make a huge difference." She turned to Dane. "Any last words?"

The sympathetic look she cast him made him take a deep breath. "Nope. Let's do this."

Karen handed Julie a piece of paper, which she unfolded. "And the total is . . . $5,210.26!" She lifted the paper high in the air. "Way to go, Wolverines!"

Dane groaned. So much for sympathy. The kids roared their approval, clapping, yelling, and stomping. Five boys brought out a chair and grinned as they helped Dane sit on it.

Julie brought the microphone over and held it to his mouth. "Principal Parker?"

"I'd like a recount."

Everyone laughed.

Dane looked up at Julie. "Can't you help me out here?"

"I'd like to, sweetie, I really would," she said into the microphone, playing to the crowd. "But there's nothing I can do."

She held the microphone out to him, and he said, "Well, if you don't do something fast, you're the one who's going to have to live with the results."

The kids were laughing, anticipating.

"Hmm," Julie said. "Did I ever mention that before you, I used to have a thing for Bruce Willis? And Dwayne Johnson? And Vin Diesel? I'm actually okay with the bald thing. You'll be in good company."

"If I find out this was your idea, you're dead meat."

She giggled and motioned for Karen McDonald's sister, a cosmetologist, to come forward. Julie shushed the kids who wanted to do it themselves, and ordered them to bring out the clippers, which were connected to a long extension cord.

"Drummers?" Julie called. "Drum roll, please."

Two members of the marching band drum line started drumming while a friend of theirs played "Taps" on the trumpet.

Resigned, Dane sat still as he was draped with a cape and as the clippers were applied to his scalp until every bit of the hair on his head was buzzed off. Everyone took pictures, the flashes blinding him.

When the last bit of hair dropped to the floor, the kids cheered loudly.

Dane was brushed off, the cape removed, and he was helped to his feet. He felt the top of his head, and Julie handed him the microphone. "Yep, I'm bald, all right. Is everybody happy now?"

Amid more clapping and laughter, Julie smiled at him, then held up a hat. As everyone laughed, he took it and put it on. "The things I do for you."

She smiled. "All for a good cause."

He decided Julie's smile was worth the shaved head. "Come on, you're dancing with me. I mean it. If I have to look like this, you have to stand beside me."

She grinned up at him. "How can I refuse such a gracious invitation?"

Seventeen

Months Later

"Please, Ms. Ashburn? Come on, it's the last day of school. Let us watch it one more time."

Julie laughed. "Okay, fine. I guess I'm easily persuaded." She opened the laptop on her desk, navigated to YouTube, and typed in *couple gets engaged during girl's first skydive.*

The kids gathered around and watched as Julie came on screen in an airplane, dressed in a jumpsuit, and grinning like crazy.

"You ready?" Dane asked, his helmet camera moving when he looked her up and down.

She raised her thumb to show she was indeed ready.

"No wait. Wrong finger."

She looked confused. "What?"

"*Wrong finger!* Here, let me help you."

The camera angle switched, and Chad laughed as his helmet camera filmed Dane getting down on one knee in the airplane.

Dane took her hand. "Julie, I love you with all my heart. You really are my stars, my moon, and the sun I revolve around. Will you marry me?"

Julie, visibly shocked, burst into tears, yet somehow she smiled at the same time. "*Oh my gosh! Oh my gosh! Yes! Yes, I will!*"

Dane slipped the ring on her finger and kissed the back of her hand. "Okay, time to go."

Still looking at her ring, Julie said, "Wait, what?"

Dane turned her around and buckled her to his body, helped her to the door, and they jumped out the open door together.

The camera angle switched again, and there was more footage of Julie flying through the air, still admiring her ring rather than the view. Dane laughed as he looked over her shoulder, filming the whole thing.

The kids laughed. This was the part that got everybody every time. Thousands of hits and messages left under the video attested to the fact that Julie, mesmerized by her ring, was hilarious.

She couldn't help but laugh too.

When they landed and finally got unbuckled, Dane took Julie into his arms and kissed her. It was pretty sweet and could still make her cry. The teenage girls sighed.

Of course, Dane picked that moment to walk into the classroom.

"Watching the video again? Someone break out the Kleenex," he teased.

Julie couldn't help but laugh, because he had, indeed, caught her in tears.

The bell rang, and the kids took off. "Good luck!" Julie yelled after them. "Do well in college!"

When they were gone, Dane leaned down and kissed her. When he pulled away, she asked, "What do you think you're doing?"

"School's out, teacher. I'm getting ready for my honeymoon."

She raised a brow. "You have to get married first."

He grinned. "Let's get that out of the way tomorrow, shall we?"

She narrowed her eyes. "Out of the way? You—"

He kissed her again, and, slowly relaxing, she melting against him and kissed him back. He pulled away to smile down at her. "I still owe you another skydiving trip."

"Yes, you do. You distracted me last time, so I barely remember it."

He chuckled. "Thousands would attest to the fact that you don't remember it at all. But I promise to make it up to you. I have something for you."

"Yeah? What is it?"

He pulled out a letter and handed it to her. She grinned. "Another one?"

"I can't seem to help myself. I start thinking about you, and I reach for a pen."

She started to open the letter, eager to read his words.

"Come here." His deep tone, the tender look in his eyes, and the slight smile on his handsome face had her momentarily forgetting the letter. She moved into his arms again. As he held her close, he whispered into her hair. "We're going to have a wonderful life. You know that, right?"

She breathed him in. "I have to say, I'm pretty much counting on it."

ABOUT DIANE DARCY

Diane Darcy is a *USA Today* bestselling author. She loves to read and write lighthearted and funny books. She's a member of the Heart of the West and RWA. She was a finalist for Romance Writers of America's Golden Heart® Award. She's written romantic comedies in several different genres: some historical, some contemporary, all lighthearted and fun. She makes her home in Utah with her family and dogs and is hard at work on her next book.

You can find her online at www.DianeDarcy.com

A Thousand Words

by Sarah M. Eden

Other Works by Sarah M. Eden

Seeking Persephone

Courting Miss Lancaster

The Kiss of a Stranger

Friends and Foes

An Unlikely Match

Drops of Gold

Glimmer of Hope

As You Are

Longing for Home

Hope Springs

For Elise

ONE

1867—Omaha

The call of "Post has arrived" echoed up the stairwell of the boarding house Shannon Ryan called home. Few things set her heart to pounding quicker than those three words. For six months, the post had been her one connection to the man she loved with every inch of herself. She'd not seen his coffee-brown eyes and lopsided smile in half a year. She'd not heard his voice whisper her name as he used to. She'd not had the comfort of his hand in hers or of his arms holding fast to her. She had only the post.

Bedrooms emptied as the left-behind women like herself rushed down the stairs to the parlor, anxiously hoping for a letter from their husband or sweetheart. America, the land of possibilities, hadn't lived up to its promise for the Irish. They'd moved farther and farther west, hoping for a job and a place to live, only to find the well of opportunity bone dry. Many of the men had found work building railroads, jobs that didn't suit the tastes of most Americans, who weren't yet desperate enough to take their chances with high explosives and deep ravines or to brave long days of back-breaking labor.

Mrs. Brooks, the boarding house mistress, read the name on the front of each letter. Some women squealed with excitement at hearing their names. Others simply smiled wide. They clutched their letters to their hearts and waited. Shannon held her breath as the pile of letters grew smaller.

Please, Patrick. Do not disappoint me again.

She'd not received anything from him in two weeks. Another happy woman claimed her letter, then another did, until one letter remained.

Theirs wasn't a large boarding house. Only one other woman stood empty handed like Shannon did. Though it was hardly a charitable thought, Shannon sincerely hoped the last letter was her own.

Mrs. Brooks read off the last name: Anna Doyle.

No letter from Patrick. Again.

Shannon kept her posture upright and unflinching even as disappointment spread like ice water through every corner of her body. She and Patrick had decided before he left with the rail crew that they would send each other letters, but not every week, so they could save as much of their pay as possible. He meant to find a town somewhere in the West where they could settle down, and then he would send for her. Between the money he would earn laying rail and what she could earn there in Omaha cleaning houses, they would have enough to marry, secure a house, and start a life together.

The plan was a good one; she still thought so. But she hadn't at all understood how the silence between them would eat away at her. She hadn't realized how lonely she would be.

Mrs. Brooks pulled a folded sheet of parchment from

the pocket of her dress. All of the boarders had remained for this moment. The work of building a railroad was dangerous, even deadly at times. The crew bosses sent word of injuries and deaths. No one knew when Mrs. Brooks received these notices, but she always delivered them on the days the post arrived.

She smoothed out the paper and set it on the end table nearest the door, then walked out of the room. The task of telling her boarders who among them no longer had a husband or loved one was distasteful to Mrs. Brooks. She never undertook it personally.

Of all fifteen women in the boarding house, only Mary MacGillis could read. She read to her housemates the letters they received, and she had been tasked with reading the fatality report. 'Twas the only reason Shannon could think of to be grateful she couldn't read a single word.

Mary took up the sheet of paper. The parlor turned as quiet as a tomb. Many of the women held one another's hands, holding their breath. Shannon stood by herself. The women she'd formed friendships with in the early weeks after Patrick's departure had all moved out, whether because their men had sent for them, had returned because of injuries, or had died. She was so very alone now.

Mary's eyes scanned the paper. "The crew's still in Nebraska, though only just," she said as she read. "They've laid a great deal of track. There've been a few injuries and a few deaths."

Not a soul moved or breathed or blinked.

Please not my Patrick. Please. Please.

Mary looked up at Anna. "Thomas had a burn to one of his arms but is recovering."

Relief chased worry across Anna's face. Her friends pulled her into their arms, offering support even as they waited for word of their own men.

Mary silently read on. She always skipped over the reports for men not connected to any of them.

She met Mary Catherine's gaze. "John's broken his arm. He'll likely be riding back to Omaha with the next post."

"He's lost his position?" Mary Catherine paled, and her hand, still clutching the letter she'd received, dropped protectively to her swelling belly.

They all knew how things worked with the railroad. So long as a man worked and worked long and hard, he was kept on. An injury that kept him from his work usually meant he lost his job. Mrs. Brooks had an arrangement with the railroad. They paid Mrs. Brooks a stipend for each woman she boarded who had a connection to the rail crew, so Mrs. Brooks only rented to women in that situation. Should a man on the crew lose his position, the woman he'd left behind lost her room.

"There's been some deaths," Mary said. "But none belong to any of us, praise heaven."

Several of the women crossed themselves. Relief touched every face. Shannon pressed her open palms together, taking a long, slow breath. Her Patrick was whole and yet living. She could endure another wait for a letter knowing he, at least, hadn't been taken from her.

The women queued up, awaiting their turn at having Mary read the loving words sent to them from out on the rail. Mrs. Brooks kept the letters until late in the evening for just that reason, when the women were all in for the night, with no jobs to go to or chores to be done about the place. The reading took quite some time.

Shannon slipped from the parlor and quickly climbed the stairs to her room at the very top of the house. Her room was small and poky, with hardly enough space for one bed and a wash stand. But choosing it meant she had a room to her own self, something none of the other women had. She had a place of quiet and refuge where she could sing if she felt the urge, or simply sit and quietly watch the sun set outside her tiny window or weep when her heart was aching.

She closed her door behind her, shutting out the world.

Six months she'd been alone, waiting, hoping, praying. All of her family were back in Boston, working in the same factory they had since fleeing dire poverty in Ireland when she was very little. She'd come west with a group of young people, looking for a future away from the crowded, disease-ridden shanties the Irish called home in the dingy cities of the east. 'Twas on that journey she'd fallen in love with Patrick, and he with her. But she'd never dreamed she'd be so long alone.

From under her mattress, she pulled out her bundle of letters. The other women had a far bigger collection, but she cherished the few she had. She sat on the edge of her bed and carefully untied the twine wrapped about her precious pile.

One by one, she unfolded them, feeling the peace return to her heart. Patrick couldn't read or write. Neither could she. The men usually dictated their letters to a foreman or to one of the lucky few amongst them who'd learned the trick of writing out words. Her sweet Patrick wrote to her in his own way. He drew pictures.

Each of his letters was a series of sketches he'd drawn of the places he'd seen, the animals he'd encountered, the other men on his crew. He had a talent for capturing the feel of a moment, for pulling her into the experience as though she'd been there herself.

She'd lovingly studied the sketches again and again as the weeks had turned to months. She felt as though she'd experienced the westward journey with him. Someday, when she joined him there, she wouldn't feel like a stranger but almost as if she were coming home.

From the middle of the stack, she pulled out her favorite sketch. He'd drawn in such detail a flower, one unlike any she'd seen. It likely grew wild in the vastness of the open West. His sketch was so lifelike, she could almost smell the fragrance, could imagine the softness of its petals and thin leaves in her hands.

He'd known she would love the flower and had sent her that bit of beauty from across the miles separating them. He hadn't forgotten her. She took comfort in that and reassurance in her loneliest hours. Someday they would be together again. Someday.

Two

"Look lively, Paddy Doodle," the foreman called. "You've a caller."

Patrick had long ago quit objecting to the nickname he'd been given. Protest 'twas of little use; the name had stuck. He took the drawing he was working on in one hand, along with his sketching pencil, and stood. The familiar-looking man standing at the foreman's side was far too clean and not nearly tired enough to be a worker. He likely made his living sitting at a desk. Wouldn't that be lovely? A roof over his head when days were wet or hot or cold, never worrying about explosions and falling rock, no canyons to build bridges across.

"This here is Patrick O'Malley," the foreman said to the fancy man of business. "Paddy, this is Mr. Houston, from the town of Sydney."

Patrick recognized the name right off. He'd given Mr.

Houston a drawing of his son quite a few weeks back when they'd laid the rail there.

"'Tis a pleasure to see you again, Mr. Houston. What brings you so far down the line?"

"You do, actually."

That was hard to believe. Mr. Houston was a man of business; that much had been clear early on. Why would a man of means make such an inconvenient journey for the sake of a poor Irishman?

Mr. Houston chuckled. "I am in earnest," he said, "though I can tell you are convinced I've gone mad."

"Not mad, sir. 'Tis an odd thing, though, to make such effort for someone as unimportant as I am."

Mr. Houston kept right on smiling. "It may seem rash, but I assure you I've given it a great deal of thought. I had hoped to find you still working for the railroad and to find your hands still intact."

"My hands, sir?"

"I've worried that you'd meet with an accident and that your talent would be lost." He held up the sketch Patrick had done. "You have a rare gift. One, I confess, I hope to capitalize on."

"I don't understand." What interest could Patrick's sketches possibly hold for Mr. Houston?

"Do you have any other samples of your work?"

"I do." He held his pad out.

The man flipped through Patrick's sketches, neither commenting nor explaining his curiosity. "These are every bit as good as I expected them to be." Mr. Houston sounded relieved.

"I thank you, Mr. Houston. It's an odd hobby for a rail layer, to be sure."

Mr. Houston flipped through them once more, nodding. The foreman's face was unreadable. Patrick kept a close eye on both of them. If they meant to make off with his sketches, they'd find themselves with something of a fight on their hands. Those sketches were for his Shannon. He'd not let them go easily. He was a full two weeks behind in sending her a picture as it was. There'd been so much to see, and he'd spent days and days trying to get his drawings just right.

"I mean to start a newspaper in Sidney, the only one in these parts. I'd have distribution all up and down the railroad to the towns springing up," Mr. Houston said. "I could use a sketch artist on staff to add a visual element to our stories. I'm offering the position to you, if you're interested."

"That'd be depending on the details of the job, Mr. Houston. 'Tis not only my welfare on the line," he said. "I've a girl in Omaha I mean to marry once I've settled someplace. If the salary'll support her and me both, and if the position is stable enough to send for her, I may be of a mind to accept your offer."

"A wise response." Mr. Houston looked impressed. He turned to the foreman. "Is Mr. O'Malley one of your drinking men? I've seen a few too many Irish off these rail gangs to imagine that isn't a risk."

"Not at all, Mr. Houston. O'Malley never takes up with the others in their drinking or carousing. We can't even talk him into a game of cards. He's laced as straight as they come."

"Very good." Mr. Houston rattled off a quick list of working days and wages, then offered the job once more. "Starting immediately," he added.

Patrick had learned young to trust his instincts. He took a moment to listen to what his mind and heart were saying. Both gave him no reason for concern. Sidney had grown significantly during the few short weeks the rail crew had been camped there. It was near an Army fort, which helped ensure its safety as well as giving it a greater promise of longevity. Not many places so far from civilization were as sure a thing as that town was.

"I believe I'll be accepting your offer." Patrick held out his hand, and Mr. Houston shook it firmly.

"Gather your belongings," Mr. Houston said. "We'll ride back as soon as you're ready."

Patrick didn't need prodding. His possessions were few and easily gathered. He packed his gunny sack and reported to Mr. Houston's buggy in less than ten minutes. Mr. Houston arranged with the foreman to have the wages owed Patrick delivered to the newspaper office in Sidney.

To Patrick's surprise, the foreman looked a bit disappointed to see him leave. "Take care of yourself, Paddy Doodle." *Paddy Doodle. Was there ever a man given such a ridiculous name as that?*

"I intend to," he answered, leaving off his objections.

Quick as that, Patrick was no longer a rail worker. During the ride back to Sidney, he let that fact sink in.

"Do you read, O'Malley?" Mr. Houston asked.

There was no point lying. The truth'd be clear easily enough. "Not a lick, sir. Not even my own name."

"Well, never mind that. We'll have you literate in no time. There's a school just started up in town, and the teacher holds classes one evening a week for adults." Mr. Houston drove parallel to the tracks in the opposite direction the crew had built them. "The paper will sponsor your classes, but you're expected to attend and learn."

"I'll gladly do so, sir. There's never been any opportunity to learn before."

Mr. Houston gave a half smile. "I had a feeling about you, O'Malley. It seems I was right. You are talented, which is good, but you seem to be a hard worker, which is even better. Don't disappoint me."

"I won't. I swear to you."

They were a full two hours riding back to Sidney. Though more than a month had passed since the tracks were laid and the work of laying more had been steady and unceasing, the crew hadn't gone any farther than that. Mr. Houston expertly drove his team and buggy through the somewhat bustling streets of Sidney. The town had grown since Patrick had last been there. He'd lived long enough in Boston to be familiar with large, busy cities. This was nothing compared to what he'd known there.

"You can have a room above the newspaper office," Mr. Houston said, "until you find a place of your own."

"Are places available at a reasonable rent? I've not much money to m' name."

"Some land outside the town is available. Stake a claim and register it, and, so long as you meet the requirements over the next years, it's yours for the taking."

"Homesteading?" He'd heard quite a bit about that from others on the rail crew.

"Precisely. You won't grow wealthy homesteading around here. But so long as you have a job with the paper, you won't depend on the land to sustain you."

Land of his own in a growing town. A job that'd pay regular and steady. 'Twas exactly what he'd hoped to find out West.

Mr. Houston pulled his buggy to a halt in front of a wooden structure on one of the many roads leading back from the train depot. A sign attached likely identified it as the newspaper office.

Patrick grabbed his sack and slung it over his shoulder. "Have you any idea how long it'd take to get word to Omaha and a passenger from there back to here?"

"The telegraph is laid this far already," Mr. Houston answered. "You can have word to Omaha in almost an instant. Traveling from Omaha to here will take but a day."

But a day. He'd have his Shannon again. She'd likely need time to give notice to her employer and purchase tickets, as well as gather the things she needed to make the journey. But after that, she'd be with him once more.

"Settle in tonight. You can send word to your sweetheart in the morning." Mr. Houston smiled empathetically. "Mrs. Houston will likely be so overcome with adoration at your love story, she'll be as eager to meet your future bride as you'll be to see her again."

"You'll forgive me for arguing, Mr. Houston, but I truly doubt that. I've not seen my sweet colleen in half a year." It felt even longer than that. "To say I miss her falls terribly short of the mark."

Mr. Houston unlocked the door at the top of the exterior stairs and let Patrick in. "You said you weren't married yet but intend to marry when she arrives. Did I understand correctly?"

"Yes, sir." Patrick took a quick look around the small room. The accommodations were far finer than he was accustomed to but too small and plain for a new bride. He'd have to find something better before the wedding.

"Is something wrong, Patrick?"

"Not at all, sir. I was only thinking I ought to claim a homestead before marrying. This isn't—"

"—what a man wishes to offer the woman who has claimed his heart." Mr. Houston obviously understood. "Perhaps you should wait to send for her until you're more settled."

Patrick shook his head. He knew perfectly well that wouldn't work. "Word will reach her that I'm no longer working for the railroad. She'll be required to leave her boarding house."

"Ah." Mr. Houston's brow pulled in thought. "Join my family for dinner," he offered. "My wife will likely have the entire dilemma solved before the second course."

The invitation surprised Patrick. "You don't even know me."

Mr. Houston waved that off. "I don't imagine you'll make off with the silver when I'm the one paying your salary."

"I'd not make off with it even if you weren't," Patrick assured him. "My da and ma raised me better than that."

"I would wager they did." Mr. Houston gave a quick

nod. "I'll come by in about an hour and fetch you over to the house."

"I'm appreciative, Mr. Houston. Please thank your wife on my behalf."

"I certainly will."

Patrick stood in his new rooms for a long moment after Mr. Houston's departure, trying to wrap his mind around all that had changed in one afternoon. No longer would he toil at the backbreaking job of laying track, praying he didn't injure his hands beyond using or lose his life in an accident as so many others had. It appeared that he now had stable work in a town where he could settle down. He was one step closer to having Shannon in his life again.

But what have you to offer her, then? A room too tiny for two? Where'll she lay her head at night? If this job doesn't prove steady, how will you get on?

He shook off the worry. He'd worked long and hard, saving and scrimping, waiting for the right opportunity. This was that chance.

But was it still what *she* longed for? He treasured the letters they'd sent to each other, though neither of them had ever sent words. He drew her pictures of the things he'd seen that he thought she would enjoy. She sent back images cut from discarded newspapers or advertisements, pasted together to form a picture of her life without him. They'd concocted the plan as a means of communicating without needing someone else to write out or read aloud their words. It was meant to be a bit of privacy during their difficult separation.

However, six months with no words between them left him wondering how she felt and what she was thinking. What if their time apart had lessened her feelings for him? What if she no longer loved him as she once had, or simply didn't love him enough to take a chance on this new life?

He peered out his window at the town below. 'Twas a typical Western railroad town; Patrick had seen more than his share of them over the past months. It had gone up in a flurry of activity and was growing by leaps and bounds, saloons and houses of ill repute going up long before any churches or other respectable establishments. Rail workers had spent many of their leisure days here gambling and drinking and carrying on. Many didn't come back to the crew, choosing instead to settle down and try their hands at other occupations.

As planned, Patrick took his evening meal with the Houstons. The family was every bit as friendly as Mr. Houston. Patrick recognized their youngest, the boy he'd drawn a picture of weeks ago while watching the lad play in a field with other children. Their home was finely furnished, declaring them a family of means. Patrick listened as Mr. Houston told their history. He'd been in the newspaper business all his life, being the son of a newspaper man. Realizing the uncivilized West would need news, he'd taken a chance, uprooted his family, and left Cleveland for the ever-expanding railroad. He'd found in Sidney a town exactly like what he'd envisioned.

"Once you've learned to write, we'll see if you've a knack for reporting as well as drawing," Mr. Houston said. "I'll work you hard, let me warn you."

"I've never feared hard work, sir. I certainly don't now."

Mrs. Houston's plump face smiled across the table at him. "He has a talent for knowing people's hearts, Mr. O'Malley. If he finds you trustworthy, one can be certain that you are."

"And does a fledgling newspaper truly need someone to make sketches? I can't imagine what I could contribute, or that I'd be worthy of the salary I've been offered." Patrick feared this would prove a foolish endeavor, one he'd regret giving up the steady pay of the railroad for.

"I have bigger plans than simple news sketches." Mr. Houston's eyes sparkled with a contagious excitement. "Now and then, I'd like to feature a drawing of your choice in the paper, a full quarter page. I have a feeling the papers featuring those bits of art will sell better than all the rest and that we'll find your prints hung in houses all along the rail line. If we accumulate enough, I'd like to see them printed and bound as a collection to sell at the train depot to passengers making the trek westward. I think we'd even find interest along the line as far back as Omaha or Council Bluffs. I wouldn't be surprised if those back East would be intrigued by drawings of the untamed West."

"Do you honestly think anyone'd buy my doodles?" Patrick wanted to believe it, to hope that he had a skill that would give him work and money to live on.

"I'm certain of it," Mr. Houston answered. "You have talent, O'Malley. And I have a nose for business. I think we'll make a fine team."

Perhaps given enough time, he'd be in a position to support Shannon—not simply put food on the table and a roof over her head, but give her a few fine things. He may even convince her he wasn't such a bad catch. He only needed time.

A plan formulated on the instant. He couldn't marry her until he was certain he could support her, but she couldn't stay in Omaha after her landlady insisted she move out of the boarding house. So he would send for her, but he would first find a position for her there in Sidney. She'd have money to live on. He'd arrange a place for her to stay. That would give him time to deserve her and give her the freedom she needed to break things off between them if she'd changed her mind.

Please let that not be the case. I couldn't bear it if I've lost her affection.

Three

idney. Shannon silently repeated the name of her new hometown as the train made its way West.

Her heart warmed with the knowledge that Patrick had laid the very tracks that were bringing her to him. 'Twas as if he'd done so for no reason other than to make certain they would be together again. After the fortnight she'd just passed, that knowledge was more welcome than ever.

Shannon never wanted another fortnight like the one she'd just endured. Word had come that she had to vacate her room at the boarding house, but with no accompanying explanation. She hadn't known if Patrick had found other work, or if he'd been injured or fired, or—her heart still thudded in her chest at the thought—killed. She'd wept as she packed her meager belongings. The other women offered empty reassurances, all of them knowing death was a constant and very real possibility for all of their loved ones.

She'd secured a room elsewhere in an area she'd felt less than safe, but there'd been nowhere else to go. For days, her heart had ached and broken as her mind imagined every horrible possibility. She'd wept as she worked, wept as she'd lain in bed at night. She hadn't the strength to even look at Patrick's drawings. The sight of them had only cracked her heart more fully and deeply.

A week to the day after Shannon's eviction, Mary MacGillis found her as she'd left one of the homes she cleaned. A telegram had arrived at last. Patrick was well and whole. The relief of that knowledge made the rest of his message hard to concentrate on. Mary had needed to read the telegram more than once.

Patrick was alive, and he had sent for her at last. She needed but a few days to make the preparations for her journey westward. She was finally closing the miles that separated them.

She sat on the back-most bench of the passenger car, where she could have a bit of privacy. All of her precious drawings were kept bundled and safe in her traveling case except for one. The flower Patrick had drawn for her sat unfolded on her lap. She wanted to see one in all its splendor, to know if the colors she'd imagined were correct, if its leaves were as fuzzy as they appeared. How she hoped they grew near Sidney so she could pick a few to keep in their home. Perhaps they could even be planted.

The conductor came through the car. Shannon stopped him as he passed. "How much longer until we reach Sidney?"

"It's our next stop," he answered. "Perhaps another fifteen minutes."

"Thank you," she told him, then offered another thank you to heaven. She'd be with her love in only fifteen more minutes.

She carefully folded her flower drawing and watched eagerly out the window for the first glimpse of the town. For long moments, she saw nothing but the unending expanse of openness she'd grown accustomed to during her journey. Six torturous months she'd longed for Patrick. Why must these last few minutes pull out so long?

Quite suddenly, there it was. A sprawling town, almost haphazard in its design, popping up out of nowhere. Shannon's heart leapt clear to her throat, racing and pounding as the train slowed its forward movement and pulled to a stop at the station.

She was there. At last, she was there. She jumped to her feet, clutching her drawing as she moved swiftly up the aisle and out of the car. A brisk wind met her as she stepped onto the platform. She clutched her bonnet to her head with one hand, holding fast to the flower sketch with the other. Her eyes searched for her dear Patrick.

The platform bustled with activity, mostly working men unloading and hauling away supplies. A few passengers, like herself, had arrived and either made their way into town on their own or were greeted by loved ones. The porter set Shannon's traveling trunk on the platform beside her.

Where are you, my love?

The platform emptied. She alone stood as the train pulled away. Worries and reassurances pushed one another in and out of her frenzied thoughts. Had she misunderstood her destination? Had the telegram she'd sent gone astray or conveyed the wrong time or date?

She opened her trunk and set Patrick's drawing inside, closing the lid against the unrelenting wind. She tightened the knot holding her bonnet on her head. Regardless of the reason she'd not been met at the station as expected, she wasn't of a mind to simply stand there being battered by the elements. Shannon dragged her trunk to a bench pressed up against a wall of the depot. She would wait for him there. Her Patrick would come; she simply needed to be patient.

Time passed as she sat there, though she couldn't say if it was a few minutes or an hour. Those working at the train station took little notice of her. No one seemed to be looking about for an unclaimed passenger. The telegram Mary had read said Patrick had a job working for a newspaper. If worse came to worst, she could ask around for the newspaper office and hope to find him there.

"Shannon Ryan?"

Hearing her name spoken by an unfamiliar voice in a town where she'd never before set foot was more than startling. She glanced up warily.

"Are you Shannon Ryan?" a plump woman in a fine purple dress asked.

"That I am."

She smiled on the instant. "I am sorry to arrive so very late. My neighbor agreed to keep an eye on the children, but she was running behind schedule, so I couldn't leave as soon as I'd intended to."

"Begging your pardon, but I've no idea who you are."

"Oh, dear. I did leave off that bit of information, didn't I?" Did the woman never stop smiling? "Being late flusters me so terribly. I'm Madeline Houston. My husband owns the newspaper."

"The one my Patrick works for?"

"Yes, exactly." She pulled a bit of paper from the pocket of her very stylish jacket. "He sent me with this so I would recognize you."

Shannon took the paper and found a sketch of her own self looking back at her. Warmth rushed to her cheeks as a smile touched her lips. "He has a fine talent, does he not?"

"Oh, yes. We are all simply amazed at how fine his drawings are."

She looked up once more, pressing the drawing to her heart. "But why did he not come fetch me himself? We've not seen one another in half a year. I thought he would— Surely he's missed me enough to—"

Mrs. Houston's expression filled with empathy. "The heartless old badger he works for has him slaving away up at the newspaper office without even a few minutes to himself to come see you."

"And that 'heartless old badger' is your husband, I believe you said."

A hint of mischief sparkled in Mrs. Houston's eyes. "Indeed. And he will get an earful about it tonight; I promise you that."

Shannon breathed a sigh of relief. She hadn't been forgotten or abandoned. Patrick would have come if he'd been able to. And he'd seen to it she'd not been left completely alone. She studied the sketch, running her finger lightly along the lines he'd drawn. His memory of her hadn't faded even with the passage of six months.

"The two of you are having dinner with us tonight," Mrs. Houston said. "We had best be on our way. I need to finish meal preparations and set out dishes and such."

Shannon took up her trunk once more and followed Mrs. Houston out into the wind. "I hope you'll allow me to help. I hate feeling like a burden."

"If you're offering, I am accepting." She smiled as they climbed into a buggy behind the depot. Mrs. Houston flicked the reins and set the horse at a trot. "The men won't be home for another hour at least. That will be plenty of time to have dinner ready and still allow you to freshen up a bit if you'd like."

"I would like that very much. As much as I'd hoped to see Patrick here at the station, there is something to be said for greeting him wearing a clean dress and with my hair combed."

Mrs. Houston nodded. "And your nerves will have a chance to settle."

Shannon smiled and let her shoulders droop. "Am I so obvious as all that?"

"Oh, my dear girl. Any woman would be nervous at seeing her sweetheart for the first time after so many months." She spared Shannon a quick glance before returning her eyes to the road. "A bit of rest and a moment's peace will do you a world of good."

Though Mrs. Houston was attentive and the Houston children sweet, Shannon found she only grew more unsettled as the day wore on. She was no help at all in the kitchen. Her feet took her repeatedly to the front windows, gazing out at the street.

The oldest of the Houston children, Hannah, who was somewhere near eight years old, dropped onto the sofa in the front parlor and sighed quite dramatically. "It is so romantic. Mr. Patrick said he sent you letters all these months."

"That he did." Still no sign of him on the street out front.

"And you sent letters back," Hannah pressed.

"I did, indeed."

"And now you'll be together again, forever and ever." Another deep, emotive sigh. "It's the most romantic thing in the whole, whole world."

It *was* rather romantic now that Shannon really thought on it. She was so ridiculously nervous, she'd not taken even a moment to reflect on the loveliness of a reunion after so many months apart.

"Do you think Mr. Patrick will kiss you?" Hannah asked.

Without hesitation, Shannon answered, "He'd better."

Hannah giggled, pulling a laugh from Shannon as well. She stepped from the window and sat beside the girl. "What punishment shall we devise for Mr. Patrick if he neglects to greet me properly?"

"We could put a snake in his bed."

Shannon grinned. "I've a feeling I ought to be a little afraid of someone who thinks of such a treacherous thing so quickly."

"Papa says I'm devious," Hannah declared proudly. "He says he hopes my little brother is a good influence on me, since Gerald never gives anyone a lick of trouble."

The littlest Houston was something of an angel. "Well, I

for one think most girls could do with just a touch of deviousness."

Hannah grinned, revealing a couple of missing teeth alongside those not quite fully in. "I like you, Miss Ryan."

"That is likely because I've a bit of devilment in me as well. It used to land me in ever so much trouble when I worked at the factory in Boston."

"Well, you're out West now." Hannah lowered her voice to a secretive whisper. "We can get away with all kinds of things here, and there aren't any stuffy old aunts or grandmothers to tell us to behave."

Shannon matched her tone and volume. "I am *very* pleased to hear that."

Hannah rubbed her hands together, clearly already making plans for some shared bits of mischief.

The sound of men's voices floated inside from the front walk. Shannon's heart returned to its earlier place in her throat.

"Does that sound like your father, dear?" she asked Hannah.

"That's him. And he'll have Mr. Patrick with him."

My sweet Patrick. Shannon stood up, feeling her knees quake beneath her. The door opened.

"I have already arranged for the paper to head east on the train on Monday to be sold at depots along the line." The man who stepped inside was unknown to her. "I'll need that cutting ready by Sunday."

"And you'll have it. I promise you that."

Patrick stepped inside. *Her* Patrick. Her sweet, lovely Patrick.

Shannon could hardly breathe. She couldn't move even the tiniest bit. He was even more handsome than she remembered. His face was darker, more lined than it had once been, no doubt the result of endless days working in the sun. And the work had changed his build as well, with muscles filling out his once-lean frame. She only hoped that any changes he saw in her were good ones.

Hannah skipped to her father's side. "We've been waiting for hours and hours, Papa."

Mr. Houston ruffled Hannah's hair. "Take Mr. Patrick's hat and jacket, Hannah, and hang them up for him."

But Hannah didn't immediately obey. She stood, staring up at Patrick, something Shannon could certainly understand. Was there a finer looking man in all the world? She sincerely doubted it.

He smiled at the child. "Have I a smudge of dirt on my face or something, Miss Hannah?"

Oh, heavens, that smile of his. How I've missed it.

Hannah jerked her head to the side. Then did so again. "Miss Hannah?"

But Hannah kept motioning rather awkwardly with her head in Shannon's direction. Bless the girl's heart. After a moment, Patrick seemed to realize what Hannah was attempting to tell him. He turned. Time slowed unbearably. Shannon clutched her hands in front of her, trying to hold back a sudden and unexpected flood of emotion.

His beautiful brown eyes met hers. He froze. "Shannon," he whispered. "Oh, saints above. My Shannon."

He dropped his hat and jacket right onto the floor and rushed to her. In an instant, his arms were around her.

"Shannon. Dearest, loveliest Shannon."

She clung to him, trying to believe the moment was truly happening. She'd dreamed of him for six lonely months.

"Are you real, love?" he asked. "Are you truly, truly real?"

"I am, indeed."

He set his hands on her upper arms, holding him away from her a bit, looking her up and down. "Heavens, I've missed you."

He brushed his hand along her cheek. Having him there, holding her again, Shannon felt as though she were breathing again for the first time in ages.

His hand dropped to hers. "And you've met the Houstons."

"They've been very kind."

That seemed to relieve his mind, though she couldn't say why. "Then this'll work out, will it not?"

"What will work out?"

"Mrs. Houston didn't tell you?"

"Tell me what?" Why in heaven's name were they discussing Mrs. Houston when they'd only just been reunited? The man hadn't even kissed her yet.

"They mean to offer you a position looking after the children."

Perhaps Patrick's new job didn't pay well enough yet. She wasn't unwilling to work. And she did like children. But could this not have waited? Mr. Houston had dragged Hannah from the room, leaving them alone, together. And Patrick stood there speaking to her of jobs.

"And they have a room for you to stay in."

"A room for *me*? And what of you, Patrick? Will you not be with me?"

He yet held her hand, rubbing it between both of his. She loved the warmth of his hand but wished he'd put his arms around her again. "I have my own room, above the newspaper office."

"But, we—" She couldn't seem to make her mouth say what her mind was thinking. They were supposed to be together now. They were going to be married and live the rest of their lives with each other, not in separate rooms in separate buildings. "How long is this arrangement meant to last?"

"I can't rightly say. Until we know for certain what we mean to do with our futures." He no longer looked her in the eye.

"But I thought—" Her voice broke. She took a breath to steady it again. "I thought we'd already decided our future."

His brow pulled tight. He released her hand and paced away. "Things can change when two people are apart for six months. I think it'd be best to make quite sure we know what we want."

All this time she had thought *she* was what he wanted. That a life together was what they both wanted. Had she been so wrong? Surely not. "If you think it'd be best to wait before making a permanent decision, then I suppose that'd better be what we do."

He nodded firmly and even smiled a little. A very little. "I think it'd be wise."

He walked at her side to the dining room and sat beside her at the dinner table. She caught him watching her from time to time, but otherwise he seemed rather indifferent to her being there. Arrangements were made for her to begin working for the Houston family. Shannon let the discussion simply wash over her, unable, or perhaps unwilling, to accept what they meant.

She'd imagined Patrick meeting her at the station with the preacher already at his side. She'd even accepted that necessity would have required a day or two of waiting. But never had the possibility of an indefinite wait entered her mind.

She followed him to the Houstons' front door after dinner. He'd insisted on returning to his room to turn in early, not remaining behind for a visit. He wished her a good night and pressed a very quick kiss to her cheek. That was it. That was all she was to receive from him.

She stood in the front parlor, shocked into stunned silence, her heart aching at the change in him. The hopes she'd been clinging to over the months began to crumble right in front of her. Something was wrong, and she couldn't begin to guess what.

Four

Patrick was nearly out of his mind. Shannon had been in Sidney for three entire weeks, living at the Houstons' home. Out of respect for her, and wanting to see to it that she had time and space to decide if she truly wished to marry him still, he'd kept himself to only a quick visit now and then and to sitting in the front parlor with her on Sundays.

He'd not held her in his arms since the day she'd arrived. He'd only allowed himself to take her hand on occasion. He hadn't even kissed her. In an effort to clear his mind, he chose to walk out to his claim despite Mr. Houston's offer of a horse. He needed to spend the pent-up energy threatening to blow him to bits at any moment. Inevitably, when he arrived at the spot where he'd begun building a dugout house, he found himself unable to focus long enough to get much work done.

He was there again, looking out over his land, empty and unimpressive as it was. He hoped to someday put in a garden plot and a barn for animals. It'd likely be a dugout just as the house was. Even the saloons in town were a finer sight than his barebones bit of earth.

This is what you have to offer her, is it? A hole in the ground you mean to pass off as a home? Lumber was scarce in that area, most of it shipped in by rail, making the price of it too dear for a man of limited means. *You dragged her all this way so she could hitch her wagon to your falling star. She deserves far better than you, you worthless bag of bones.*

He pulled off his hat and wiped at the trickle of sweat making its way down his face. The paper's circulation was growing, just as Mr. Houston had predicted it would. But there was little money in the endeavor. Patrick pulled a wage, but a small one. Should the paper grow significantly, Mr. Houston meant to increase his salary, but that was likely months, if not years, down the road.

The sound of horse's hooves pounding the dry earth spun Patrick about. He seldom had visitors. His nearest neighbors dropped by on occasion when he was there working. But the horse, approaching at an almost comically slow pace, wasn't carrying any of the nearby families. 'Twas carrying Shannon. As far as he knew, she hadn't ridden a horse in all her life.

Patrick moved swiftly toward her, being quite careful not to spook the animal.

"Are you daft, woman?" He took the horse's rein the moment it came within reach and brought it to a full stop. "You might've been thrown, left in a broken heap on the trail somewhere."

"I've no intention of arguing with you over something that didn't happen. Now help me down, will you?"

The horse was calm enough. He stepped over and held his arms up for her. She set her hands on his shoulders and carefully lowered herself into his arms. She was safe on the ground once more, and he really ought to have released her. But he couldn't. His arms simply refused.

Her hand slid from his shoulder to his cheek, her thumb brushing along his jaw. "You've neglected your razor, Patrick. Stubbly as a hedgehog, you are."

Saints, if she kept touching him that way, he'd simply melt right there in front of her. "'Tis Saturday. I don't bother cleaning up when I'm spending my day out here."

Her hand slipped from his face, trailing slowly down his neck, coming to rest open against his heart. "I've the day off myself," she said, her voice low and mesmerizing. "I'd like to spend it with you, if you don't mind."

He most certainly didn't mind. Though with her there, he'd likely get little work done. Indeed, he couldn't seem to pull two thoughts together. Every sense was aware of nothing but her. His arms clung to her, keeping her but a breath away from him. His eyes refused to see anything beyond her honey-colored hair and eyes of deepest blue. The air filled with the scent of her. His mouth ached for one taste of her lips.

He closed his eyes, trying to bring himself back from the brink of madness. 'Twould be the easiest thing in all the world to pull her the rest of the way to him and kiss her more fervently than he ever had before. He could, without even the smallest struggle for words, beg her to stay with him always, to accept what little he had to offer her simply because she'd once told him she loved him. But she needed to know what a terrible bargain he'd turned out to be. No coercion, no pleading, no kisses to quiet the concerns she would inevitably have.

He forced himself to step back, allowing his arms to drop to his side. "You're most welcome to stay, Shannon. I'd enjoy your company. But I'll warn you, there's little to see here and nothing at all impressive."

"Well then, I'm fully prepared to be unimpressed." She gave him a smile that felt almost like a challenge. In their months apart, Patrick had nearly forgotten how fiery Shannon could be when she had a bee in her bonnet.

She stepped past him and up the dirt path a bit. Patrick took the horse's reins once more and followed close behind her. She stopped in front of the dugout. "What's this here, then?"

"It's what passes for a house around here," he said. "Wood is hard to come by, so we dig holes and build up the rest of the house with mud bricks."

"This is your home?" she asked, her back still to him.

"It is that." Pathetic as it was, it was his. He wrapped the horse's rein around an obliging bush.

"And Mrs. Houston tells me this is your land as well," Shannon said.

"It is."

Quite without warning, Shannon spun about to face him and plopped her hands on her hips. Patrick took a step backward at the fierce look on her face. Few things a man ought to fear more than an Irishwoman in high dudgeon.

"Then why in blazes did I have to climb on that great lumbering beast and come out here of my own accord? Why is it, Patrick O'Malley, that you weren't of a mind to bring me here your own self?"

"And do what? Brag about this bit of nothing I've acquired? Show you what a fine and fancy man I've become? Give you a grand tour of this house of mine?"

That didn't even give her pause. "Yes. That is exactly what you ought to have done. Don't you want me to be part of any of this?"

"Part of it? I didn't want you to even see it."

She stepped toward the dugout. Patrick deftly moved in front of her. "I'd rather you didn't go inside." He was humiliated enough as it was. She'd give up on him entirely if she saw the pathetic state of things inside. He'd nothing but a few overturned crates serving as furniture.

"You don't want me to see—to see *your* house?" Her

eyes searched his face, but for what he wasn't sure.

"It's not fit for company."

"Is that what I am, then—*company*?"

Something in that sounded wrong. "It isn't ready for you," he tried to explain. "*I'm* not ready for you."

"Oh." She blinked a few times, her lips pressed together as if holding something back. "I . . . I didn't realize."

"Things are different than I'd expected them to be, Shannon. All those months ago when we were planning and dreaming, I didn't know how things would turn out."

"And if you had known?" she asked in a small voice.

"I—"

"Please be honest with me, Patrick. I need you to be."

Be honest. He could give her that if she truly wanted it. "In all honesty, I'd have not sent for you when I did."

"Ah." Her eyes dropped. She nodded slowly. "Well, that certainly is honest."

Again, he'd gone about the explanation wrong. He couldn't seem to string the right words together. He'd never had a talent for saying what he thought or felt. "Shannon, I think that sounded different from how I meant it."

She shook her head, even smiled a wee bit. "Don't fret. I think I understood. May I ask a favor of you while I'm out here?"

"Of course. Anything."

She pulled a folded bit of paper from the pocket of her jacket and opened it carefully. "If you'd point me in the right direction for finding one of these."

'Twas one of the sketches he'd sent to her, one of his love letters. Seeing it brought back with perfect clarity the days he'd spent drawing it. When he'd seen the clump of bright yellow flowers, he'd thought of her on the instant. Shannon adored yellow and never could resist smelling any flower she came near. So he'd plucked a small handful, preserving them in a cup of water. For days he'd worked to get the sketch just right. 'Twas the drawing he'd labored over most; he'd been determined to convey every small detail for her enjoyment.

"Those grew along the line back quite a bit," he said. "I've not seen any in months. I don't think they grow out here."

She folded the paper once more. "Of course they don't," she whispered. She stuffed the drawing into her pocket. "I'm sorry to have interrupted your work day."

"Are you leaving, then?"

Her smile was clearly forced and not the least believable. "I plan to stop at the mercantile to inquire after the price of a dress length. I'm in need of a new dress. And the sewing of it will use up my free time nicely, don't you think?"

"Yes, I suppose it will." The air between them sat heavy, as though filled with a dense fog. She seemed somehow farther from him, though she stood just as close.

"Would you mind taking the horse back to the Houstons when you're done out here?" Shannon asked.

"You mean to walk? 'Tis a great distance."

But she shook her head. "It seems the longest journeys are most likely to show us things we hadn't known to be true."

"You anticipate some great discovery on the journey back to town?"

"Oh, Patrick." She sighed his name. "That discovery has already been made, and it wasn't a great one, I assure you of that."

He could feel her disappointment in him. It showed in the slump of her shoulders and the downward turn of her lips. She'd seen what little he had to offer, just as he'd feared she would.

"I'm sorry, Shannon." A quickly forming lump in his throat nearly cut off the words, but he managed them. "I am truly sorry."

Five

With a bit of prodding, Mrs. Houston managed to pull from Shannon every depressing detail of her visit to Patrick's homestead. Rather than commiserating or crying with her, Mrs. Houston, who was generally quite jovial, grew noticeably angry.

"I swear to you, Shannon, there are times when I wonder how it is that men are so infernally thickheaded." Mrs. Houston threw her hands up in exasperation. "I had a feeling this would happen. Your Patrick is a dear, dear man, but he's not always terribly bright."

Something about the declaration brought a shaky smile to Shannon's face. "I've been trying to make sense of it. If he no longer wanted me for his bride, he ought not to have sent for me, rather than bringing me here only to tell me he wished he hadn't."

Mrs. Houston's eyes narrowed. "Are you certain that is what he said—that he wished you hadn't come?"

"That was more or less what it was. He said he didn't want me there in his house, that if he'd known how things would turn out, he wouldn't have sent for me when he did."

"Ah." Mrs. Houston, it seemed, had had a revelation. "*When he did*. There's significance in that, I'm certain of it."

"Then I wish you would explain it to me, because I can make neither heads nor tails of that man's thinking lately. When I first arrived today, he held me so tenderly, as though he'd never let me go." Heat stole across her face at the memory, then fled as the rest of the visit returned to her mind. "But not five minutes later, he was telling me how *his* house was no place for me, and *his* land didn't have the flowers I was looking for, and how he didn't want me there."

Mrs. Houston sat on the edge of Shannon's bed, patting the quilt in invitation. Shannon sat beside her, her energy too far spent to do anything else. "I have a theory about your suddenly feather-headed Patrick, if you would care to hear it."

"I would appreciate it, actually."

"Men, though we love them dearly, are rather stupid about these things." Mrs. Houston patted her hand in a maternal show of empathy. "I've known Patrick for a few weeks now, and I can't say I've seen him fret over many things, save one. You."

"Me?"

"He has missed you fiercely, though I know he hasn't done a very good job of showing you that. And he has more than once worried aloud that he has very little to offer you." Mrs. Houston's mothering instinct seemed to extend to Patrick as well, though she couldn't have been more than ten years his senior. "When he asked after the position of nanny on your behalf, he did so in a way that, at the time, seemed odd. I think I understand it better now."

Shannon would give almost anything to understand Patrick better. She couldn't at all piece together the puzzle he presented her lately.

"He made absolutely certain you would have a room of your own and that the position paid enough for you to be comfortable so, as he put it, you would 'feel no pressure to make hasty decisions.'" Mrs. Houston's expression turned thoughtful once more. "I do believe, Shannon, he worries that you have changed your mind in his absence these past months, or that you would do so after seeing how humble the life he had to offer you truly is."

For a moment Shannon couldn't formulate words to express her thoughts. In fact, she couldn't entirely formulate her *thoughts.*

"He thinks—he believes my heart would grow cold because we were apart? Or—or that my heart was so fickle as to close itself off to a man because he wasn't destined to be wealthy?"

"I do believe that is the crux of the trouble," Mrs. Houston answered. "Though I am certain that in his mind, it isn't a matter of fickleness. I imagine he fears you think he is a failure or not worthy of you, or that you'd dreamed of better things than he can offer."

Shannon stood and paced away from the bed. "Of all the mule-headed things! I told that featherhead I wanted to marry him. The least he can do is give me the courtesy of believing me." She spun about, shaking a finger in frustration. "I've half a mind to throttle him until he's forced to admit that I love him."

Mrs. Houston laughed out loud. "I can honestly say I've never heard of a woman employing quite that method, but it may be necessary in this instance. You have chosen a very stubborn man."

"He's Irish," Shannon answered. "They're *all* stubborn."

"Are the women just as stubborn?" Mrs. Houston asked the question in a tone that indicated she knew the answer perfectly well.

"Stubborn enough not to let that man throw away both our happiness. I'll just march myself back out to his house and let him know what is what."

But Mrs. Houston held up a staying hand. "He needs to learn to talk with you about the things that worry him. Otherwise you'll spend the rest of your life fighting this fight."

"How do I convince him of that?" She was willing to try almost anything.

Mrs. Houston's smile turned decidedly mischievous. "Brace yourself, my dear. Tomorrow evening will be one you'll not soon forget."

Patrick dragged his feet all the way to the Houstons' home on Sunday evening. He felt utterly at loose ends where Shannon was concerned. She'd left his land Saturday morning quite obviously dispirited. He didn't know if she'd given up on him, changed her mind, or was simply angry about something. He'd probably done a poor job of explaining things, but words had never been his strong suit.

He made his way up the front walk. Beneath his uncertainty was the usual flipping in his heart at the knowledge that he'd have Shannon's company again. No matter that he felt unsure of his footing; her very presence was a balm. He spent every week looking forward to that one evening.

As he made to knock at the door, the sound of voices inside stopped him. 'Twas more than the sound of young children. 'Twas more than the three adult voices he usually heard. From the sound of it, the Houstons were hosting half the town.

He knocked, but no one answered. Twice more he attempted before admitting he probably couldn't be heard over the din. He let himself in and froze at the sight that met him. The house was nearly full to bursting. With men.

Patrick stood, unnoticed, in the open doorway of the parlor. He recognized most of the visitors but couldn't think of anything they had in common that would explain their presence there. He'd wager it wasn't a society or club meeting of any kind—their interests and professions were too varied. The only thing he could think of that they all had in common was bachelorhood.

Bachelorhood. They're unmarried. Every last one of them. The realization was followed immediately by an urgent question. *Where is Shannon?*

The children often kept her busy during his Sunday visits. He certainly hoped they were occupying her time this evening as well.

No such luck. Patrick spied her standing in the middle of the parlor, chatting quite friendly like, with a gathering of admirers. Men far outnumbered women in the West. An unmarried lass never lacked for attention. Until that moment, Patrick had never seen any bachelors hovering about Shannon. He'd assumed they'd kept a distance because of his prior claim. Perhaps Shannon herself had warned them off. If so, she clearly wasn't doing so any longer.

"We'd almost given you up, Patrick." Mr. Houston appeared seemingly out of nowhere and slapped a friendly hand on his back. "Quite the gathering, isn't it?"

"Yes, quite."

Robert Mills winked at Shannon. Gregory Hanson smiled at her. Bill Duarte eyed her with clear interest. Patrick glared at the lot of them. So help him, if any of them so much as touched her, even by accident, he'd toss the blackguard out the door quick as lightning.

Mr. Houston looked out over the crowd with more than a hint of amusement. "My wife happened to casually mention to someone at church this morning—I can't remember just who—that our dear Shannon hadn't been asked to the social this coming Friday," he said. "Next thing we know, our usual quiet Sunday evening turned into this."

He waved at the room, shaking his head. "She's a sweet girl and pretty as a picture. I'm only surprised the men didn't swarm sooner."

"Do you suppose she's enjoying the attention?" Patrick's heart dropped at the realization that she might very well be. He'd given her time and space for just that reason, so she could be sure of what she wanted. But in his heart of hearts, he'd still believed *he* was what she wanted, dugout home and all.

"Why don't you go find out for yourself, son?" Mr. Houston suggested.

"I believe I will." With that declaration he felt the fight in him growing in a way it hadn't for weeks. He'd felt little beyond utter defeat. What a fool he'd been to think himself willing to give up his lovely, wonderful Shannon.

He crossed the room, forcing his way through the pressing crowd directly to where Shannon stood. "A good evening to you, Shannon," he said.

She turned her head quickly—he flattered himself that she turned *eagerly*—in his direction. "Is that you, Patrick?" She sounded happy to see him, even a touch relieved.

"'Tis myself, indeed."

Hanson elbowed his way back to Shannon's side and took up immediate conversation. The crowd continued jostling, each eager for his turn filling Shannon's ears with flattering, honeyed words. Her cheeks were a rosy pink, her eyes sparkling with lantern light. Even as the pressing throng forced him farther from her side, he could hear her lilting voice and see the spell it wove over all around her.

After several fruitless attempts to regain his previous position at Shannon's side, he admitted defeat. He'd not have so much as a moment of her time that night; he knew it well enough.

He'd simply wait them all out. Eventually the Houstons would push Shannon's throng of admirers out the door, and he alone would be left. He'd stand outside the back door if need be.

Patrick stuffed his hands into his trouser pockets and made his way to the kitchen. It was as good a place as any to bide his time. The kitchen was not, however, empty. Little Hannah Houston rushed to his side the moment he entered.

"Are all those men still here?" she asked.

"They are," he muttered.

"And are you going to punch them all in the nose?" She sounded positively giddy at the possibility.

"I think your parents would rather I not start a brawl in their parlor, dearie."

Hannah was clearly unimpressed with his logic. "If I were going to marry someone, and he let a whole group of men court me instead of tossing them all out, I'd positively die."

He'd learned during the weeks he'd known Hannah Houston that she lived her life in a constant state of dramatics. Still, he could appreciate the sentiment. "I don't know that Shannon is unhappy with the attention she's receiving."

Hannah rolled her eyes and moved to the kitchen door, pressing her ear against it. "She was sure put out when they all started arriving. She kept asking Ma how long they'd be here and if she could just lock herself in her bedroom until they all left."

"She wasn't pleased about it, then? Wasn't she hoping one of them would invite her to the social this weekend?" Patrick had debated extending the invitation himself, but he meant to stand firm in his decision to not pressure her into anything.

"Hush." Hannah waved him off as she pressed her ear ever harder to the door.

He moved up beside the door himself and lowered his voice. "Has nobody asked her yet?"

"Oh plenty just tonight, but she's turned them all down."

Excitement bubbled inside. "Did she truly?"

Hannah shot him a look of utter annoyance. "Why would she go to the social with someone other than you? What kind of a person do you think she is?"

"She's a fine person," he answered, his tone more heated than it ought to have been. Though he knew Hannah liked Shannon, even a hint of disparagement against his beloved's character was enough to ruffle his feathers.

"Then I suppose you're only interested in people who aren't fine, since you don't even kiss her goodnight when you're here." Hannah looked him up and down dismissively. For a ten year old, she could certainly put a man in his place. "Maybe one of these men will kiss her good, and then she won't look so sad all the time."

"They won't if they know what's good for them."

"Good grief." Hannah pressed her ear to the door again.

So did Patrick, but he couldn't make out a single word, only the ongoing dull roar of so many conversations. *You don't even kiss her. She looks so sad all the time.*

Shannon did often look sad—when she wasn't spitting mad at him. Could that truly be laid at his feet? He was doing the right thing by her. He wasn't forcing her to accept what little he had to offer. He was sacrificing for her happiness and hoping, in the process, to secure his own.

Why, then, did they both seem so miserable?

Six

Mrs. Houston's plan hadn't worked. Patrick had stayed for not more than a moment Sunday evening before leaving as though it bothered him not at all seeing his intended surrounded by would-be suitors. Shannon had not seen him even once the past two days. Mrs. Houston told her not to fret, but she was fretting. So help her, she was fretting. Perhaps throttling the man really was her best option.

Shannon returned to the Houstons' home after a brisk walk with the children. The wee'uns had so much energy, she couldn't expect them to remain inside all the day long simply because her aching heart wished for a quiet corner in which to mope.

"Go wash up for lunch, loves," she instructed them.

The youngest two rushed up the stairs. Nothing

motivated them more than the promise of food. Hannah remained behind.

"Is your heart so, so broken?" Hannah asked. The dear girl was living every one of her tragic romantic fantasies by watching Shannon's life fall to bits.

"I have full confidence I will survive, Hannah."

"But Mr. Patrick is never here."

"Believe me, I have noticed." Shannon pressed on, cutting off Hannah's continued emoting. "Up the stairs with you, girl. Wash up like you're supposed to."

"Yes, Miss Shannon." Hannah *hmphed* all the way to the first floor landing. She stopped and looked over the railing down at Shannon. "If Mr. Patrick does something truly tragic, you'll tell me, won't you?"

"I will invite you to witness the tragedy for your very own self."

"Oh, good!" Hannah clapped her hands together and spun around in a gleeful circle.

Shannon left the girl to her celebrations and headed to the kitchen. Mrs. Houston was there already, preparing lunch. "May I help?" Shannon asked.

"You have helped so much these past weeks." Mrs. Houston smiled at her over the pot of soup. "In Cleveland, we had a nanny and a cook. We've had to live more frugally since coming here, at least until the paper is more successful. I confess, doing all of this myself is far harder than I expected it to be." A flush of embarrassment touched Mrs. Houston's face. "You probably think I am unforgivably incompetent."

"Nonsense." Shannon pulled a small stack of bowls from a cupboard and set them on the table. "'Tis never an easy thing to adapt to a life so different from what one has always known." She set out spoons as well. "I remember very little from our first years here in America, but I clearly recall how much my parents struggled. Nothing was the same as it had been."

"And America didn't exactly make things easy for your

people, did we?" Only someone as kindhearted as Mrs. Houston would feel compelled to apologize on behalf of her entire country.

"One thing you can say for the Irish, we do rise to the occasion."

"Oh, speaking of which" —Mrs. Houston moved to the kitchen door and pulled a folded bit of paper from a basket hanging there—"this arrived for you."

"What is it?" But she knew the answer the moment she took it from Mrs. Houston. "Someone's sent me a letter?"

"Indeed." Mrs. Houston wiggled her eyebrows. "And I am entirely certain it is a love letter."

"Which of the beaux you arranged for on Sunday is writing to me?" How she wanted the letter to be from Patrick!

"You can't fool me, dear girl. It is a letter from your Patrick, just as you're hoping."

Shannon pressed the very edge of the letter to her lower lip and closed her eyes. Her Patrick. "I lived for his letters the past six months. I felt closer to him when looking over his letters than I have since coming here."

She felt Mrs. Houston's hand rest on her shoulder. "Go read your letter, Shannon. Take as long as you need."

She didn't need convincing. She sat on her bed, laying the letter on her lap. It was quite a bit thicker than any of the others had been. *What have you sent me, Patrick?* She needed this letter to be one of healing and love. She needed to know he still cared.

She nervously unfolded the letter. She had, on occasion, received two drawings from him at once. This appeared to be at least a half dozen. Her breath caught at the sketch on the very top of the stack. Though her memories of Ireland were extremely vague, she'd heard enough stories of her homeland to have a clear picture in her mind of what it looked like. The sketch Patrick had made of a thatched cottage set against a background of rolling hills and stone fences was Ireland. She knew it as surely as she knew the beating of her own heart. Standing in front of the cottage was a small girl, likely not more than four years old, her dark hair hanging in braids.

Shannon carefully set the drawing on the bed beside her and studied the next paper in the stack—a boat with tall sails, making its way across a rough sea. Shannon had made the awful voyage across the Atlantic when she was only five years old. She'd never forgotten the sounds and smells of that journey. Looking closer, she noted the same little girl from the cottage sketched on the deck of the ship.

The next sketch brought a smile to her face. Though she and Patrick hadn't grown up in the same Irish area of Boston, she knew from his stories that their childhoods had been remarkably similar. He'd drawn what she would guess was the overly crowded, rundown neighborhood of his early years, one that looked startlingly similar to her own. And there again was the young girl, looking much the same but older.

Her heart fluttered as a warm wave of understanding rushed over her. This was her life. Patrick had sent her drawings of her own life, a connection to her past and to the people and places she missed. 'Twas precisely the kind of tenderhearted gesture she would have expected from him before the odd aura of indifference of the past few weeks.

Next was a sketch of the boarding house where she'd lived while he was away. And there she was, looking out the uppermost window. *Oh, how I missed you when I was there.* Somehow he had captured that forlorn expression even without having been present to see it.

He drew her in the window of the passenger car of the train she'd ridden on her way west, on her way to him. Only one paper remained. What had Patrick drawn there? The Houstons' house with her, once again, standing alone? That would be fitting, though heartbreaking.

She took a breath, rallying her courage, and looked down at the final page of his letter.

'Twas Patrick's house, the one he was building out on his land, the one he'd not let her set foot inside. But he hadn't drawn anyone alone at a window. He'd drawn himself—she recognized his face in an instant—standing with his arms around her, holding her as though she was the greatest treasure in all the world. He'd sketched his home with the two of them together and placed the picture at the end of her journey.

She jumped from her bed, clutching the final drawing, and rushed back out to the kitchen. "I need to borrow your horse." Her voice was nearly frantic.

"I can do better than that. The buggy is hitched up and ready to go, and Mrs. Green is here to watch the children." Only then did Shannon realize Mrs. Houston had her jacket on and stood at the ready.

"You knew?"

"Not any particulars," Mrs. Houston said. "But my husband did say Patrick requested the day off. I had a feeling that letter was him finally coming to his senses and showing you what was in his heart."

"I need to go out to his home," Shannon said. "I think he is there, waiting for me, probably wondering if I'll even come."

Mrs. Houston smiled. "Let's not leave him in suspense any longer, then."

The ride out of town felt so much longer than it truly was. Shannon resisted the urge to plead with Mrs. Houston to drive faster. At last, the dugout came into view. But she didn't see Patrick.

"He has to be here," she whispered, fighting the urge to cry. She never cried, but too many endless days of heartache had taken a toll.

"I am certain he is here," Mrs. Houston said. "Go on over and peek inside."

She climbed down from the buggy, still holding the drawing Patrick had made of the two of them together.

Carefully, quietly, she moved toward the house. If he wasn't inside, her heart would break. Relief flooded through her when she spotted him, his back to the door, hanging something on the opposite wall.

She turned back to Mrs. Houston, still sitting in the buggy, and waved. Mrs. Houston waved back, then set the horses in motion once more, heading back toward town. The noise was enough to finally pull Patrick's attention to the door.

His eyes widened when he saw her there, but his expression turned wary in the next moment. "Good day to you, Shannon."

"I received your letter." She held the drawing up in front of her, the final scene facing him. "This was my favorite part."

He moved to where she stood, uncertainty filling every line of his face. "That's all I have to offer you. A tiny house half in the ground, fields that will likely not be very fertile. You've known so much hardship in your life, and all I can give you is more of that. I don't want you to feel trapped or—"

She pressed her finger to his lips. "This was my *favorite* part. Us. Together. 'Tis all I've wanted from the first time I met you. Not fancy houses or wealth or fine things. Just you, Patrick O'Malley. Just you."

He clasped his hands over hers and kissed her fingertips. "I've been a bit of an idiot."

"A *bit* of an idiot?"

His beloved smile returned. "An enormous idiot."

"Then it is a very good thing for you I adore enormous idiots. They're m' favorite kind."

He took her face in his hands and pressed a lingering kiss to her forehead. "I had intended to ask you to the social this weekend, but I suspect we're going to miss it, love."

"Are we, now?"

"We are, indeed." His arms wrapped around her waist.

Shannon slid her arms around his neck, leaning in to his embrace. "And why exactly are we going to miss it?"

"The way I figure it, I'd best marry you before you change your mind about loveable idiots." He kissed her temple, then the very corner of her mouth.

"I think you'd better," she whispered. "But first, I need you to do something for me."

"Anything, my love. Anything at all."

"Kiss me like you mean it."

He did without hesitation. His kiss was fervent and deep, six months of longing and loneliness finally coming to an end. Shannon held him as tightly as her arms would allow, refusing to let him go. Too long she'd been without him. His final love letter had brought them to that moment, not to the end of a journey but to the beginning of a brand-new one, together.

ABOUT SARAH M. EDEN

Sarah M. Eden is the author of multiple historical romances, including *Longing for Home*, winner of *Foreword* magazine's IndieFab Gold Award and the AML's 2013 Novel of the Year, as well as Whitney Award finalists *Seeking Persephone* and *Courting Miss Lancaster*.

Combining her obsession with history and affinity for tender love stories, Sarah loves crafting witty characters and heartfelt romances. She has twice served as the Master of Ceremonies for the LDStorymakers Writers Conference and acted as the Writer in Residence at the Northwest Writers Retreat. Sarah is represented by Pam van Hylckama Vlieg at Foreword Literary Agency.

Visit her website at www.sarahmeden.com

Twitter: @SarahMEden

Facebook: Sarah M. Eden

Between the Lines

by Annette Lyon

Other Works by Annette Lyon

Band of Sisters

Coming Home

The Newport Ladies Book Club series

A Portrait for Toni

At the Water's Edge

Lost Without You

Done & Done

There, Their, They're: A No-Tears Guide to Grammar from the Word Nerd

One

When Jane Martin arrived at the meeting of the Aid and Cultural Society, everything appeared to be perfectly normal. No one could possibly have thought differently. As usual, the members were sitting and, in some cases, standing, in a circle, but everyone knew who was really in charge: Emma Tanner. She stood at the front of the classroom in the schoolhouse, their typical meeting spot, while everyone listened to her going over the agenda. Jane sat at a desk and listened quietly with her ankles crossed and her hands in her lap.

They'd already discussed the success of the results of the canvassing project, during which they'd collected money to send to an orphanage in Africa. They'd covered the plans for an upcoming benefit concert to raise money for repainting the town hall. Now Emma was listing off who would perform what at the benefit.

Finally the society was doing something cultural. Jane was entirely supportive of charity activities, but combining service with culture, as the benefit would do, would be particularly gratifying. As usual, Jane said little or nothing, instead observing those around her and daydreaming about what she might perform at the benefit in four months.

And yes, at times, her mind strayed to envying Emma, whose golden hair was always the most elegant hair in the room. Jane had always yearned for such hair; in primary school, Emma always had the thickest, shiniest braids. Rumors had circulated that Emma's mother used olive oil on her daughter's hair to create the effect. Jane's practical mother never allowed such nonsense related to one's appearance. Such concerns weren't proper or Christian, she'd always said.

Now that they were grown, of course they no longer wore two long braids, but Emma looked even prettier with her hair crimped into waves and swept back into a simple chignon. Those waves! Jane's drab, limp hair would never hold a wave much longer than it took to make it. Her destiny most surely did not consist of ever having a beautiful or elaborate hairstyle. No, hers lay flat, in spite of efforts to use decorative combs to hold her hair in place, and in spite of efforts to tease sections so they'd stand off her scalp, and in spite of many other efforts, her hair looked as if it belonged atop the head of a stern old school mistress of fifty instead of a nineteen-year-old eligible young woman.

"Let's see," Emma said, consulting her notes with a paper in one hand and a pencil in the other, which moved along her list. "Evangeline, do you still plan to do a poetry reading?"

"Most certainly," Evangeline said, her face lighting up. She'd always been pretty too, but unlike Emma, Evangeline had been so kind to Jane that there were days she'd forgotten how plain and simple she looked in comparison with her classmates, or how the boys admired the other girls, but never her. Evangeline looked about the circle of two dozen or so members of the society. "I'm thinking of performing one of Keats' works. He wrote such *beautiful* poetry."

Keats was a wonderful choice, no question. Ever pragmatic, Emma, who had not a single romantic bone in her body, nodded and jotted a note. "As soon as you decide which piece, let me know. Of course, I'd like to have a program that's balanced with topics and lengths and such. The sooner I know who is doing what, the better I can make the program sing." She smiled at Evangeline, although the look in her eye seemed a bit patronizing. Jane shifted in her seat, hoping she wouldn't get the same look.

"Oh, yes," Evangeline said. "I'll choose my selection tonight and tell you what it is first thing tomorrow." She nodded, then wiped away a wisp of hair that had escaped the loose bun of her chestnut hair.

Thomas Allred raised his hand, and Emma called on him as if she were his schoolteacher rather than his peer. "Could I do one of Shakespeare's sonnets?"

Emma's mouth closed tightly in thought before she said, "A sonnet is *awfully* short, and Shakespeare's works are overdone."

"True," he said. "But if all of us perform long works, the benefit will last all night. A happy and alert audience is more likely to applaud and donate more." He seemed to completely ignore her other argument about Shakespeare being overdone. "Besides, better a short but excellent performance from me than something dull and lifeless by someone else." He grinned, as if he knew full well that he was being silly. But the descriptors repeated in Jane's head.

Dull and lifeless—like my face. And my hair. She reached up and smoothed it, hating how drab it—and she—was. Yet her eyes strayed to Thomas, the only boy in town who'd never teased her. He'd even stood up for her against a couple of boys throwing snowballs her way one winter several years back. She'd always been grateful, and a corner in her heart had always belonged to him and the strawberry-blond cowlick over his forehead.

What did Thomas Allred look for in a girl? She forced her eyes away from him so no one would suspect she felt anything for her former classmate, but the question still rang in her mind. What did he think of her? Of the other girls? She'd seen him escort girls home from dances, but he'd never seemed to have his eye set on one girl in particular. The fact that he wasn't set on one girl might have comforted another young woman in her shoes, but not Jane. He wouldn't ever look her way. No man ever would.

Jane had figured that much out six years ago, when it became common for the school children to pass notes behind Miss Sterling's back, bearing messages about which boys had eyes for which girls and vice versa. The idea of having her name on such a note, and thereby drawing the attention of the entire class to herself, would have been embarrassing, whether or not the rumor was true.

Far more humiliating, however, was the absolute knowledge that she was in no danger of ever seeing her name on one. No one would ever have thought to write her name on one, not even in jest. And they never had. She might as well have not existed, for all the attention paid to her. As she looked about the room at her former classmates, memories of the past flooded back of feeling ugly and unimportant—unless the class had a game involving math or Latin, in which case they all wanted her on their teams because she was smart in those subjects. Jane mentally shook herself away from thoughts of the past. Dwelling on such things never resulted in anything but a sour stomach and a headache.

Instead, she decided to lose herself in imagination, for in the mind, all things were possible; even Jane Martin could be beautiful in fantasy. She could be noticed for something other than brains and a strong work ethic. So she sat there and built a castle in the sky, complete with her very own prince, who, after declaring his undying love, tilted her head back and leaned forward to kiss her. Their lips had almost met when the jab of an elbow in her side brought her back to earth.

With a start, she looked about the room, only to see chuckles rippling around the circle. At Jane's side, Martha Prater laughed openly. It had to have been *her* elbow Jane had felt the tip of digging into her ribs. She smoothed her skirts and tried to ignore the heat building in her face, which undoubtedly translated into hot pink spots on her cheeks.

Do not give them the satisfaction of seeing you embarrassed.

She cleared her throat and turned to Emma. "I'm sorry, what did you say?"

Emma tilted her head and chuckled, but then with impatience and a fist at her hip, said, "Will you or won't you play the piano for the benefit?"

A chorus of "Oh, do," and, "You play so well," and, "Really" followed from several girls.

Honest or not, the flattery did its work. Jane nodded agreement. "I will. I've been practicing a piece by Rachmaninoff, *Prelude in G Minor*—"

"Perfect," Emma said with a nod. She scribbled a final note, then hugged her writing tablet to her chest as she looked around the circle. Jane swallowed, unable to speak up to tell Emma that she hadn't gotten the full title out. Emma went on. "I have one last item on the agenda—something I think you will all enjoy."

Perhaps it would be something else cultural. Emma finally had Jane's attention, at least for the moment, as well as the attention of everyone else in the room.

Emma looked from side to side several times in an aggravating manner of anticipation. "As many of you know, I have an aunt who lives in Canada. She wrote recently asking if our association would be interested in writing letters to members of a similar group she heads in Toronto."

"As . . . letter . . . friends?" Andrew Barton asked, as if searching for the right term.

Emma nodded, and Violet clasped her hands. "That sounds delightful," she said. "I've always wanted a letter friend. I've heard that famous novelists often have letter friends, ones they've never met their whole lives, but they're dear friends all the same." Violet got a far-off look of wonder in her eyes, which Jane studied. Did Jane herself look like that when drifting into daydreams of castles and princes? No time to think of that now.

Emma hurried on. "She sent me a list of names and addresses, which I have here. I've already spoken with Mrs. Allred about it, and she's quite pleased with the idea."

Everyone looked at Thomas, whose parents ran the town's post office. He raised his hands in protest. "This is the first I've heard of it," he declared. "But I'm sure they'll put me to work on it one way or another."

"Splendid." Emma smiled and smoothed her hair, which hadn't a single hair out of place. She tore two pages from her notebook and set them and a pencil on the table behind her. "For those interested, be sure to clearly print your name and address. You'll be assigned someone to write to soon. I would recommend mailing a letter at least once a week, especially at first, so you can get to know your new Canadian friend. Eventually, we could help with charitable and cultural events and maybe someday meet them face to face."

"That would be delightful," Evangeline said, but then her brow furrowed. "We won't be writing to any *French* Canadians, will we?"

A ripple of laugher went around the circle, making Evangeline frown, but they all understood her question. Evangeline's marks in French had never been good.

"No French-speaking letter writers," Emma assured her. "We will all be writing in English, although don't be surprised to see slight differences in spelling and punctuation written by our Canadian friends. And that ends tonight's meeting. Let's sing our song, and then you can all sign up."

The group stood and sang their anthem, officially ending the meeting, after which most members moved as one toward the desk. They lined up and chatted as they waited their turn to add their names to the list. Jane hung back even after half of the group had signed up, pondering the concept of writing to some unknown Canadian.

The idea had a certain appeal: she might be able to confide in a total stranger about the inner workings of her heart and mind, after a time. Not if the recipient laughed at her romantic notions and "silly" daydreams. She stood and got in line near the back, deciding to give letter-writing a try.

"Are you signing up?" Thomas asked from in front of her. She startled; she hadn't realized he was there. Plus, she hadn't stood this close to him in years, so she hadn't realized how tall he'd grown, nor how nicely his shoulders had broadened from all the farm work he did. And to think he'd once been part of a group of five unruly, undisciplined boys who brought frogs to school. He'd never put one in her lunch pail, however.

As with so many other things, that was one more occurrence to be both relieved and saddened by—the mean boys' biggest, hardest snowballs were always aimed at the girls they had liked best. She never got hit, except when a snowball missed its mark of Susanna Billingsly and brushed the sleeve of Jane's coat. That hardly counted. For a moment, Jane almost wished Thomas *had* thrown a snowball at her during their school years.

"So . . . are you signing up?" Thomas pressed.

Again Jane's mind had drifted off. She found herself nodding three times quickly before she found her voice. "Yes. Yes, of course. A letter friend would be a delight to have, don't you think?"

One of his shoulders came up and then dropped. "I

suppose. I'm not much in the way of a letter-writer, although it seems to be an important art. If necessary, I shall learn." He added his information to the paper and handed the pencil to Jane, shooting her a brief smile as he put on his hat and left, whistling.

I wouldn't mind being hit by a snowball if it meant Thomas had a hankering for me. The thought flitted across Jane's mind before she realized it, and again she felt her cheeks flush as she stepped forward to take her turn signing up.

Two

wo days after the Aid and Cultural Society meeting, Thomas sat at the post office desk behind the front counter, sorting incoming mail. The door clunked open, and light, high-pitched footsteps sounded, indicating a woman in heeled boots, like his sister Dorothy wore. He looked up to see Emma Tanner before him, twisting a handkerchief in her hands.

"Emma," he said, standing. "Is there something I can help you with?" She'd worn the same horrified and embarrassed expression as the time, ten years ago, when Toby Gillis put a toad in her lunch pail.

"I hope you can help. Oh, I don't know." With a harrumph, she dropped onto the bench by the door and sighed.

"What's the matter?" Thomas asked, setting the stack of letters aside. He rounded the counter to help as a gentleman should, if he could.

Emma shrugged. "It should be nothing, but I do feel so dreadfully foolish." She looked at the handkerchief in her fingers, which was wrinkled from all the wringing. "Aunt Bertha promised that her group had more than enough people to write to ours and that some of our members might be even asked to have two letter friends."

When she didn't go on right away, Thomas raised his eyebrows and tried to coax her on with the word he could feel hanging in the air. "But?" he prompted.

She let out a groan. "But they don't have enough people to write us back. Almost, but not quite. I thought we would have more interested members from the Canadian group." She groaned and covered her face with her hands. "What kind of president am I when I rush into decisions without confirming details first?"

He leaned his back against the counter, arms folded. "What exactly is the problem?"

"The list Aunt Bertha sent—you remember, the letter that arrived yesterday—is short three writers." Her voice rose in pitch, ending with a wail as if she'd singlehandedly brought about the end of the world. "What have I done?"

Thomas studied her carefully and thought through her words. "Let me see if I understand. Some of our members won't be able to have a pen friend?" Was that all?

"I feel awful!" Emma raised the handkerchief and dabbed at both eyes. "I've already decided that I'll forgo my letter friend; it's the only right thing to do, under the circumstances. But how will it look for the president herself to not have a letter friend of her own, when it was her aunt who arranged the whole thing?" Her face contorted into a number of shapes, all of which telegraphed distress. "And that still leaves two more people in our society without someone to write to." Her tone seemed to imply that such a thing was just shy of being savage, that every good American had a letter friend hailing from their northern neighbor.

To his credit, Thomas didn't laugh at her distress. He didn't so much as crack a smile. "So you need others to step aside, to not have a letter friend. Is that correct?"

Chin lowered, she looked up at him through her lashes. "Yes . . ." she said slowly, dragging the word out.

"I'll step aside," he said. It wasn't as if he'd particularly yearned for a letter friend.

"Would you?" Emma stood, hands clasped before her. "But . . . but there's more." She sank to the bench again and opened her purse, which Thomas hadn't noticed before, and she withdrew a stack of papers. "I made nearly every match so far. Somehow, I couldn't seem to find the right match for Jane Martin."

"She's the last person without a letter friend, then," Thomas clarified.

Emma nodded, eyes pinched. "I can't bear to hurt that poor bird of a girl. What should I do?"

"I'm sure we have a letter friend request somewhere in the post office—sometimes people send requests asking for a letter friend."

"Often?" Emma asked hopefully.

"No, not often," Thomas admitted. Probably not in years, for that matter. "I'll ask my mother, and I'll assign that person to Jane."

"But she'll know it's not from Aunt Bertha's club."

True. He squinted one eye as he thought. "I'll try to come up with a letter friend request from Canada. She need never know it's not from the same group." At the society meeting, Emma had mentioned the city her aunt's club was from, but he couldn't remember it. With any luck, neither would Jane.

"You'd do that? Arrange it all, and no one would ever know how foolish I've been?" A flash of guilt crossed her face. "But wouldn't that be lying? Lying is horribly evil; I couldn't bear to think that I was being dishonest." Yet her eyes remained trained on Thomas with an odd, hopeful expression.

"I'll take care of it; no worries. Maybe I'll walk up to Montreal myself and find someone for her to write to."

"To Toronto," Emma inserted. "And you could never walk that far."

"Then maybe I'll write to your aunt Bertha to find someone else for Jane to write to," Thomas said, confident he could make this work. Anything to make Emma and her anxious feathers calm down and go home. Watching her wringing her hands in the post office made him uneasy, like he had an itch he couldn't reach. "That's her name, isn't it? Aunt Bertha?"

"Yes, but she doesn't have anyone else," Emma said.

"All the same, leave the list here. I'll write out official invitations for everyone, and I can help you hand-deliver them to everyone tomorrow so no one is the wiser if Jane's letter friend ends up being from a different city." He was promising Emma an awful lot, but if it got himself free of her, doing it all would be worth the effort.

A smile broke slowly across Emma's face until he could see her teeth, and her eyes lit up like electric lights as understanding dawned. "With private invitations, our members will be unlikely to compare addresses as they would at a meeting." Her grin smoothed into a flirtatious smile, and one eyebrow went up. "And you'll help me deliver them?"

"Sure," Thomas said, his voice suddenly going up in pitch. He had no desire to be the object of Emma Tanner's affections. "You can take half, and I'll take the other half. We'll get them all delivered in no time."

Her smooth smile wavered for a moment, but in the end, her relief at getting out of a difficult situation must have outweighed the fact that he hadn't flirted back. "You're a good boy, Thomas Allred."

He laughed. "Boy?"

"Fine." She lifted one shoulder in a shrug. "A good man."

"I aim to please."

Emma stood and handed him the pages, which were covered with lines and arrows showing who was matched with whom, but it was nearly illegible, she'd scribbled so much—entire sections were scratched out and redrawn—to the point that it looked like a web made by a drunken spider. Deciphering who was supposed to write whom would take all night.

"Thanks again, Thomas," Emma said with a wave as she headed to the door.

"Come tomorrow afternoon, about three, for the invitations?" he called after her. "That's when Dorothy takes over."

Emma nodded, her entire bearing far brighter than a moment before, as if a storm cloud had blown away from above her head. "I'll see you tomorrow then." She headed outside, letting the door close behind her, the bells at the top jingling against the wood.

Through the window beside the door, Thomas watched her walk down the road. He couldn't help but also watch men on the street, both familiar ones and strangers alike, tipping hats her way and calling to her or simply turning their heads as she passed to admire her looks. Emma Tanner was undoubtedly beautiful. So why didn't *he* find his heart pounding when she came near him? Unlike Ernie Holdaway and several other members of the society, Thomas had never found himself at a loss for words around Emma Tanner. Maybe something was wrong with him, but somehow he couldn't fathom being attracted to a woman solely because of a pretty face and fine eyes. He'd tried to imagine what marriage would be like with such a wife on his arm. Pure misery, that's what. Sure, at church and social functions he'd be the envy of the town, but inside their own walls he'd be liable to pull out both of their hair if his wife was concerned entirely with reputation and appearance and spent her day ordering everyone about.

As Thomas returned to his chair at the desk, he shook his head, knowing full well that in spite of being the president of the Aid Society, Emma Tanner didn't have a truly charitable bone in her body. Or maybe she had a tiny one, like one from her toe. The thought made him smile as he spread out her papers on the desk. She wasn't a bad person, but she wasn't purely altruistic, either. He looked over the papers and attempted to read her spiky, messy handwriting. With effort, he figured out most of Emma's scratchings, and he guessed some, but when he was done, the final problem remained: there was no one to write to Jane Martin. He searched the desk and shelves of the post office for any letter friend requests but found none.

Could he ask someone else to give up their letter friend without Emma losing face? He'd have to swear that person to secrecy. *Not a good idea.* Thomas sat in his chair again and tapped the desk with the tip of a pencil for several minutes, thinking. He hadn't seen a request for a letter friend in ages, but perhaps his mother knew of someone. He went to the front door, hung the sign that read *Will Return Soon,* and went out back to the family's living area to the sitting room. He found his mother in the rocking chair beside the fireplace, which wasn't yet lit, but which would need to be soon to ward off the oncoming evening chill.

She glanced up from her knitting and smiled. "Thomas. Is your shift over already?"

"Not quite," he said, crossing to her. "Have you seen any letter friend requests lately? Are any waiting a reply?"

She lowered her needles to her lap. "Oh, no, dear," she said with a shake of her head. "Were you hoping to have a friend to correspond with?"

"It's not for me," he said. "It's for the Culture and Aid Society."

Turning her knitting in her lap to begin a new row, she

tugged on the ball of yarn sitting in the basket at her feet. "I haven't seen any letter friend requests in ages. The last one was, oh, two, three years ago?"

It hadn't been that long; he was quite sure of that. But Mother's memory had started to fade. If she didn't remember one, he wouldn't be able to find one even if it existed. "Ah, well. Thanks anyway. Nothing to worry about." He leaned down and pecked her cheek.

She smiled up at him and patted his face, then nodded to the corner wood pile by the fireplace. "Would you mind bringing me some wood from outside?"

"I'd love to, Mama. And I'll get a fire started for you too."

"You are such a dear boy."

He laughed at that as he headed for the door.

"I know, I know," she called after him. "But you'll always be my sweet boy, Thomas."

His heart warmed. "Yes, Mother, I will. Always."

As he gathered the wood and carried it inside, and then as he set to starting a small fire to warm his mother's feet, the wheels in his mind turned and turned on the problem of the letter friend and Jane, until, just as the flame caught, a simple, obvious solution presented itself.

He would write to Jane. She wouldn't know it was he, of course. He could easily imagine a fake address she would write to. He'd slip her letters to himself when she dropped them off at the post office. He'd probably have to tell Dorothy about it in case Jane mailed a letter during his sister's shift. Yes, this would work. He would write letters in return and deliver them to her as if they'd come from Canada. Technically that would be dishonest, but surely Jane would tire of the exercise, stop writing, or if worse came to worst, he could have the imaginary letter friend move to some remote location, one with unreliable postal service. No harm done. Emma would save face, and Jane would have her letter friend.

The fire grew before him in the grate. He stared at it as thoughts warred in his mind. He might as well have had an angel on one shoulder and a devil on the other—only he didn't know which voice was the angel. They both seemed like the right choice. Which should he choose, remain entirely honest but disappoint Jane and embarrass Emma, or create a tiny, inconsequential lie, one which would likely fall into nothingness within a few months anyway, and spare both Jane's feelings and Emma's pride?

He stood and brushed off his hands. He found himself caring far more about Jane's feelings than Emma's. Why? He hardly knew her as anything but the girl who'd attended school and church across the room since he was a boy. Thoughts and worries tumbled in his head as his mother's needles clicked rhythmically behind him. He slowly admitted the reason he didn't want Jane's feelings to be slighted: she'd been the object of plenty of peer disdain over the years. He'd seen her ignored and teased by school girls for no reason other than that she was easy prey. Now as a young woman, she didn't seem to have any friends in the Aid Society. He found himself wishing he'd stood up for her in the past. He wouldn't let her be pushed aside again.

But could he make it happen? The idea of creating a fictional persona to write to her sounded nonsensical, but the more he considered it, the more merit the idea had. Yes. He would adopt a pen name and write to Jane. He'd be kind. He'd listen to the chatter of the young ladies at club meetings and elsewhere to know what kinds of things they would like to read about in a letter from a male friend. It would last a few weeks, and then he'd find a way to end it. No one would ever have to know.

His mother looked at the fire and reached her fingers toward its warmth. "Thank you."

"You're welcome, Mama." Thomas' feet carried him back to the post office, because his mind was elsewhere. Even though closing time wasn't for another forty minutes, he flipped the sign over the window to read *Closed,* then locked the door.

He returned to the desk, knowing he should finish the day's work, but all he could think of was Jane Martin, of how quiet and shy, even melancholy, she often seemed. Before he lost his courage and turned yellow bellied, he opened a drawer, pulled out a sheet of ivory paper, and began to write with Dorothy's blue fountain pen. By the time he finished his letter, he'd need to come up with a proper nom de plume.

Three

10 Weeks Later

For once in Jane's simple, often disappointing life, fortune had finally smiled upon her. She sat in her room, door closed, and held in her hand her *tenth* letter from Charles Percival Wharton—her *tenth* in as many weeks, while all of the other ladies in the society were still waiting for their third. The others couldn't blame their friends' slow response times on the postal service, now that planes delivered air mail so quickly. Some of the Aid Society members had yet to receive a single letter. Half of the members wrote to ladies, and most who wrote to men seemed to have found their letter friends to be stuffy old bores.

But not Jane. Somehow, she had been given the name of a man who was not only an eligible bachelor, but one who was also wealthy, educated, and utterly charming. He appeared in her daydreams instead of princes now. They hadn't yet exchanged photographs, so she didn't know precisely what he looked like beyond his own description, something she was certain he'd been all too modest about. Sure, he mightn't be as tall, dark, and devastatingly handsome as her mind had conjured. Such concerns mattered little when one considered that Charles had the honor of a knight and the heart of a poet. And somehow, through their correspondence, she'd found a voice to her thoughts about so many things, subjects she could talk to no one else about.

After holding the letter in her hands and relishing the anticipation for several minutes, she finally broke the seal. Unable to contain her excitement, she stood and paced the eight-foot length of her room, back and forth, as she reread just the greeting: *Dearest Jane.*

Dearest! He'd called her *dearest!* He didn't seem to be the teasing type. She didn't think so, anyway. So he had to mean it. Who would have ever thought that a man would call her *dearest?* She read the full letter, determined to finish the whole thing before stopping again, although of course she began from the first word.

Dearest Jane,

What a delight to receive your latest letter! It arrived at just the right moment, after a dreadful thunderstorm, which made me feel most in need of a cheerful friend's visit by a roaring fire. In spite of our relatively short acquaintance, I feel like I can already predict what you are thinking. You had some melancholy feelings yourself when you composed your last letter. Am I right?

Any letter from you cheers me so, and this was no exception. Your words always have a way of doing that. I never suspected that our friendship would come to mean so much to me, and in such a short span. Surely the time will come that another man will win your heart, but I hope that when that day comes, that man, whoever he may be, will allow you simple correspondence with an old friend.

He went on to talk about his ailing mother's health and how he worried about her memory failing. How he cared for her and the family the business, which he never did spend much time talking about. Jane often wondered what type of business it was so she could picture Charles working at his desk doing whatever it was he did—for he had mentioned a desk. She knew that much. He replied to several anecdotes she'd shared, then shared some of his own. Finally, near the end of the seven pages—seven delicious pages, front and back—she reached a portion where he discussed some of his favorite writers and asked if she enjoyed reading as much as he did.

His list of favorites included several works with which Jane was somewhat familiar with but had never read: *Pilgrim's Progress*, *The Diary of Samuel Pepys*, and *Roderick Random*. She was eager to find copies of each and read them so she could share her thoughts on them with her Charles, who had quickly become the dearest friend she'd ever had—in some ways, the only real friend she'd ever had.

He closed his letter with a short final paragraph.

Please write as soon as you can. I know you will, of course. You always do, and I anticipate each letter, as I keep saying. Do tell me about your reading habits and which writers you enjoy.

Yours,

Charles

Even though it was a nice, plump letter, it ended far too soon. Jane had the urge to sit at her desk and write him immediately, but she stopped herself with the thought that she had nothing to say, not yet. She had to find those books he'd recommended and read them quickly. Perhaps she could take in a play at the theater so she could tell him about it; he'd mentioned how much he enjoyed the theater.

She sat on her bed and reread the letter, committing as much of it to memory as she could so she could recall entire sections at will. She lifted the ivory paper to her nose and inhaled the musky scent of Charles's cologne, which he always dabbed on the corners. She closed her eyes and smiled with contentment. She could live her life this way forever, she was quite sure—sharing her innermost thoughts and feelings with a friend with whom she didn't have to pretend and who didn't expect anything else from her. Who didn't know she was plain and therefore had no preconceived notions about her.

If their friendship was to continue, she'd need to find a way to prevent him from ever insisting on exchanging photographs. As much as she yearned to know what he looked like, she wouldn't pay the price of sharing her dull appearance in exchange for that knowledge. No, sending him a photograph was a completely unacceptable proposition. She slipped the letter into her desk drawer beneath the ribbon holding the stack together. She smoothed her hair and checked her reflection in the mirror on the wall. Her cheeks seemed slightly pinker than usual, making her slightly less drab. Almost pretty. Not quite, but almost.

One more thing Charles does for me, she thought with a smile.

As she headed downstairs to the kitchen to help her mother with supper, Charles remained in her thoughts. She rolled out two pie crusts, deciding to somehow mail the second pie to Charles and hope it arrived in one piece. He deserved a pie, and more. Or perhaps she should try mailing something less fragile, like cookies.

She hadn't realized such men existed, ones who genuinely wanted to know a lady's opinion, even if he disagreed, which he sometimes did. They'd gotten into playful arguments over the merits of a certain Dickens novel, for instance, an activity she couldn't have imagined ever engaging in before, let alone enjoying.

She put the second crust into the tin and pressed it into place with care. How long would their long-distance friendship last, realistically? Another few months? A year or two? While some people managed to carry on such friendships for years and years, she worried that Charles would soon tire of her. She'd run out of interesting things to say, and his attention would be drawn away by the Emma Tanner of Toronto.

As she fluted the edge of the crust, she frowned. She hadn't revealed that she was plain, that she had no extraordinary talents and tended to follow instead of lead. That she'd never stand out in a crowd unless it happened to be part of a competition involving calculus or a Latin conjugation.

Enjoy this while it lasts.

Four

For the first time in memory, Jane sat in the Aid and Culture Society meeting with the plan to *say* something specific. When Emma would ask for input or suggestions for upcoming activities, Jane would raise her hand and suggest they go to the theater while the touring troupe of *Peter Pan* was in town for the next week. Jane felt as if her heart was in her throat; she could hardly breathe for nerves. In one palm she held the folded note she'd written up with the suggestion, a small piece of torn paper that grew moister by the minute. If Emma didn't ask for suggestions soon, Jane might very well leave without saying a word. Again.

She'd never dared speak up with something like a suggestion before. Normally she sat quietly, answering with affirmative replies when required, signing up for whatever charitable activity or performance was on deck. Today was different. Charles had given her the courage to speak up. She'd determined that she must attend the play so she could report on it in her next letter, as she had yet to finish all three of the books he'd recommended, which she was determined to do, and she had to have something new and fresh to write about.

But speaking up in the meeting would be hard; she wished it weren't necessary. Alas, it was; attending the play alone was absolutely out of the question. She'd feel as if she'd been abandoned by a beau or not popular enough to attend with a friend. And she would face all of that in front of hundreds of people. No, she could speak up here, with only twenty or so young adults to avoid that kind of humiliation.

Looking about the room, she counted how many were in attendance. She reached seventeen before pausing in her count; Thomas Allred had his eyes trained right on her. He sat directly across from her, so there was no mistake. Odd. She blinked in surprise, and he smiled back, making her smile in return. She reined in her smile quickly, however; how forward of her to smile at a man. She was no flirt.

At long last, Emma opened the floor to other business, and Jane forced herself to stand right away, before anyone else got up and she lost her nerve entirely. Especially now that the Allred boy kept looking at her. Why was he doing that?

Emma's eyebrows went up with apparent confusion at seeing Jane stand. "Leaving already?"

Jane had to swallow a knot forming in her throat. Emma had all but handed Jane a way to escape. She could walk out now, pretending that doing so had been her plan all along. As the thought crossed her mind, her hands tightened into fists, and the note dug into one palm. No, she had to speak up. For Charles.

I must have something worth writing to him.

"I have a suggestion for a future cultural activity," Jane managed, so quietly she wasn't sure anyone had heard.

Emma leaned against the desk at the front of the room and folded her arms. "By all means, tell us." She gestured to the floor before her, telling Jane to come forward and make her presentation.

Why couldn't Jane have simply made her little speech from her spot at the edge of the circle?

Go, and go now. Her gaze flitted nervously across the room and landed on Thomas again, who *still* had his focus on her and his smile aimed her direction. Odd. He'd always been kind and polite to all of the girls, but he'd never given Jane this much attention, not ever. Still smiling, he nodded encouragingly. Why he gave her attention today after more than a decade of virtually ignoring her, she had no idea, but his friendly expression calmed her frantically beating heart just enough for her to walk to the front of the room.

She cleared her throat and tried to speak loudly. "You all may have seen the announcements in the paper of a touring theater troupe in town. They're performing J. M. Barrie's *Peter Pan,* which was later adapted into a novel."

Several nods and murmurs in the affirmative. Thomas' smile turned into an all-out grin. Did he enjoy the theater, then?

Or is he making fun of me?

His expression and rapt attention disconcerted Jane; for several seconds, she lost her train of thought entirely. Instead of her suggestion for the club, all she could think of was that Thomas had an aquiline nose, bright blue eyes, and strawberry blond hair with the slightest bit of a wave. That he likely needed a haircut, but how he looked handsome in a disheveled kind of way when his hair was longer and a bit messy, as it was today. And how had she not noticed before?

When Jane didn't go on—how long had she been silent, staring at Thomas?—Emma continued for her, taking the note from Jane's hand and reading the details. "The Saturday matinee has the most affordable price, but the Thursday show has the most tickets available." She looked up. "I suppose we should put this to a vote. Who wants to attend the play as a club?" Emma set the note on the desk beside her, then looked around the room with an air of someone who had no interest in the affair.

Jane looked about too, willing hands to go up. *Don't make me go alone. Mother would never come along, and I have no other friends to invite. This was a horrid mistake.* She had to attend; she couldn't let Charles down. *But alone? Oh, I'll die.*

Finally, one hand went up. Thomas'. All eyes turned to him, several people wearing surprised expressions. "I'd like to go. I've always wanted to see that play. I hear it's quite fun."

From beside him, Priscilla rolled her eyes. "Isn't it for children? We're a bit old for fairy tales, don't you think?"

"I don't think anyone is ever too old for a good story," Thomas said to Priscilla. Then he deliberately turned to face Jane, to Priscilla's clear dismay. "I can go either day. You choose." His response was so unexpected, so kind, that Jane had to scramble for words. When she didn't answer immediately, his eyes dimmed. "Unless you don't want to go only with me. I can fully under—"

"No," Jane interrupted. "I'd be happy to go with you. How about the Thursday evening show?"

"At seven?" Thomas grinned broadly. "It's a date."

A date? Not really. Jane shot him a quick smile of gratitude, nodded, and returned to her seat. Her face felt awfully hot, but for the first time in memory, she didn't particularly care if other people noticed her blushing.

Five

Thursday evening, Thomas arrived at the theater with forty-five minutes to spare, wanting to be certain he didn't miss Jane's arrival and that they were in plenty of time to buy tickets. He went straight to the box office, where he purchased two. He'd prefer it if she didn't attempt to pay him back. Paying for her ticket would feel more like they were actually courting. But he'd gotten the tickets for practical reasons too: he wanted to buy them both, because the tickets could be sold out later, or worse, he and Jane could end up sitting apart. As he slipped the tickets into the breast pocket of his vest, he thought of openly courting Jane, something he'd wanted to do ever since they'd started exchanging letters almost three months ago. Ever since he'd realized what an extraordinary, beautiful woman she was. How had he not noticed before? The signs had always been there; he saw them at society meetings, now that he looked for them.

He'd been so blind. Now, every letter captivated him. He'd realized with stunning surprise that shy Jane Martin had grown up beside him into an intelligent, beautiful woman, and she'd done so without him knowing it. She'd always been quiet. As he paced before the theater, he wished she'd spoken up at least a little so he'd have known earlier what a jewel lay beneath the surface of her quiet demeanor.

Thomas checked the sidewalk for her in both directions and across the street. When he didn't spy her, he pulled out his pocket watch. Only fifteen minutes had passed since his arrival. Of course she wasn't here yet; the play wouldn't start for another thirty minutes.

What would he say when she did arrive? Maybe it was a good thing she wasn't here yet; he had time to compose himself. He shoved his hands into his pockets and once more paced before the glass doors of the theater, back and forth, consumed to distraction over what he'd say to Jane. More importantly, how could he win her over so she'd see him as something beyond another member of the Aid and Culture Society? She clearly cared for Charles, who was technically Thomas, although he'd worked on creating a voice for Charles that sounded refined and intelligent. But he *was* Charles. She just didn't know it. Yet. How could she find out—and not hate him for it?

Anxious, he tugged on the hem of his vest, not that it needed straightening. Then he adjusted his cravat, which he'd already tied to perfection at home an hour previous while his best shoes had dried from being polished. He wanted everything to be just right. His challenge for tonight and beyond included far more than Jane finally seeing see him as something other than another boy from their school years. In a very real sense, he was competing with the image of himself he'd created on paper in the form of Charles

Percival Wharton. What a stuffy name Thomas had invented. He was growing to hate Charles.

His eyes were trained on the ground as he paced in thought, brow furrowed. When a pale yellow dress appeared in his view, he caught himself, nearly tripping as he came to a stop to avoid careening into the woman. He sputtered an apology and looked up, his words cutting off at the sight of Jane. Her hair was down, reaching just past her shoulders, and gently curled. She wore a matching yellow headband that went across her forehead and had a beaded leaf design on one side. Her cheeks had more color in them than usual, which could have been from the cold, but he wanted to believe it was because of their impending evening together. Even her lips seemed to have a bit more color than usual. She looked angelic. Had she, too, spent extra time getting ready tonight? The idea made his stomach twist pleasantly.

"Hello, Thomas," she said. With a gloved hand, she indicated the box office. "Shall we buy our tickets?"

"Yes. I mean, no." His fingers seemed all thumbs as he fumbled in his pocket. Finally he produced the tickets. "I already bought them. Mezzanine, right in the center."

Jane smiled, her eyes brightening. In response, his mouth curved into a smile of its own. Had her eyes always sparkled so?

"That was very thoughtful of you," Jane said. "Thank you."

"You're—you're more than welcome," Thomas stammered, grateful that the sudden tightness in his throat had eased enough for him to speak. "Shall we?" He reached for one of the doors' large handles and pulled it open, then gestured for her to go inside.

She thanked him and passed through. He followed, feeling a strange mixture of emotions. So far, things were going swimmingly. But after their letters and the deep conversations they'd had in written form—wherein they'd both shared so much straight from the heart—acting so formal, and as if he didn't know her heart, drove him to distraction.

He had half a mind to take her by the shoulders, proclaim, "*I* am Charles," and kiss her soundly right there in the lobby. He couldn't do that, of course. Aside from the potential of embarrassing Jane by kissing her in public, he couldn't bear to think that she'd hate him for pretending to be someone else. He needed to find another way to gently let her know. Or perhaps he could win her over as himself, and Charles' letters could simply fade away.

They showed their tickets to an usher, who gestured up a staircase on one side of the lobby. They made their way up and looked for their seats. Jane walked ahead, and the entire way, Thomas couldn't help waves of guilt from washing over him, replacing the pleasant thumping of his heart and flipping of his middle he'd enjoyed a moment before.

I've been lying to her.

But I didn't mean to. It wasn't supposed to last, and it wasn't supposed to turn into this.

He'd expected to write one or two quick letters as a harmless way to smooth over Emma's ruffled feathers and make sure Jane didn't feel jilted.

"Is this right?" Jane asked, pointing to a seat.

"It sure is," he said.

She took her seat, and he took the one beside it. They sat so close, he could smell her perfume, which had a hint of something he couldn't quite put his finger on—hazelnut, perhaps? Vanilla? Whatever it was, he knew it intimately from the scent of her letters, and the smell had become dear to him. Except for his conscience nagging at him, he would have been quite happy to sit there all night, eyes closed, inhaling her aroma.

But he was also wearing his cologne. Did she recognize it? He calmed the worry by assuring himself that many men wore the same cologne. She'd never suspect.

Jane flipped through her playbill and read parts. "Are you familiar with the story of *Peter Pan*?"

"Somewhat," Thomas said, banishing thoughts of her perfume and cologne and his deceit. He was grateful that the house lights would soon hide his face, including any expression or blushing that would betray his guilt. Plus, he'd be able to breathe in her perfume without anyone noticing. "I read the novel that was published after the play, but it was years ago, and I'm sure I've forgotten a lot of it. I'm curious to see the original on a stage."

She gazed stage-ward. "I'm sure it'll be wonderful."

"Yes," he said, his voice going softer as he took in her profile. She was beautiful, with soft curves, almond-shaped eyes, and skin that could have been mistaken for porcelain if she hadn't had a smattering of tiny freckles across her nose and the tops of her cheeks—freckles he'd come to be quite partial toward.

He continued to marvel at how he'd lived so close to her for so long without being conscious of her beauty. Yet he knew the reason well enough: "flashy" girls like Emma, Priscilla, and several others created a different kind of effect. Their clothing, hair, jewelry, and hints of makeup tended to outshine the simple, natural beauties beside them. The attention inevitably stayed on them. Jane had slipped past his awareness until he'd seen her without the baubles and noise of the other girls masking her real self.

Jane turned to face him. "Thank you for coming with me," she said, leaning toward him and speaking quietly, something Emma and the others would never do. They would speak loud enough for audience members rows away to hear. "I wanted to see the play so very much, but I couldn't bear to come alone." She didn't know, of course, that he now knew all about her shyness and lack of confidence around other women.

"It's my pleasure, I assure you," Thomas ventured. "I never knew we shared a common interest in theater." There.

He'd made an attempt to connect their interests. A first step toward a courtship, perhaps. A tiny one.

"Truth be told," she went on, "a friend wrote to me about how much he enjoys the theater, and in my last letter, I promised to see this production and report on it."

Everything this evening seemed to return to Charles. Thomas's teeth ground together with illogical envy.

"I had to see it," Jane said. "I'm sure you understand."

He had to force his jaw to unclench. "Of course," he said, working on keeping his voice pleasant. Who'd have ever thought that he would become rabidly envious of a fictional man he'd invented? More, a man who had the same opinions, thoughts, and feelings Thomas himself held? Who, in all reality, *was* Thomas, except for the name, a fake mailing address, and an occasional high-brow phrase? It made little sense, yet the envy was there, changing into grief and hopelessness. He'd lost her heart to someone else and had no chance of winning it.

Worse, he'd concocted a situation where Jane's heart was bound to be broken, because Charles was a figment of his imagination.

Except that Jane actually sat beside her beloved Charles—Thomas *was* the man in the letter, but she didn't know that, of course. A distinct disadvantage.

The house lights finally dimmed. He breathed out heavily and settled in to watch the Darling children in their bedroom. Although he'd anticipated seeing how the novel differed from the stage play, his attention kept wandering to Jane, who remained rapt, as if she was taking in every detail and committing it all to memory so she could write about it. Her next letter would likely include a long description of everything about the play, from the sets and costumes to the actors. Surely she'd leave out the detail about going to the play with a male friend. For the first time since the beginning of their correspondence, he dreaded getting a letter from her.

I was there, he'd want to say in reply. *Right beside you.*

Melancholy consumed him. He watched Jane out of the corner of his eye. Against the glow of the stage lights, her skin seemed almost alabaster, flawless. He couldn't continue to pretend. He had to say something. Perhaps at intermission, he could find a way to tell her the truth. She'd *have* to stay for the end of the play, and when it ended, she would have had time to think through it all. If she'd become angry, her emotions would have had time to settle during the final act. Perhaps by the time the curtain fell, she'd realize that he truly cared for her as Charles did, because he *was* Charles.

Yet he'd come to know that Jane had more fire in her than that. She might well stalk out, incensed, and she'd never again speak to him. He'd never get another one of her delightful, thought-provoking letters.

Tinker Bell came on stage, or rather, the ball of light representing her did, and soon the audience had to clap to save the fairy. The children in the audience wore broad smiles, and their eyes were wide with the pure magic of the moment. They looked as he'd often felt upon receiving Jane's letters. In a sense he supposed that he'd felt as if he'd been experiencing magic too, a magic extending beyond friendship to love. Jane had turned his life inside out by writing so honestly and beautifully and . . . He couldn't explain it. He quite simply loved Jane and couldn't wait to receive her next letter. He often wrote his letter the same day he received hers. He couldn't mail them back the same day, of course. He had to pretend that the postal system was sending their letters over hundreds of miles. As it was, he deliberately smeared the postmarks so she wouldn't be able to tell where they really came from. Waiting those extra days was necessary for maintaining the mirage, but doing so was pure torture. He'd wanted a chance to be alone with her for weeks now, and here they were, but she was thinking of Charles.

Thomas gave up trying to follow the play. Jane's

attention seemed so caught up in the action on stage that she wouldn't notice how he was no longer looking at the stage at all but had even turned his head to gaze upon her. He'd hear all about the play from her anyway. For now, he pondered on how to cross the barrier between them. He decided against doing so tonight. It had to be another time and in another place. He'd need to ponder how to tell her the truth while retaining her friendship. And do so while retaining the chance to create something *beyond* friendship. Perhaps such a thing wasn't possible. His chest felt heavy at the thought, and his mouth went dry.

At last, the curtain fell. Intermission had arrived. Jane turned to him and caught his gaze already on her. To his relief, she smiled. "Isn't Captain Hook remarkable?"

"Quite." Thomas managed, although his voice sounded off pitch and tinny to his ears. "Care to take a walk about, stretch your legs a bit before the second half?"

"Sounds delightful." Jane stood, and together they walked back down the stairs to the lobby. She excused herself to go to the powder room, during which time he agonized as he'd never known was possible. The angel and devil warred again, one voice whispering that he should tell Jane everything, because she would understand, and because she deserved to know. The other voice countered that he couldn't do such a reckless thing, that telling the truth would hurt her too much, and she'd hate the sight of him forevermore if he so much as breathed a word.

Before he could come to a decision, Jane reappeared, looking beautiful and fresh and glowing. Thomas opened his mouth to tell her—well, something about the truth—but she spoke instead.

"I cannot wait to tell Charles all about this. He's my letter-writing friend I mentioned. He loves the theater so." She clasped her hands and looked about the lobby area, at the chandeliers hanging above them, seeming to admire the intricate carvings and woodwork.

"Oh?" Thomas managed. "Charles?"

"Surely you've seen our letters pass through the post office. We exchange letters every week."

"Yes. Yes, of course," he said, hating the pink flush her cheeks got at simply mentioning Charles. "Have you exchanged photographs?"

"Not yet," Jane said. "He seems quite well versed in the theater and would enjoy a report on *Peter Pan*. Although I'm sure he's visited much grander theaters than this one, as beautiful as this is."

"Perhaps," Thomas hedged. "Perhaps not."

"Isn't the actress who plays Wendy splendid? And the actress playing Peter—I don't know how she does all that flying."

"On wires," he said, distracted.

She tapped his arm playfully, which effectively cut off Thomas's voice box. He wanted to hold her hand. To hold all of her in his arms.

"I know she's on wires, silly," Jane said with a laugh. "I meant how she makes it look effortless. Imagine all of the practice she'd need to make it look just so."

"You're right, of course," he said, although he'd hardly heard a word after she'd touched his arm.

He decided to forget about unveiling Charles tonight. First she needed to see him in a favorable light. She needed to like Thomas for himself first. Perhaps then he could reveal his true identity. Yes. That was a good plan, and quite possibly the only one that would work. He held out an arm for her to take; then they headed back up the stairs to their seats.

"So tell me more about yourself, Jane," he said as they walked along. "We've known each other an awfully long time, but I don't think we really know each other, not really. Aside from theater, I don't know what else interests you." A slight fib, as he'd learned much about Jane over the last while, just not under his own name. "Do you by chance enjoy poetry? Personally, I enjoy Wordsworth and Coleridge." He felt slightly evil for deliberately leading the conversation into a place she loved.

Jane's step came up short, and her eyes went wide. "Those very poets are my favorites too!"

Thomas grinned. "You don't say?"

"What are the chances . . ." she said, her voice trailing off.

He thought hard about how to continue the conversation for the few minutes left until the lights were to go down. He'd found a way to make her like him, at least a little. Perhaps he could continue along these lines, showing her how much they had in common and how well he understood her, and then Charles could stop writing, leaving Thomas alone for her to care for, without ever needing to reveal the truth.

They settled into their seats once more. For the rest of the production, he thought of all the things he could work into their conversations.

She loves daffodils over roses.

She loves the scent of baking bread, but kneading the dough is a nuisance.

The perfect crystal star adorns her family's Christmas tree. She found it on a trip to New York.

She loves reading John Donne. Remember to read more of his poetry before bringing him up.

Ice cream in any flavor.

The list went on and on. Occasionally, he looked over at Jane. Sometimes she noticed, looked his direction, smiled, and returned to the play. For a good portion of the final act, he gazed at her hands resting in her lap and wished he could offer to cradle her hand in his, to kiss the back of it and hold her palm to his cheek.

All in good time. This evening is only the beginning.

Six

Jane felt a twinge of regret at how short her letter to Charles was today. Granted, she'd filled four pages, but she usually wrote three times that, easily. She'd mostly recounted the play from earlier in the week and her impressions of it: how the actor portraying Hook was pure genius, as was Peter, but she thought the Darling boys weren't as strong as the rest of the cast. How the sets and costumes were beautiful. And how she was eager to visit the theater again soon.

She did *not*, however, mention that she'd seen the production with a male friend, or that her eagerness to see another play, or perhaps a moving picture, had as much to do with wanting to spend time with Thomas again as it did with writing Charles. She had secretly enjoyed the night at the theater, especially the way Thomas had treated her, as if she mattered and had interesting things to say. She'd even felt beautiful for a few hours.

As she reread her letter, her omission about Thomas needled her. She couldn't end the letter on a note that was silently about another man. She groped for and found a different topic to close with.

I've long been interested in Victorian poets, but I have yet to read much of Elizabeth Barrett Browning. My next reading adventure, I've decided, is to read all of her works. After that, I'll turn to her devoted husband's. The Brownings, of course, will eternally be one of history's most celebrated couples; it seems only right that a lover of poetry would not have a complete education or collection unless he or she has been fully immersed in their poetry.

Besides, it's not often a reader gets the chance to see how life events influence a writer's work. In Elizabeth's case, or so I hear, her writing changed dramatically after she met and married Robert. Such a fascinating story!

I must go now; I have a pressing engagement. But I promise to write again soon, and with luck, my next letter will be much longer.

Faithfully yours,

Jane

She stared at the way she'd closed the letter. Was she indeed *faithful*?

Charles and I are friends. We are nothing more, at least for now. Even if I've thought of more with him.

Except that for the last while, ever since the play, her thoughts had often strayed to Thomas. If he and Charles could somehow be woven into the same person—the intellect and culture of Charles, with the fun, sweet personality of Thomas—such a man might well be her perfect match.

Deliberately, she blew on the ink, then slipped the pages into an envelope and sealed it. She'd mail the letter on her way to meet Thomas at the park, where they planned to take a walk before visiting an exhibit at the museum. Jane hurried out of her room and down the stairs. She snatched her shawl from the coat rack on her way out the door, eager to see him again.

She walked quickly to the post office, but when she reached it, her step slowed, and she looked at Charles's letter in her hands. She still hoped to meet Charles one day, and she still felt that same thrill whenever she received one of his letters, which had become even more intimate and devoted of late. Save for his last letter, which had been shorter, as hers was today. But she had gotten the distinct impression that he would soon declare his love for her, and she was eager and willing to do the same in return.

Yet here she was, about to meet up with Thomas. *Was she being unfaithful to Charles?* She shook her head and reached for the door.

We haven't officially met, for Pete's sake. He's not my beau.

The twist in her middle continued as she stepped inside. A glance of the front desk had the butterflies flitting about in her middle. She smiled, hoping to see Thomas sitting at the desk, yet knowing he didn't work the afternoon shift today. Of course he didn't; they had plans to meet in the park in only fifteen minutes. Even so, her heart drooped the slightest bit when she spotted his sister, Dorothy, behind the desk instead.

"Hello, Jane," she said cheerfully. "Can I help you with something?"

"Just mailing a letter," Jane said, holding the missive out, which already bore the required postage.

"I'll be sure he gets it," Dorothy said, then blushed. "I mean, I'll be sure it gets into today's outgoing mail." She looked distracted as she returned to her work sorting incoming letters.

"Thank you. Have a nice day." Jane turned toward the door. As she pulled it open, however, Dorothy's words rang in Jane's ears again. What had she meant by she'd be sure "he" got the letter? Yes, the letter was addressed to a man, but Dorothy herself surely wouldn't be traveling to Toronto anytime soon. Odd. Perhaps she was used to saying such things in the course of her work, and the wrong phrase came out. Yes. That had to be it.

Jane strode to the park, putting Charles out of her mind now that she anticipated seeing Thomas. He was usually early to their meetings, which had become almost daily since their evening at the theater about a week ago. She found a bench, where she sat and tried to enjoy the slight breeze, sunlight, and squirrels chattering in the trees, but she couldn't help looking about, expecting every person who rounded the corner to be Thomas. Her heart rate picked up as she waited. And waited some more. She checked her watch. He was late. Only two minutes late, but that was the equivalent of ten minutes late for Thomas.

What was keeping him? Perhaps he'd forgotten. Jane smoothed her hair with one hand, making sure her curls and pins were in place. She pinched her cheeks to give them a little color. And she tried to be patient. It didn't work. She should have brought along her new poetry book to pass the time, but she'd left it at home, not wanting to tell him why she was reading it. He tended to get a far-off, distracted look whenever she mentioned Charles.

Finally he appeared at the end of the lane. Jane stood quickly and made her way to him, grateful and relieved to see him. And yes, there was the crazy tumbling in her middle upon seeing his disheveled hair and his crooked grin aimed right at her. She could still hardly fathom how she'd never paid him mind until recently. He was strikingly handsome, and he had a way of looking at her that made her knees feel no stronger than tapioca pudding.

He held out his hands for her to take, smiling broadly himself. "Jane," he said, drawing her nearer. "I'm so sorry I'm late. I was delayed—post-office business." He shook his head as if dismissing some worry, yet something in Jane's chest twisted. She'd just been at the post office. She hadn't seen him there. Surely he knew she was aware of his work schedule; they planned their outings around it.

I'm worrying over nothing, she thought. *He lives right behind the post office. If there's ever any trouble, of course he's called to help. He was probably at home looking over records or something.*

Just because *she* had a secret, keeping her friendship with Thomas from Charles, and felt disloyal over it, didn't mean that everyone else was hiding something.

"Don't you worry at all," Jane said, smiling broadly. "You're only a few minutes late, and late for the first time." She took her place beside him, slipping her arm through his and resting hers in the crook of his elbow. "Shall we?"

"Please."

Together they walked the paths of the park, passing other couples, groups of friends chatting, and the occasional mother with a baby carriage. She and Thomas nodded to each in turn. They talked about what they expected to see in the art exhibit, which led to talk of their favorite artists. They both liked Rembrandt and his contemporaries and agreed that Van Gogh had been a mad genius.

They walked in comfortable silence for a few moments; Jane enjoyed every step, feeling at once entirely comfortable with Thomas, yet jittery all over, but in the best way possible. Her heart pounded crazily against her ribcage like a hummingbird trying to escape.

She let her mind wander among the clouds as he talked about the latest book he'd read, *Ben Hur*. Her thoughts returned to earth only when he asked a question. "Have you read it?"

"*Ben Hur?*" she asked, making sure he hadn't brought up another title while she'd daydreamed about walking with him through a meadow of daisies. "I'll put it on my list to read."

"Do. You can borrow my copy. You'll enjoy it, definitely. And I'll put the Brownings on my list of writers to read soon, just as you have." Thomas kept walking, but Jane's feet felt like they had stepped into tar; they wouldn't move. He took another step or two until he looked over and realized he'd lost her. He turned back, eyebrows raised in curiosity.

Jane's mind spun as if there were a puzzle she couldn't quite put together. "I never told you about the Brownings."

Thomas blanched, and his eyes suddenly widened. "Of course you did, I—" But his voice cut off, and guilt was written all over his face. Guilt which could mean only one thing.

She marched forward, shaking. "You've been reading my letters to Charles! He's the only person I've ever said a word to about the Brownings." She stood there, daring him to deny it. Wanting him to, silently begging him to. But his cheeks only colored. Suddenly his tardiness made sense. "You had to have read the letter I just mailed, and *that's* why you're late." Anger boiled in her middle and coursed through her veins. "How *dare* you? I thought—I thought you were my *friend*." Her first real friend. Her eyes welled up with tears, but she fought to keep them back. She would *not* cry. She would not be made a fool by Thomas Allred.

She waited for an answer, any answer that would put her out of her misery. But his mouth only opened and shut, and he shook his head helplessly.

"Deny it if you can," she said, wanting to add, *Please.*

His face had gone ashen with an emotion she couldn't pinpoint. Shame? Regret? Embarrassment? Not that it mattered. He'd betrayed her confidence and pretended to be her friend. Why he'd done so, she'd never know. But she could put an end to it at least.

"Goodbye, Mr. Allred." Jane spun on her heels and stalked off. After a few yards, tears fell in hot tracks down her cheeks. She kept her back ramrod straight and didn't lift a hand to wipe the tears away. She had to maintain what little dignity she had left.

But when she reached home and had escaped to her room, she collapsed on the bed and wept, caring nothing for how many tears she shed. What a fool she'd been! *This* is what Dorothy meant—that she'd give the letter to her brother. How many other people knew? She'd never be able to walk the streets of Provo again without wondering who was snickering at her expense behind their polite nods and smiles.

And the Aid and Culture Society! Thomas had probably bragged to his friends there, or at the least told some of the other girls.

Oh, I can never show my face there again!

After some time, Jane's tears slowly dried up. She got off the bed and looked at herself in the mirror. Her face was puffy and had splotches of red all over. She looked as bad as she felt.

How would she be able to tell Charles, or ever write to him again, knowing her words would first be read by someone else?

Jane paced her room, crying for a spell and refusing to come down to supper when her mother knocked on the door and called her down. "I'm not hungry, Mother, but thank you."

Her mother opened the door a crack. "Will you come down anyway? You have a visitor."

Jane froze in place, then slowly rotated to look at her mother. "Who is it?"

"Thomas Allred. He says it's urgent, and I believe him. He looks quite ill."

"Good," Jane said shortly. At her mother's horrified expression, she sighed and shook her head. "Tell him I'm unwell and can't see visitors."

Her mother opened her mouth briefly, but at Jane's terse shake of her head, she relented. "I'll tell him," she said and quietly clicked the door shut.

The nerve of the man trying to talk to her now, after his lies had come to light!

She fumed, marching to her bedroom window, where she peered through a crack in her curtains and watched Thomas walk away. Part of her wanted to call him back so she could demand answers, but the other part reminded her in no uncertain terms that he was not to be trusted.

She'd almost come to the conclusion that she loved Thomas and that Charles would always be nothing more than a dear friend. How wrong she'd been. After ten minutes of pacing and ranting against Thomas under her breath, Jane finally calmed down enough to see reason. Somehow she would continue to write to Charles, even if that meant giving her letters to Thomas' mother, Mrs. Allred, the postmistress herself. Jane could still attend school in Salt Lake to become a secretary. No one would know her there.

It's that or never leave the house for the next decade, she thought miserably as she pictured life as a cloistered nun. Her eyes strayed to her bookshelf, which had a collection of the Brownings' poetry. She straightened her back and decided to be the woman Charles believed her to be. She'd study the Brownings' work, then write Charles a nice, long letter all about it.

She fetched the book, then settled on her bed with two pillows at her back and began reading. Robert Browning had plenty of satirical and dark poetry, with men killing off their wives and such. Yet he had a softer, and often tragic side, too. After an hour, she turned to Elizabeth's work and read until the room grew dark and she had to turn one of the family's new electric lights to keep reading.

She lost complete track of time as she immersed herself into poetry. Most of it was a balm to her wounded soul, especially Robert Browning's satirical pieces. She pretended that the duchess who was murdered was really Thomas. The fictional act had a feeling of justice in it, and she had to smile.

Then she came to one of Elizabeth's poems, and all of her confused emotions, including the feelings she'd felt for Thomas, which she had started to call love, all came flooding back. The end of one poem in particular cut her to the center.

I must bury sorrow
Out of sight.
—Must a little weep, Love
(Foolish me!)
And so fall asleep, Love,
Loved by thee.

A tear splashed onto the page. Only then did she realize she was crying. She still cared for Thomas. Or at least, she cared for the man she'd believed him to be.

Another knock at her bedroom door startled her. Once again, her mother cracked the door open, but Jane shook her head and wiped her cheeks with both hands. "I'm not seeing him."

"He's not here," her mother assured her, opening the door further and coming inside. She crossed to the bed and sat on the edge, then took Jane's hand in hers. "I don't know what's happened between you, but whatever it is, I'm terribly sorry."

Jane leaned into her mother's embrace and cried hot tears. When she pulled away, her mother was holding out an envelope. "He did drop this off, though."

Jane just stared at it as if it might be a viper.

"I think you should read it," her mother said. "If you could have seen his face when he gave it to me, you'd know how tormented he is." At Jane's snort, her mother insisted. "Just read it. Will you do that much?"

With a deep sigh of resignation, Jane held out her hand for the envelope. "I'll read it. I promise."

"Good." Her mother leaned in and kissed Jane's cheek. "Let me know if you need anything."

"Thanks, Mama," she said with a weak smile as her mother shut the door behind her.

What could he possibly have written? And what could he say that could make any difference? With the desire to get the misery over with, she opened the envelope and slipped out a piece of stationery that looked oddly familiar—ivory, with one deckle edge. The writing was similar too—a dark blue fountain pen, and long, slanted strokes.

Jane's heart sank uneasily. What did this mean? This letter was from Thomas, wasn't it? Not from Charles? She cautiously read the short letter.

Dearest Jane,

For you have become dear to me, although I hadn't expected it when this all began. Please let me explain everything, and let me do so face to face. All I'll say here is that everything I ever wrote to you as Charles was true, and everything I ever said as myself was true too. And whichever identity you choose to see me as, the deepest truth is that I love you.

Her eyes widened. Thomas *was* Charles? How was that possible? She gazed into the darkness out her window and tried to comprehend what it meant. She'd told *Thomas* the deepest thoughts and desires of her heart? As anger threatened to mount, she thought through what he'd written. *He'd* shared just as many private thoughts and feelings with *her*. And he said they were all real.

And that he loves me. Her mind spun, trying to create order out of the chaos her world had been shattered into.

I did wish for one man made up of Thomas and Charles, she thought. *Oh, the irony.*

There was more writing on the page. He had written out the entirety of number 43 from Elizabeth Barrett Browning's *Sonnets from the Portuguese*.

> *How do I love thee? Let me count the ways.*
> *I love thee to the depth and breadth and height*
> *My soul can reach, when feeling out of sight*
> *For the ends of being and ideal grace.*
> *I love thee to the level of every day's*
> *Most quiet need, by sun and candle-light.*
> *I love thee freely, as men strive for right;*
> *I love thee purely, as they turn from praise.*
> *I love thee with the passion put to use*
> *In my old griefs, and with my childhood's faith.*
> *I love thee with a love I seemed to lose*
> *With my lost saints. I love thee with the breath,*
> *Smiles, tears, of all my life; and, if God choose,*
> *I shall but love thee better after death.*

All my love,

Thomas

Beautiful words, but did he mean them? Oh, how she wanted him to mean them and to believe he felt them. But it was easy to quote words written by someone long dead. She noticed a post script.

P.S. Meet me at the park tonight at nine o'clock. I beg this one favor of you.

Should she go? Jane could hardly think. The clock said she had an hour to decide. She got off the bed and paced for a moment but then went to her writing desk, where she opened the drawer containing all of Charles' letters, bound with a pink ribbon. And Jane spent the next hour rereading the letters with the understanding this time that the writer behind them had been Thomas all along.

Her Thomas.

If he really did care, if this wasn't some joke, then maybe she could meet him.

And if he didn't care, perhaps going would help her sort that out as well.

If I don't go, I'll always wonder.

Decision made, Jane went to her vanity table. She fixed her hair and powdered her nose, although she wished the powder would cover the splotches. She finished her attempt at beauty with a thin layer of pale lipstick. Perhaps it would be too dark for him to be horrified by her appearance. She checked the clock. It was already time to go.

Seven

Thomas sat on the bench at their usual meeting place at the park, his head in his hands, his fingers grabbing chunks of hair. He'd been there ever since leaving the note with Jane's mother. It had been a long hour. Would she come? And would she give him a chance to explain? If so, would she believe him? Would she be so cross that all hope for a relationship was already gone? The thought of losing her was more than he could bear. Someone might as well shatter his heart into a thousand shards.

At long last, he heard footsteps against the dirt and gravel of the path. He looked up, his heart aching with anticipation. Dark as it was, and with a lamppost behind the woman, he couldn't quite make out who it was at first. He stood, and waited, and hoped as the figure drew nearer and her features resolved. Jane.

"I'm so glad you came," he said, breathing a sigh of

relief. But her wary expression made him regroup. Of course she was still angry. Hurt. And it was his fault. He went to her side and held out his arm. "Shall we?" he asked as he had several times before.

She didn't take his arm. "Not for the moment, thank you," she said in a painfully polite voice. She walked forward with her hands clasped before her.

He nodded. "Very well, then. I suppose I deserve that."

"Yes, you do," she said as he caught up to her.

"You must believe that I never expected this." He glanced over and noted her jaw tightening, so he hurried to go on. "I never meant to hurt anyone. I did it at first as a favor to Emma so she could save face because there weren't enough letter friends for everyone. I didn't expect that I'd come to—" His voice cut off. He wanted to say the words he'd written. To tell her face to face that he loved her. But he couldn't get another word out, not unless she spoke first.

"Emma knows, then?" Jane asked, distraught.

"No. She thinks I found you a letter friend from a different area of Canada. Not that they were from me or that it became—" Again his voice failed him. He cleared his throat. "On my honor, Dorothy is the only person who knows, and I told her only to be sure that your letters weren't actually shipped off to Toronto."

"Why would you care if they had been?" Jane asked. "They'd eventually be returned when the postman couldn't find the address."

Thomas took a few steps before replying, weighing his words and hoping he'd pick the correct ones. "It mattered because I could not wait for your letters. You can't possibly understand how hard it was to wait long enough between them for me to dare to send one back so it would look like your letter had gone to Canada, and then his—I mean mine—had traveled back."

Jane's face softened slightly, and she tilted her head toward him. "Really?"

"Before our letters, I had no concept of how truly wonderful you are, in every way. We've practically grown up at each other's sides, yet you were hidden to me." He stopped and turned toward Jane. He reached for her hands, and—glory!—she let him take them. "Jane, you have become dearer to me than any woman I've ever known. I wanted to find a way to put an end to the letters, to let you know the truth, but . . ."

A slow smile crept across Jane's face. "I think I understand."

"You—you do?"

She nodded. "Ever since *Peter Pan*, I knew you were different. At first, I wished you were Charles, and I felt guilty for wanting to be with you instead of him."

The moment hung suspended in time as they gazed into each other's eyes. Thomas softly grazed her jaw with his thumb. "You are so beautiful . . ."

Jane caught her breath. "What . . ." No other words came out, but her cheeks flushed the most fetching shade of pink.

"I can't get your eyes out of my mind. Or your freckles. You have just the right number, you know. Your smile is warmer than the sun. Shall I go on?"

She smiled shyly and lowered her gaze as if hearing a compliment about her appearance for the first time. "I just never—"

He reached forward, and with one finger, he lifted her chin so their gazes met again. His heart pounding, he found himself murmuring part of an Elizabeth Barrett Browning poem. "'Eyes in your eyes . . .'"

Jane's smile spread, lighting up her eyes. She was even more beautiful when she smiled like that, especially now, with the lamppost's golden light making her look like an angel. She leaned closer, enough that he could almost feel her breath. There was her perfume again. "'Lips on your lips . . .'"

she whispered, finishing the line, but her voice went up as if it was a question.

He pulled her closer and complied, pressing his lips to hers softly at first, then, as she responded, more fervently. He held her tightly, unwilling to let the moment go as the warmth of joy and love erupted inside him.

Mrs. Browning's sonnet repeated in his mind. He knew he'd spend years counting the ways he loved beautiful Jane Martin.

ABOUT ANNETTE LYON

Annette Lyon is a Whitney Award winner, a two-time recipient of Utah's Best in State medal for fiction, plus the author of ten novels, a cookbook, and a grammar guide as well as over a hundred magazine articles. She's a senior editor at Precision Editing Group and a cum laude graduate from BYU with a degree in English. When she's not writing, editing, knitting, or eating chocolate, she can be found mothering and avoiding the spots on the kitchen floor.

Find her online:

Website: http://AnnetteLyon.com

Blog: http://Blog.AnnetteLyon.com

Twitter: @AnnetteLyon

Blackberry Hollow

by Heather B. Moore

One

1908—England

Lucy Quinn reread the solicitor's letter as she sat in a jostling carriage that was taking her and her mother to Quinn Manor. She couldn't quite believe the words of the notice she'd received three weeks before, even though she was now traveling with her mother to said Quinn Manor, located in Stanmer Park, several hours south of London.

As sole heir, you have inherited Quinn Manor, including all of its properties and possessions.

The place was built in the early eighteenth century, Lucy had learned in her research of her father's family. Her father's death three years before had apparently left Lucy as the only direct descendant. Her uncle Jonathan Quinn, the eldest brother, never had children and had recently passed away.

Lucy had never met any of her father's English family, as she'd been born in New York, although she'd been named after her great-great-aunt Lucille Quinn, who'd never married and who had died in her thirties. Curiosity about the ancestor she was named after and, of course, interest in learning more about her other relatives, were two reasons for making the long journey.

She glanced over at her widowed mother, who had finally dozed off. It seemed her mother had more questions than Lucy herself did. But one thing was certain: Lucy wanted to see Quinn Manor before she sold it.

Lucy turned to look out the carriage window and let out a sigh as she peered at the countryside rolling by, where the colors of green were touched by the autumn oranges, yellows and reds. It was beautiful in its own way, as was her home in New York. Lucy definitely enjoyed her family's stately three-story home on a wide avenue where shops, restaurants, and theaters were only a short carriage ride away.

She was American through and through, so although the notion of living on an English estate was quite romantic, it was far from practical. Not to mention her practically engaged status with Robert Jamison. He had offered to come on the trip, but last-minute business had kept him in New York. Robert was always busy, it seemed, though when he did pay her attention, she felt like the luckiest girl in the world.

Robert had sent along some articles for her to read while she was in England. "Your sketching is nice, but not really a conversation piece," he'd told her more than once. It was only natural that Robert expected his wife to be well-versed in economics and politics. Lucy didn't mind Robert's suggestions—she wanted to be the best companion, and if that meant reading boring articles on the state of the American economy so she could have intelligent conversations about it, then so be it.

As she thought of the sketch papers and pencils she'd

also brought, she allowed herself a secret smile. She'd find the time to read Robert's articles, but she also fully planned to never forget this trip—and drawing it would be better than writing about it.

Lucy kept her gaze on the window as they turned off the main road onto a narrow lane. Majestic trees lined this lane, seeming to reach the cloudy sky above. It was September, before the legendary English rainy season, but even so, the sky did not look promising.

Her mother stirred next to her. "How long have I been asleep?" Mrs. Julia Quinn's hat was askew, and her brown eyes were a bit dull from sleep.

"Maybe an hour," Lucy said, then stifled her own yawn.

People said Lucy looked a lot like her mother with her brown eyes, wavy brown hair, and fair skin that freckled in the summer.

Her mother straightened, fixing her shawl about her shoulders. "We must be arriving soon, right? I had no idea this place was so far from London."

Lucy turned her attention to the window again. In truth, she wasn't exactly sure how far Quinn Manor was from London, but the fact that they were now on a lane more like a country path gave her some hope they'd soon arrive.

The carriage slowed, approaching a rather large gate, nearly as tall as the carriage.

She reached for her mother's hand. "I think we've arrived."

Sure enough, the carriage came to a stop, and the driver climbed down. Through the window, Lucy watched him push open the gate, then climb back up onto the driver's seat. They jolted forward again, and Lucy couldn't keep her eyes from the estate.

A massive lawn, littered with autumn leaves, led up to a two-story manor that looked like a painting from a storybook. A gorgeous fountain sat in the middle of the still-green lawn, and closer to the house was a mass of rose bushes, all intently blooming as if competing with each other. Dark green ivy climbed the edges of the home, reaching for the dozen windows. To the left side of the house stood a forest of trees, their leaves brilliant shades of orange, yellow, and red, bright even beneath the clouds.

"Oh, Mother," Lucy whispered. "I cannot sell this place."

Her mother's scoff brought her back to reality. "You'll say that until the winter sets in, then find yourself spending the days huddled by a fire." She smoothed her skirt, then repositioned her hat. "Your father always said there was nothing modern about this manor. No electric lights or radiators. It would cost a fortune to renovate. Besides, what would Robert think? You can't very well be married to a man on another continent. I'd never have any grandchildren."

Lucy knew her mother was right, but for now, Lucy wanted to pretend she would stay longer, perhaps forever. The manor was small according to English standards. But this property was perfectly charming.

Perhaps she could convince Robert to move to England, or this could be their summer home, and they'd fashionably travel back and forth between continents. Yet even as she thought it, she knew Robert would not be content away from his thriving stock broker company. He was always in the middle of things—vibrant and intelligent, with ambitions for politics—and he was the last man Lucy could picture living a quiet life in the middle of the English countryside.

No, Lucy would have her two weeks here. She would sketch the beautiful scenery to her heart's content, and then she'd meet with the solicitor in London before returning home. Papers would be signed, and once the estate sold, Lucy would have a sizable inheritance. It was exciting to consider. She'd be a self-made woman marrying the most famous bachelor in New York City.

Not a bachelor for long, though. Lucy was certain Robert was close to proposing. This trip had set that back, of course, but once she returned, it wouldn't be long before she was booking a reception hall.

I am a lucky girl.

Two

Calvin Bevans scowled at the broken fence along his property line. It seemed he'd be spending his time off doing manual labor. The cracked wood extended for a couple of dozen meters, and there would be much to do in repairing it. First task—order new wood.

He hesitated before turning away and walking back to his house. This part of his land bordered the Quinn property. Perhaps they had replacement wood stored. If Calvin were to study his father's well-kept ledgers, he might be able to discover who had originally built the fence to see if there was extra wood stored somewhere. But such a study would take hours. Calvin was tired of paperwork. Besides, he was sure his father had built it. It seemed that the Bevans Estate had always been saddled with the majority of the upkeep. The history between the two families was not friendly.

The sun peeked out from behind the clouds for a

moment, reminding Calvin that he was on vacation. His job as a barrister kept him at the townhouse in London most of the time. He'd used his summer vacation to watch some of the 1908 London Olympic Games, so he put in extra hours to make up for that and wasn't able to check on his ancestral estate until now.

It had been neglected for too long.

Calvin continued along the property line, hoping he wouldn't find any more damage. It seemed that hiring a man a few days a month wasn't enough . . . Calvin would have to pay for more work. Since he'd been a young boy, he knew he'd inherit his great-grandfather's estate, and Calvin had always looked forward to it. He supposed he looked at it from a status viewpoint, rather than with the reality that he would be sinking money into a place that would only require more and more money. It never ended.

Calvin was too busy to enjoy it besides. The house was enormous—much too big for just him and a couple of servants. He rarely invited guests on his sporadic vacations, because, frankly, his closest university friends had all up and married. They were starting families of their own, leaving Calvin behind.

Logic told him that at thirty-one, he wasn't all that old; in fact, in London he spent after-hours with other barristers who were older and still single. But each one of them had a strange quirk. One was nearly bald except for some excessive ear hair; another bachelor friend had a horrible stutter, and a third seemed to hate all women.

Calvin fit into none of those categories . . . He believed himself to be a pleasant fellow and not too terrible-looking. He certainly didn't hate women. *Nothing is wrong with me. So why do I feel like I'm dragging my feet in life? Turning circles, and getting nowhere?*

He'd reached the far edge of his property that sat atop a hill. A wooden sign, which looked like it had been carved a century ago, read *Blackberry Hollow*. Calvin had been fascinated with the hollow as a child, but it had been a good many years since he'd ventured there.

Calvin gazed at the tangled blackberry bushes, and he was surprised to see a plethora of large berries, fully ripe and practically falling off their branches. He strode down the hillside and picked a few, then popped them into his mouth. The sweetness burst in his mouth, making him crave his mother's pies. Both of his parents were long gone, and his sister wasn't around to make them either. She was living in London, busy being a mother.

Out here in the blackberry patch, Calvin suddenly felt quite alone in the world.

He walked slowly up the far side of the hill and stood there for a moment, looking over Quinn Manor. He'd read about the passing of Jonathan Quinn in the papers, and Calvin's housekeeper had informed him that a niece from America had inherited the place. He supposed it would be auctioned off now. It was hard enough for a born and bred English gent to keep up with an old estate, so he wondered whatever an American woman would do with one.

He was about ready to start down the hill, when, across the quietness of the countryside, he heard the distinct sound of a pair of horses and a carriage. He paused and watched as a carriage came into view. Curious, he stood in his spot and waited as the carriage pulled up to the manor and two women were helped out by the driver.

Calvin didn't recognize the driver or the women, and so he assumed they must be the Americans. He wasn't close enough to distinguish much about them, except that one seemed to be older—the mother, perhaps?

The older woman followed the driver toward the house, but the younger woman walked to the front of the carriage, looking in Calvin's direction. He didn't think she could see him, at least not directly.

She set out toward him, surprising Calvin so much, he didn't move. She'd soon enough find the stone wall she'd have to walk along to reach the gate before she could reach his property and the hollow.

The older woman called out, her voice faint, and words indistinguishable. The younger visitor stopped and turned, then answered back. After a final glance behind her, one that landed almost directly where he stood, the young woman walked back toward the house.

Calvin let out his breath—not realizing he'd been holding it. His heart had been hammering like a school boy watching a horse race. And he'd been doing absolutely nothing but observing an American woman walk toward him.

Three

I t was like a dream, or, more accurately, like a description from a travel book. The man on the hill looked as if he were part of an advertising bill for estate living in England. Behind him sprawled a mansion that could have housed a dozen families. With the clouds in the sky, the mansion looked a bit forlorn and gothic, which only intrigued Lucy more.

Perhaps the man on the hill was a ghost. But when she had set out toward the hill and he had moved, Lucy had known he was real. A thrill had run through her as she thought about meeting a neighbor of one of her relatives, someone who could tell her about her uncle and the history of Quinn Manor. He could tell her of weddings held here, of births, funerals, parties, summer picnics . . . But she'd have to meet the neighbors later. Perhaps they'd invite her to English tea.

The thought made her smile.

"Who was that man?" her mother asked as she approached.

Lucy glanced over her shoulder again. He was gone. "Our neighbor, I assume. You didn't give me a chance to find out."

"Oh, Lucille. You can't go traipsing about talking to strange men."

Lucy laughed. "There's no reason I can't introduce myself. Besides, he's only strange until we learn his name."

The driver had set their luggage by the front door, and Lucy knocked. "We'll find out soon enough who he is from Mrs. Yates."

Her mother pursed her lips as the door was opened by a stout woman wearing a black dress.

"Mrs. Yates?" Lucy said.

"Yes," the woman said, her voice formal, but there was warmth beneath it. "I assume you are the Quinns from New York?"

Her mother answered. "Yes, it's wonderful to finally be here." She was already looking past Mrs. Yates into the hall.

"Peters will bring in your luggage," the housekeeper said. "Come in and sit by the fire, and I'll bring you some tea."

"Thank you," Lucy said as she followed her mother inside. The quiet from the countryside seemed to extend into the house, and Lucy marveled at the stillness. A dark wood staircase rose to the second floor, and hanging above it all was a gorgeous chandelier. Her mother was eyeing everything as well, more for the value of each item, surely, than from appreciation.

But that's why they'd come, Lucy reminded herself, to sell the house and decide if there was anything they wanted to keep before scheduling an auction. Mrs. Yates led the way into a sitting room with a cheerful fire. Vases of fresh-cut roses sat on tables dotted throughout the room.

Lucy's mother sank onto one of the sofas. "What a lovely room," she said. "Are the flowers from the gardens?"

Mrs. Yates beamed. "They're watched over quite particularly—we've always prided ourselves in our roses at Quinn Manor."

Crossing to the fireplace, Lucy studied the portrait hanging above the hearth. She'd seen a miniature of it in her father's possessions. Her father was a young boy in the picture, about ten, and his brother about thirteen. Between them stood a pair of hunting dogs. But now, she saw something new. The two boys were standing on a hill . . . one that looked like the hill she'd seen their neighbor standing on.

Her thoughts turned to the man she'd just seen. She supposed she'd meet him soon enough. "Who lives to the north?" Lucy asked when Mrs. Yates bustled back in, carrying a tray full of tea things.

"That would be the Bevans family, except it's only Calvin Bevans III there now," Mrs. Yates said in a disapproving tone. "A bit reclusive, he's always been. Sent off his sister, let go most of the help, and now the place is falling apart."

Lucy settled onto the sofa next to her mother and reached for a tea cup from the tray Mrs. Yates had set on the low table. "Did he lose all of his money or something?"

"I don't rightly know," Mrs. Yates said. "I don't make it my business to guess, either." She set out two small plates and put a scone on each. "As much as I hate to see this manor sold and all the memories with it, it would be better than having it go downhill like the place next door."

"Do many of the estates in this area belong to the original families?" Lucy's mother asked.

Mrs. Yates clasped her hands in front of her. "Not many. They've been bought up by rich investors—some of them Americans. Over time estates have been renovated and used as vacation homes."

"Well, we certainly don't have that kind of money," Lucy's mother said with a laugh.

Mrs. Yates gave a curt nod, and Lucy knew the two women would get along fine.

"Perhaps you can show us the items you believe we should keep in the family," Lucy's mother continued. "And if there are a few things you'd like to keep yourself, for sentimental reasons, that can be arranged as well."

Mrs. Yates smiled—the first Lucy had seen from her. "That would be wonderful, ma'am."

A bell chimed from someplace in the hallway. "Mr. Peters is taking care of the driver, so I'd best answer the door," Mrs. Yates said and left the room. A moment later, a male voice echoed through the hallway and into the sitting room. Lucy was immediately on alert. "Do you think it's him? Our neighbor?" she whispered to her mother.

Lucy stood, thinking Mrs. Yates would be ushering him into the room at any moment, but the front door shut, and the house went silent again. From where Lucy stood, she could see the driveway and the man leaving. His back was to her, but she was certain he was the same man she'd seen before.

She was about to find Mrs. Yates when the woman hurried into the sitting room. "Well, that's that," she said, brushing her hands together, her face flushed.

"What happened?" Lucy asked.

The housekeeper let out a sigh. "Mr. Bevans won't bother you now. You can expect a peaceful stay and plenty of quiet to make your decisions about the house."

"You sent him away?" Lucy blurted. Her mother sent her a sharp look—one Lucy knew well. It meant to hold her tongue and her questions would be answered.

"We don't look kindly upon the Bevans. Not after how Calvin Bevans Sr. treated Lucille."

"Lucille? The woman my Lucy is named after?" her mother asked.

Lucy walked over to the sofa again and sat down, intrigued to hear the story about the Bevans and the great-great-aunt she was named for.

"Yes, that's the one," Mrs. Yates said. "Lucille was hopelessly in love with Calvin Bevans Sr. But she was never good enough for him, living in a simple manor house and all, and he married another woman who brought a sizable fortune to Bevans Estate."

Lucy knew that Lucille had never married, but she hadn't known that the woman was in love with the owner of the neighboring house. Lucy tried to remember what her father had told her about Lucille. "She continued to live here, then? Even after the eldest Mr. Bevans married?"

"And had three children," Mrs. Yates said. "Lucille had the purest heart. The woman even became friends with Calvin's wife. But in the end, it was too much for Lucille. Her heart gave out with grief before she was thirty."

It was a sad story, and the fact that it had started to rain outside made it even gloomier. Her mother continued asking questions, and Lucy rose and walked to the tall windows. The rain pelting on the panes obscured some of her view, but the estate was still charming. Her thoughts turned to the current Calvin Bevans. What would he say to the story about Lucille and his great-grandfather? Odd how, even after so many years, the housekeeper at Quinn Manor wouldn't welcome a Bevans into the home.

She turned to interrupt her mother's questioning about the furniture. "Are there any portraits of Lucille?"

"Oh yes," Mrs. Yates said. "On the second floor and in her old room, of course. We call it the blue room now—it was her favorite color and all."

A slight chill spread through Lucy, but she ignored it. "Can I visit her room?"

"Of course. This house belongs to you—and everything in it. Even Lucille's trinkets."

Lucy smiled and looked over at her mother, hoping she felt adventurous.

"Go on," her mother said. "You won't rest until you explore, but I'm too cozy sitting here. I can see everything in the morning."

In agreement, Mrs. Yates nodded toward Lucy. "Take an oil lamp with you. The sun is nearly set, even though you can't see it. The fires have been laid and lit in your bedrooms, so they should be comfortable by now."

Four

C alvin paced the length of his study as the light faded from the already dark room. It was ridiculous that a feud more than fifty years old was still in effect. All of those involved were dead. Still, the housekeeper of Quinn Manor had refused to let him inside to be introduced to the visiting Americans.

But that wasn't what had disturbed him the most today. He'd returned from his walk to a letter from Sylvia waiting on his desk. This meant she was on her way to see him now. His older sister could be an angel one moment, then the very devil the next. And it didn't help that she had married into extravagant money. Enough to turn Bevans Estate upside on its head and do a complete renovation without a dent in her husband's pocketbook.

Calvin settled on a cracked leather chair on one side of the mahogany bureau. It was littered with statements of accounts he'd gone over more than once. He could afford to make a few basic repairs, ones he'd set into effect this week, but that was the extent his money would stretch. His parents hadn't passed on debt, yet his father's investments had gone bad and hadn't been able to carry the estate through more than a few years.

But Calvin's pride had stopped him from borrowing one pound from his sister. Bevans Estate had been left to *him*. It was up to him to preserve the place, and if his business continued to thrive, then in about five years he'd be able to start serious renovations. Unfortunately, his sister's impatient nature had driven a wedge between them. So much so, that she hadn't been to the estate in over a year.

That was about to change . . . It seemed Sylvia was on her way, and by Calvin's calculations, she'd be there as soon as the next day.

Five

Lucy rested her hand on the latch to Lucille's room. Her heart pounded with both nervousness and excitement. She lifted the oil lamp higher, then turned the latch with her other hand. The door swung open, and Lucy was greeted with musty, cold air. She took a few steps inside, looking around in the dimness. Lucy practically tasted the dust as it irritated her throat.

A bed sat near the window, and next to it was a vanity dresser with bottles of what looked like perfume. White drapes covered the double windows, but the rest of the room seemed blue, although it was hard to distinguish the color in the almost darkness. Above a lounge chair, which sat opposite the bed, hung a large portrait.

Lucy crossed to it and held the lamp to the side of the frame. The woman in the picture looked sort of ethereal. Her hair was pale, and her skin more so. But her eyes were strikingly dark—Lucy couldn't tell if they were brown or dark blue or green. The woman sat on a chair, and a hand was on her shoulder.

Lucy raised the oil lamp to see a man standing behind Lucille. He didn't look like one of the dark-haired Quinn men she'd seen in the portrait corridor. This man was tall, with fair hair. Leaning forward for a better look, Lucy had an odd thought. Perhaps the man wasn't the woman's brother or father. Perhaps the man in the portrait wasn't a Quinn at all.

That would mean it could be Calvin Bevans, a strange idea. Why would Lucille have a portrait of her and the man who'd married another?

Lucy turned and looked at the bed. Had Lucille fallen asleep each night looking at that portrait? If so, it wasn't too far-fetched to think that the poor woman had died of a broken heart. After taking another look around, Lucy left the room.

She found her own room easily enough, where the fire had warmed the chamber, just as Mrs. Yates had said it would. Her luggage was already there, so after lighting every oil lamp in the room, Lucy set about unpacking. Without electric lights, the place was positively dim—but it was still intriguing. And thinking about Lucille made the history of the house all that more mysterious.

Lucy put away her underclothing in the bureau, then hung up her dresses in the closet. They were wrinkled from traveling but would likely smooth out with the moist English air. Nestled in her clothing was Robert's package. She smiled as she reread his farewell note to her. His handwriting was so bold and sure. He reminded her to pay special attention to a couple of the stock-market articles he'd included.

She leafed through the pages, deciding that if she read one per day, she'd finish by the time she stepped onto New York's shore. She'd like to be able to give him a good report when she returned, perhaps even impress him. Lucy smiled as she removed her sketchbook from beneath some folded clothing. It wasn't wrinkled or bent, and the pencils had all stayed untouched in their square tin.

By the time Lucy had finished unpacking and had gone into her mother's room to do the same for her, she realized there was still more than an hour before supper, and apparently her mother was going to remain in the sitting room with Mrs. Yates.

Lucy found herself with her sketchbook on her lap, drawing the outline of her room, then filling it in with details of the furniture. She marveled that everything in this house belonged to her. Every chair, every vase, even the frames around the window panes. Surely a new owner would rearrange things, so soon her sketches would be all that remained of how the house was organized.

She continued to sketch until the supper bell rang, when Lucy set her things aside and went downstairs. Dinner was a quiet event, with just her mother, so Mrs. Quinn insisted that Mrs. Yates join them. "Peters is welcome too," Lucy's mother said.

"Oh, he is content in his little room at the back of the house." Mrs. Yates turned to Lucy. "What did you think of the blue room?"

"You were right," Lucy said. "There isn't much to see with an oil lamp. But I was curious about the portrait over the sofa. Who's the man in it?"

Mrs. Yates clucked her tongue. "Mr. Bevans himself. It was their engagement portrait."

Lucy raised her brows. "They were engaged to be married?"

"They were, but Lucille called it off. She took her last breath with the portrait staring down at her." Mrs. Yates pursed her lips and stirred the creamed potatoes on her plate with a fork.

"What a scoundrel," her mother said, and Mrs. Yates gave her a significant look.

Lucy let the information sink in. "Well . . . I supposed we can explore the rest in the morning."

Her mother offered a half-smile, then turned her attention back to the silverware she was holding. "It will be a difficult thing to decide what to have sent home and what should stay with the house and be sold."

Mrs. Yates gave a slow nod. "I've made a list of what you need to particularly consider."

"I'm looking forward to going over it," Lucy's mother said. "After a good night's sleep."

Her mother retired early for the night, and Lucy tried to fall asleep too but found herself lying on the stiff bed, the image of Lucille's portrait in her mind. Why had Lucille kept such a bold reminder of her former fiancé?

When morning came, Lucy wasn't sure how much she'd slept, but as soon as the room started to brighten, she stepped into her slippers and made her way to the blue room. Her practiced, artistic eye took in everything with a quick glance. She walked around the room, wondering about the aunt she was named after.

Lucy sat on the sofa as the sun's rays filtered through the white drapes, casting a white-yellow glow in the room, making the room appear almost heavenly. The pale blue carpet extended nearly to the windows, although in one corner it looked a bit warped, like the carpet had been damaged.

The layer of dust on the dressing table seemed a part of history as well, as if it held memories in place. Lucy examined the various bottles. Would the perfumes even have a scent anymore? She used her sleeve to pick one of them up, and the dust that bloomed made her sneeze. She set the bottle down and walked to the window. The view was of the rear gardens, which looked a bit scraggly.

Lucy assumed that there wasn't too much of a need for a large garden with only a few inhabitants. She moved back, her slipper catching on the edge of the carpet, where part had rolled up. When Lucy stepped away, she felt unevenness, as if the floor beneath was warped.

Lucy knelt down and smoothed the carpet into place, earning her another sneeze. That's when she felt a bulge under the carpet. She lifted it as far as she dared and, with her other hand, felt around. Her hand touched something smooth and cool. She flinched, pulling her hand back. When nothing moved or made a sound, she reached beneath the carpet again and pulled the object out—a satchel.

The leather was cracked and worn, as if it had seen decades of use. Lucy held it in her hands for a moment, then rose to her feet and walked to the sofa, where she sat. The satchel had probably not been opened since the owner put it there. Based on its location, Lucy guessed that the person didn't want it easily found.

She hesitated a moment, her heart pounding, before she untied the thick leather cord holding it closed. As she lifted the flap, a dozen thoughts flitted through her mind as to what she might find. When she pulled out a bundle of what looked to be letters, Lucy's pulse increased. Holding her breath, she unfolded the top letter.

The handwriting was definitely male.

Dearest Cille,

I cannot believe the words of your note. You surely don't mean to break off our engagement. Meet me at Blackberry Hollow at sunset. Please do not end this.

—C

Lucy stared at the words. From the letter, which must be from Calvin to Lucille—or "Cille"—it seemed that she had broken off the engagement. But why?

She opened the next letter, but the date was three years later. Before reading it, she sorted through the other letters, spreading them on the carpet and organizing them by date.

When she came to a letter dated only a few days after the first one, Lucy started reading.

Dearest Cille,

I do not sleep. I cannot eat. When you told me your kiss at Blackberry Hollow would be our last, I didn't believe you. Now that you haven't replied to any of my letters and refuse to see me, I wonder if perhaps I've fallen asleep and am only dreaming. Or living a nightmare. I don't care if you can't ever have children. I wouldn't want you to attempt it because of your weak heart. Even if my cousin inherits Bevans, at least I will have lived my life with the woman I love. You are more important to me than the possibility of any children.

Earnestly yours,

—C

Lucy's eyes pricked with tears. Her great-great-aunt had sacrificed her happiness because of her inability to have children. Lucy read through several more pleading letters from Calvin, each similar in tone. The dates told her that he gradually wrote less and less frequently. She came to a space of about six months when there were no letters at all. She picked up the next one.

Dearest Cille,

I caught a glimpse of your blue cloak in the back gardens this morning. It seems that blue is still your favorite color. Do you read my letters? Or are they burned the moment they cross the threshold? Or perhaps you do cherish them, just as I cherish any glimpse of you.

I heard that you were ill over the holidays, and I sent up dozens of prayers to heaven. Seeing you outside walking this morning was the most joyful thing I've felt in a long time. You are well and safe.

Cille, my heart is yours and always will be. It has been more than a year since I held you in my arms at Blackberry

Hollow, and more than a year since I've heard your voice. I understand now. Perhaps it's time passing, or maybe it's knowing that even as you suffered through another illness, you did not send for me.

I realize now that you are determined to live your life without me in it. I have grieved over this. But mostly I have denied it. Yet now, I've decided that at the end of this month, I will travel to London for the Season, and I will find a wife.

Unless you tell me not to.

Send but one word, and I will remain here, always yours.

—C

Six

Calvin paced the threadbare rug of the front parlor. He'd heard his sister's carriage before it had come into view, which, one might argue, was impossible, but every nerve in his body was taut, and his senses had risen to those of a hunting dog. He stopped in the middle of the floor, his eyes focused on the window as the carriage drew closer.

He barely breathed as he watched the driver hand his sister out of the carriage, followed by her eldest daughter, a girl of about six or seven. His breath released when he realized no one else had arrived but his sister, her daughter, and a maid. No husband. No infant son. That was a relief. His brother-in-law, Phillip Worth, pretty much let Sylvia do anything she pleased.

Calvin strode out of the room and into the hallway. He opened the door himself; there was no butler anyway. Sylvia was coming up the steps, and her eyebrows lifted in faint surprise, but her smile was quick.

"Brother, you're here," Sylvia trilled. Her daughter, Gwen, clung to her mother's skirts.

"Why wouldn't I be?" he said in an exceedingly patient voice. "You knew of my plans and where to write me."

Sylvia reached him and pecked him on the cheek. He was assailed with the scent of something floral. "I thought you might have fled once you opened my note." Her smile broadened.

That infernal smile. No wonder his sister had attracted, then married, the wealthiest bachelor in London. "I was tempted," he said.

"Say hello to Uncle Calvin," Sylvia said, prodding her daughter forward.

It appeared Gwen wanted to do anything but greet him. She gave a small smile, then, in a voice with the strength of a mouse, said, "Hello, Uncle Calvin."

"Hello, Gwen," he said as kindly as possible.

Her face reddened, and in an instant, she was back behind her mother's skirts.

Sylvia sighed. "We'll take our tea now, and after Gwen's nap, we can talk."

Calvin opened the door wider to let them in. Then he went to tell Mrs. Rollings about the expected tea, knowing she was already up to her arms in preparing bedrooms. But it gave him an excuse to get away from Sylvia's tirades, which had already begun when she walked into the parlor and found that the fire had not been lit. Calvin saw no reason to light a fire when the sun was out.

Less than an hour later, with tea finished and Sylvia and Gwen miraculously cloistered in their room, Calvin had to escape the house. Ever since the letter informing him that his sister was on her way, everything in the house had looked rundown. More so than usual, and to the point that it bothered Calvin as well.

But he simply didn't have the funds to start renovating yet. It would be so easy to let his sister help, but then Bevans Estate would be a product of Sylvia, not of him.

Calvin shoved his hands deep into his pockets and strode from the house. He'd ordered wood for the fence that morning, and now he needed to walk the rest of the property to see if there was anything else that needed immediate attention. Something moved over by Blackberry Hollow—a swatch of color among the autumn colors—a hue that didn't match. He paused in his step, then changed direction and walked toward the hollow. Who would be there, except for the Americans who'd arrived the day before? Calvin slowed his step as he drew closer, realizing that what he saw through the trees was a woman in a lavender dress, sitting on the hill and writing in a book. The American. He hadn't had a good look at her before, but there was no doubt. A large hat with feathers sat next to her in the grass. Her honey-brown hair was full and wavy at the top. She had it swept up into a knot, showing off an elegant neck as she bent forward, intent on her writing.

Calvin realized she wasn't writing, but sketching. Every so often she glanced up, then down, and drew some more. He didn't know how long he'd been watching her until she looked over and gasped.

"I'm sorry," he said.

She scrambled to her feet, dropping her pencil and clutching the book to her chest.

He walked up the hill, intent on meeting her, even though he'd startled her. "I didn't mean to alarm you," he began, then realized she was smiling at him.

"You're my neighbor?" she said.

He halted, confused for a moment. Calling him her *neighbor* sounded so permanent. "Yes, I'm Calvin Bevans."

She lifted her hand and grasped his. Her fingers were warm, despite the cool English air.

"I'm pleased to finally meet you." She looked over her

shoulder in the direction of Quinn Manor. "And I apologize about Mrs. Yates."

Calvin nodded, his throat feeling thick. Dropping her hand, he stepped back. "A lot of history has passed between the families. I don't entirely blame Mrs. Yates, but I don't see any harm in welcoming you to Stanmer Park."

She peered up at him, still smiling, and he found himself smiling back. It was hard not to. This woman's smile was so unlike his sister's too-bright one. This one made him feel . . . interested. Her brown eyes seemed to sparkle, but perhaps it was the sun playing tricks.

"I've set about correcting Mrs. Yates this morning on the relationship between your ancestor and mine," the woman said.

This was not what he expected to hear. "What have you corrected her on?"

"Many misunderstandings have happened over the years," she said, her voice breathless. "Probably the best way to explain is to let you read the letters for yourself."

Now he was curious. "What letters?" She kept fidgeting with her book, and he wondered what she'd been drawing.

"Love letters from Calvin Bevans Sr. to my great-great-aunt Lucille." She tilted her head. "Come with me to the house. You can read them there."

Calvin hesitated. "I'd better not. Mrs. Yates may throw me out again."

"She won't," the woman said. "She may even ask for your forgiveness."

Calvin stared at her. "The misunderstandings were that significant?"

"They were."

His mind took only seconds to make up. "All right. But only if you tell me your name first."

"Why, I'm Lucille Quinn." She flashed another smile and touched his arm. "But everyone calls me Lucy. And . . . it's ironic that you, Calvin Bevans, are standing here with me,

Lucille Quinn—with the two of us bearing the names of our ancestors—because Blackberry Hollow was their secret meeting place."

The earth seemed to shift beneath his feet. Her hand rested on his arm still, and it sent waves of warmth through him. He blinked a few times, trying to clear his thoughts. Blackberry Hollow had been some sort of secret meeting place? "I'd love to read the letters," he said, his voice sounding faraway to his ears.

When she dropped her hand, his senses returned. He walked with her to Quinn Manor, and she asked a few questions, which he was sure he must have answered satisfactorily, as she didn't give him any strange looks. With each step taking him closer to the manor, he felt more and more strongly that his life was about to change significantly.

Seven

Lucy pretended to be busy sketching, but truly, she was watching expressions flit across Calvin's face. It was fascinating to observe him read. She soon found herself sketching him, even though people weren't her favorite subjects. She drew him sitting in the upright chair, leaning forward, his elbows on his knees, as he read letter after letter.

She sketched the fireplace to his side, then the small table with the vase of roses. She drew his three-piece suit, his winged-collared shirt, and the cuffs on his trousers. And finally, she drew the way a wrinkle had appeared between his eyebrows as he concentrated. His hair was blonde, curling at his collar and longish in front, and it kept falling across his forehead. More than once, he brushed it back. At Blackberry Hollow, she'd noticed his blue eyes. How could anyone not? They were a deep blue, like a lake on a summer's day.

She wished she had her colored pencils in the sitting room with her. She'd have to blend a couple of blues and greens to get the color of his eyes just right. With Robert, she'd never had to blend colors. His hair was black, his eyes plain brown . . . not that she'd made a habit of sketching him. When she had once, during a summer picnic, he'd laughed at the drawing and told her to stick to sketching flowers in the meadow.

"Well," Calvin said, startling Lucy.

She snapped her sketchbook closed and met his gaze. Her heart pounded as if she'd been caught doing something wrong. Yet she'd only been sketching him . . . She looked at the letter he held. "Quite the romantic tale, isn't it?"

"Although a tragic one." He looked toward the fire.

Lucy didn't know him well enough to guess what his expression meant. But his profile tempted her to start another sketch of him. Instead, she reached for the final letter on the table near her chair. "There's one more letter. It's written by Lucille, but she never sent it."

Lucy handed it over, and Calvin unfolded the letter and read it aloud. She leaned back in her chair, listening to his deep, mellow voice.

My Dearest Calvin—

You will never see this letter, but I wanted to write to you one more time, and then I will put this away with all of your letters I've saved. I knew you would come to my bedside. I had been praying for it. Although I didn't want your last image of me to be of a weak and ill woman, I could not depart this life without saying good-bye to you in person.

I envy the years you have to live and mourn the years that I am losing. Even though we could never truly be together, I was married to you in my heart. You have brought me the greatest happiness I could ever imagine. Knowing you were close by, and knowing that you cared for me, helped me endure.

All my love forever,
Lucille

Calvin looked up. Lucy realized her eyes had teared. She blinked back the tears and tried to smile.

"Do you know," he began in a quiet voice, "my great-grandfather had a gravestone made for Lucille in her memory and had it placed in our family cemetery? It's surrounded by a half dozen rose bushes and a low stone wall. It's as if she has a private garden at Bevans Estate."

Lucy looked toward the fireplace and flickering flames. "She gave up a lot for him."

"It couldn't have been easy for him, either—to marry another woman with her so near at hand." He gathered up the letters into a pile.

Lucy and Calvin fell into silence for a few moments. She thought about how everything might have been different if Calvin Bevans Sr. hadn't married another woman. The man sitting across from her wouldn't be alive.

"I supposed he was right in marrying to have children," Lucy said. "The house has stayed in the family, and you and your wife will pass it on to your children."

A smile touched Calvin's face. "You sound like my sister." He handed over the letters, and Lucy set them on the table next to her.

"My bachelorhood and lack of funds are my sister's greatest angst," Calvin said. "She arrived this morning, here for a few days to set me straight, no doubt."

Lucy laughed, then covered her mouth. "Sorry, I didn't mean to laugh. But you look perfectly capable of handling your own affairs."

"Thank you." His gaze assessed her, and she found herself staring back into those lake-blue eyes. "What are you drawing?" he asked.

Heat rushed through her face. "Oh, I'm sketching the rooms and gardens of Quinn Manor. I don't want to forget my visit." She couldn't hide the wistful tone in her voice. "I was amazed to inherit such a place . . . I mean, an English estate! I know it's small compared to Bevans, but it's beautiful and peaceful. I feel like I've walked into a storybook." She took a much-needed breath. "Sorry, I've been rambling."

Calvin chuckled. "I don't mind. I agree with everything you've said, and even though I grew up here, I'll never tire of the place. If I could get all of my work done outside of London, I'd live at Bevans fulltime." He told her about his business in London and how he hoped to renovate the estate in a few years.

"Will you live here after the renovations are complete?" she asked.

"I would love to, but it would be difficult to run the business from here. I must be close to London unless I can find some profitable investments that allow me to cut down on the number of clients."

"My fiancé knows all about investments," Lucy said. "I could have him write you with advice."

"You're engaged?" Calvin said.

For some reason, his question made her flustered. "Almost. It's only a matter of time before he proposes."

Calvin simply nodded.

"Robert's a stock broker. He runs his own firm and is incredibly busy. That's why he's not with me now. He sent along articles for me to read about the market so I'd understand his world more." Lucy realized she was clenching one of the letters in her hand. She set it down and picked up her drawing pencil. "He's very knowledgeable; he wouldn't lead you astray."

Calvin leaned forward in his chair, his eyes intent on hers. "If he's well versed in the foreign markets, I'd be happy to hear his advice."

"All right." Lucy flushed at the intensity of his gaze. "I'll write him."

Calvin glanced at her hands. She was fiddling with her drawing pencil. "Can I see your sketches?"

Lucy hadn't expected his interest. "They're quite amateurish. In fact, it's such a small hobby, I don't think I'll continue after we marry. Robert says we'll be too busy with entertaining. He aims for a political career someday, you know." She looked away from Calvin's gaze. "I don't want to forget anything about Quinn Manor, so I'm drawing the rooms and the grounds."

"You're in love, aren't you?"

The question sent a jolt through Lucy. She hadn't exactly considered herself *in love* with Robert, although everyone said they were perfect for each other. "I . . . ."

"Admit it," Calvin said, amusement in his tone. "No one would blame you for falling in love with Quinn Manor, even if it weren't your inheritance."

Oh . . . he meant the estate . . . not Robert.

"I am in love with it," she said in a quiet voice, realizing she didn't want to sell the place. She wanted to live inside the storybook. She suddenly felt melancholy, caught between two worlds—a new, fascinating one, which had captured her heart, and the old, familiar one, which was very dear to her too.

Calvin rose from his chair and crossed the few steps that separated them. Towering over her, he extended his hand. "I'd love to see your drawings."

Lucy's heart thumped. She'd never shown a stranger her sketches before. Robert and her mother hardly paid attention to them. She looked up at Calvin. "They're simple, really."

He smiled, his fingers still extended, and Lucy reluctantly handed over the sketchbook.

Calvin settled in the chair next to hers. With this arrangement, she could see the drawings as he turned each page. Her stomach knotted.

The earlier sketches were of the ship they traveled on to England. Then the hotel they stayed in the first night. When

Calvin reached the picture of Blackberry Hollow, he paused for a long time. He glanced over. "You're very talented, Miss Quinn. Do you paint as well?"

Her face heated at the compliment, although she knew he was just being kind. "Some watercolor, but I like sketching the smaller details, and watercolor tends to bleed everything together."

He turned the next page before she could remember to stop him. The sketch was of him reading the letters. Even though it was rough, it was plain who was in the image.

Calvin looked over again, his brows raised, wearing a half smile.

Lucy reached for the book. "You weren't supposed to see that."

He didn't surrender it. "Why not?"

"I—I don't normally draw people, and it's not finished—"

"Will you finish it then?" His eyes held hers.

She hesitated. Mostly because her heart was pounding way too hard, and she didn't exactly trust what she might say. Finally, she exhaled. "All right."

Eight

Walking the grounds with his sister as she explained all of the improvements the estate needed was not exactly Calvin's favorite way to pass his day. Added to the torture was the feeling that he'd spent hours in the company of a woman who was becoming more and more intriguing to him by the moment.

In his mind, he could still hear Lucy's laughter. He pictured her bent over her sketchbook, concentrating, with her full lips pressed together as she drew. Her brief glances at him as she sketched him watching the fire. At first, it had been disconcerting to know he was being scrutinized, but the longer he'd sat and she'd worked, the more fascinating he'd found it—that an artist was re-creating him.

What did Lucy see when she looked at him? At the time, when she'd finished, she'd said she wasn't ready to show him—that she wanted to add some color first. Even though he was curious, even impatient, to see the result, he'd agreed to wait. If only to secure another meeting with her.

Calvin barely listened to his sister as she went on and on about resurrecting the orchards, which he wholeheartedly agreed with. Lucy would love to draw the orchard in its different seasons.

"Stop that," Sylvia said.

Calvin looked over at his sister. "What?"

"You haven't even been listening to me, have you?" Sylvia's eyes, which everyone said matched his, looked like a thundercloud.

Calvin sighed. They were near the house now, yet he could hardly remember anything from the past half hour. "I agree with all of your suggestions. But I'm not changing my mind, Sylvia. I can't let you pay for the renovations; this estate is my responsibility."

She folded her arms. "You are stubborn like Father was."

"I'll be able to start in a few years," Calvin tried to amend. "There's no hurry."

Sylvia's stormy eyes filled with tears.

Calvin froze. She'd never cried about it before. "What's really going on? Why are you so determined to make changes *now*?"

She wiped at a tear that had fallen onto her cheek. "It sounds foolish, really . . ." She glanced up at him, then looked down at her clasped hands. "Marriage has been so *boring*."

Calvin stared at her, then laughed.

When she turned away, crying more, he bit back his laughter. "I'm sorry," he said. "I didn't mean to make light of your distress."

She sniffled, her shoulders shaking, and Calvin realized his sister was laughing. "I'm terrible . . . I've turned into a horribly spoiled woman." She turned around, wiping at the tears spilling down her cheeks. "I have everything I could ask for—cooks, nannies, servants—it's all rather revolting, if one really thinks about it."

Calvin was smiling, but he also understood this side of his practical sister.

"I mean, I could lie in bed all day and do nothing but eat sweets if I wanted to. Phillip would still adore me, and my children would still be spoiled." Her eyes finally dry, she took a deep breath. "I want to do something that *matters*, Calvin. And this place matters to me. It's where I grew up. Phillip's houses are gorgeous, but this place—it has my heart."

His home had Calvin's heart too. He pulled his sister into his arms. "I understand. Perhaps I can allow you to do one, very small project."

She squealed, then hugged him hard. He laughed as he drew away.

"You will not regret it." She pinched his cheeks. He hated it when she did that, but he didn't have time to complain, because his niece, Gwen, came screeching out of the house.

Calvin wasn't about to decipher what the little girl was screaming about. He'd never heard her speak more than a few shy words, so this running girl, braids flying behind her, as she clutched something in her hand, was a shock.

"What is it, dear?" Sylvia ran toward her daughter.

Calvin hurried after his sister, fearing her child had been hurt. Or perhaps she was sick. But did little girls scream and run when they were ill?

"He ruined it! I hate him!" Gwen yelled.

Sylvia was holding Gwen now, who waved a piece of paper.

After much crying, and some coercing from Sylvia, Calvin finally gathered that Gwen had spent "all day"— which could have only been half an hour—drawing a picture of the "horsey in the stable" when Jupiter, one of Calvin's hunting hounds, had bumped into Gwen. She'd fallen, and the picture had become soiled and wrinkled.

Calvin understood the disappointment, but did all children carry on this way? He took the picture and smoothed it out. The dirt was barely noticeable after he gave it a good brush-off. Not much could be done about the wrinkles, though. "Would you like to draw another picture of the horse?"

To his surprise, the suggestion sent Gwen into another fit of wails. He met his sister's helpless gaze over the girl's head.

"Or . . . perhaps *I* could draw you a picture?" Calvin said. Even more dismay. "I'm not such a bad artist," he tried again. "Perhaps you'd like my picture. I could add in the dog as well."

More crying.

"She wants *this* picture fixed," Sylvia murmured.

Suddenly Calvin had a possibly brilliant idea. "Gwen," he said, crouching down so he could look her in the eye. She must have noticed his confident tone, because she turned her head to look at him.

Calvin's heart hitched at the sight of her puffy, red eyes. "I know someone who can fix it."

Gwen's eyes widened, and for the first time, Calvin noticed that she had her mother's eyes, which meant he had something in common with his niece.

He held out his hand. "Come with me."

Amazingly, Gwen put her small hand in his. A day earlier, he wouldn't have done anything like this, but ever since Sylvia had cried about wanting to do something that mattered, Calvin had unexpectedly wanted to help her little girl smile too.

"Calvin," Sylvia whispered, walking next to him as he led them to Quinn Manor. "What are you doing?"

He merely grinned. He'd told Sylvia nothing about their American neighbors or of the forlorn love letters between their ancestors, and certainly not of the drawing session he'd sat for Lucy.

When Mrs. Yates answered the front door, Calvin braced himself out of habit. But when she smiled and greeted them, Calvin quickly recovered. "Is Miss Lucy Quinn available?"

"Yes, she's in the back gardens, I believe. I'll have her come in and meet you in the sitting room. Mrs. Quinn is in there now."

Sylvia threw him a questioning glance when the housekeeper ushered them inside. "Who's Lucy?" she mouthed.

"She's the American who inherited the property," he whispered as they followed the housekeeper. "She's also an artist."

They reached the sitting room, and Mrs. Yates announced them to a woman who was unmistakably Lucy's mother.

Mrs. Julia Quinn rose from her seat at a small desk, where she'd been writing. "Welcome. It's wonderful to meet you."

Mrs. Yates bustled out, and Calvin stepped forward to take Mrs. Quinn's hand. He'd met her earlier that day before reading the letters with Lucy. Calvin introduced his sister and niece to Mrs. Quinn.

"How lovely to meet you," Mrs. Quinn said, smiling at both of them.

Mrs. Yates opened the door, and Lucy walked into the room, pulling off her wide straw hat. Her hair was full and wavy, knotted at the nape of her neck. Lucy's brown eyes met his, curious, then went to Sylvia and Gwen.

"Your sister?" Lucy said.

"Yes. May I introduce Mrs. Sylvia Worth and her daughter, Gwen Worth, who also happens to be an artist." He motioned to Lucy. "And this is Miss Lucy Quinn." Gwen grabbed onto Calvin's hand, which he found quite endearing.

"I'm *not* an artist," Gwen said, her fingers tightening around his.

Calvin held up the drawing he still held. "Did you not draw this?"

Gwen's eyes shone. "Yes."

He peered at the drawing closely. "It's an exquisite drawing of a horse. If a girl of only seven drew this, she must be an artist."

Gwen giggled.

"We've had an unfortunate incident," Calvin said, looking over at Lucy, who had a smile tugging on her face. "Gwen needs your help restoring her drawing. Maybe some colored pencils would help?"

"Let me see." Lucy held out her hand for the drawing. Her smile was soft as she looked at it. "I think I can help." Her eyes found Calvin's, then moved to Gwen. "Wait here. I'll return shortly."

Nine

Back in her bedroom, Lucy put a hand over her racing heart. Her heart wasn't pounding from having just climbed the stairs. Calvin had returned, bringing his sister and niece in tow . . . and Lucy had never seen anything more adorable than how Calvin proclaimed the young girl an artist. She could tell that Gwen had been crying—her small, puffy eyes, and intermittent sniffs.

Calvin will make a great father, she thought, then immediately shook her head. What was she thinking? Ever since Robert had said he wanted to wait several years to have children, she'd felt a little downcast about it. She'd told herself that was why she was so aware of how other men acted around children, nothing more. She picked up her metal tin with the colored pencils, and her gaze fell on the sketch she'd finished of Calvin—fully colored now. The colors had brought him to life, especially his lake-blue eyes, although she didn't think she had the color exactly right.

She took a couple of calming breaths before returning downstairs. Seeing Calvin with his sister and niece had impressed her—he was a man with depth, compassion, and cleverness. A man who knew how to make a little girl dry her tears. A man who made a fuss out of appreciating a small child's artwork.

Lucy found herself smiling again as she walked downstairs and returned to the sitting room. Calvin had moved a small table in front of the sofa, and Gwen sat there waiting, her tiny hands clasped in her lap.

"Coloring pencils are a great secret of every artist," Lucy said, glancing at Calvin with a smile. Her mother sat near the fire, the inventory ledger in hand, as if she meant to review her notes. But she spoke quietly to Sylvia, and Lucy could tell their conversation was about Lucille's love letters.

Lucy settled beside Gwen. "You can borrow my coloring pencils today."

"No one else knows the secret?" Gwen said.

"Only artists, so we must ask your mother and uncle not to tell anyone else." Lucy opened the tin and picked out three shades of brown. "You never want to use just one color. If you blend colors, the animal, or whatever else you are drawing, looks more real."

Lucy had never drawn anything with someone watching, so she tried to steady her nervous hands as she lightly shaded the horse, blending with the smears of dirt until they weren't distinguishable from the pencils. She picked up a darker brown and shaded beneath the belly.

"Do you want to try?" Lucy asked, holding out the pencil.

Gwen took the pencil and started to shade.

"Don't press too hard," Lucy said. "You can always go over it more than once to make it darker."

Gwen adjusted her pressure and continued shading. A

moment later, she beamed at Lucy. "I can't see the dirt anymore."

"When you get home, hold the paper over a steaming kettle for a few seconds," Lucy said, glancing at Calvin to make sure he was listening in so he could help his niece. "Then place another piece of paper over the drawing and a stack of books on top of that. In the morning, your paper will be flat again."

Gwen wrapped her arms around Lucy. "You're the best artist in the world."

Lucy laughed and squeezed her back. "We artists need to stick together." She looked again at Calvin, who seemed amused.

Sylvia crossed the room and inspected the reformed drawing. "Thank you ever so much, Miss Quinn."

Lucy rose to her feet. "It's my pleasure. I'll be here for two weeks, and I'm available anytime to help her."

"Oh, please!" Gwen said, jumping up. "Can I come over tomorrow so you can show me how to draw a house?"

"A house?" Lucy said. "Why yes. I can certainly show you that."

Sylvia took her daughter's hand. "I think Miss Quinn has plenty to do. She's only here a short time."

Lucy did have a lot to do. She had barely started exploring the grounds and had a lot of sketching ahead of her. She hadn't even gone over her mother's inventory list. But she said, "I'd be happy to teach you how to draw a house tomorrow." Lucy could hardly believe she was making the offer. But if it was a chance to see Calvin again . . .

Gwen tugged on her mother's hand. "She said it's all right."

Sylvia smiled and looked at Lucy, then Mrs. Quinn. "Are you sure?"

"We're happy to have her over," Mrs. Quinn confirmed.

"Come after breakfast," Lucy said. "The light in the morning is divine—as long as it's not raining."

"I'll pray for no rain," Gwen blurted out.

Mrs. Quinn and Sylvia laughed.

"All right, dear," Sylvia said to Gwen. "We'll come tomorrow and learn how to draw a house."

Lucy noticed the exchange of smiles between Calvin and his sister. The color of Calvin's eyes was like his sister's *and* his niece's. Apparently, lake blue ran in the family.

When Calvin's gaze landed on her, Lucy's cheeks were already pink, if not scarlet. "Thank you, Lucy," he said. "You're a remarkable person."

Remarkable? Showing a seven-year-old child how to color was simple. But Calvin seemed sincere. Before leaving, he grasped her hand and brought it to his lips, then pressed a soft kiss on her hand. The warmth of his touch traveled all the way to her stomach, tumbling her insides.

After they left, her mother started to say, "Well, that was unexpected . . ." then fell silent.

The two women stood by the window and watched Calvin, Sylvia, and Gwen walk across the property. Lucy felt a hollow ache in her chest as she watched them. Gwen was between the two adults, a hand snugly in each of theirs. It made Lucy feel alone in the world, even though her mother stood near her and Robert awaited her in New York.

Her mother walked back to the desk and took up reading through the ledger, leaving Lucy to her thoughts.

Calvin had disappeared through the line of trees at the border, and then he reappeared as he drew closer to the house. Lucy wondered what it would be like to walk about the estate hand in hand with Calvin. She immediately dismissed the idea. She should be thinking of Robert, not Calvin.

Yet, her stomach had never tumbled when Robert had kissed her like it had with simply talking with Calvin. And he had only kissed her hand. Kissing Robert was nice, but it wasn't the stuff of fables. She already knew he'd insist on separate bedrooms like his parents had.

There was nothing wrong with that, of course. Robert would make a fine husband, and she'd be at his side as he achieved success in New York City. Her mother would be proud, and Lucy's future would be secure.

Then why do I want to hurry after Calvin and show him my nearly finished drawing of him? Why do I want to study the blue of his eyes so I can get it perfect? And why can I still feel the touch of his lips on my hand?

Ten

"She's engaged?" Sylvia asked, working on a bit of needlepoint while Calvin stood by the large front windows, looking over the vast lawn of his estate.

"*Almost* engaged, she said," Calvin replied. He'd felt gloomy since returning from Quinn Manor, and his ever-perceptive sister had finally dragged it out of him. Yes, he was interested in Lucy Quinn. More than interested. But she was American. She was leaving in less than two weeks. And she was almost engaged.

"Is she in love with the man?" Sylvia asked.

Calvin nearly choked. "I can't exactly ask her that."

Sylvia was quiet for a moment. "Well, I wonder, all the same."

I do too. Yet, two issues still divided them even without the fiancé, and he hadn't considered the biggest of all. Could she ever be interested in *him*?

"This is ridiculous; I don't even know her," Calvin grumbled. He stalked away from the windows and sank into an oversized chair. The fire had been lit at Sylvia's insistence, and now he studied the flames as if they somehow had the answer.

Sylvia chuckled.

"You're enjoying this, aren't you?" Calvin said. "Watching your little brother be miserable. It must be the best day of your life."

Sylvia kept smiling.

Calvin folded his arms and exhaled. Had he been imagining it, or had there been some attraction on Lucy's part? They had seemed to get along so well. She'd been direct, not shy at all, yet she'd also been forthright about Robert. Could he ask her about her feelings for the man she was soon to be affianced to? No. It wasn't his place or his business. And what did he hope to accomplish? The odds were entirely against him.

He closed his eyes, remembering how Lucy's head had bent forward while helping Gwen. Tendrils of Lucy's honey-colored hair had escaped, framing her face. Her brown eyes had sparkled every time she looked at him, as if they'd shared some great amusement. Did Lucy know that her fair skin and honey-brown hair were the perfect combination of hues?

"I think she likes you," Sylvia said, startling Calvin.

The suggestion shot a wave of anticipation through him. "How can you say that?"

"Every time she looked at you, she blushed." Sylvia set down her needlepoint. "Women notice these things."

Calvin furrowed his brows, trying to remember. Could it be true? And if it was, would Lucy consider someone like him? She'd have to change her whole life. Then he remembered her words: *I feel like I've walked into a storybook.*

A spark of hope ignited in his chest.

Eleven

ucy sketched Calvin's house from her bedroom window. She could see only a portion of Bevans Estate from here, but it was an interesting angle. Most of the house was still in shadow, not yet captured by the rising sun, but that made it look all the more exquisite.

She thought of Calvin, possibly still inside at this early hour. Was he eating breakfast? Reading by the fire? Going over ledgers? His lake-blue eyes were never far from her mind, and she supposed they would stay that way until she got the shade right in her sketchbook.

She looked forward to seeing Calvin again . . . and as she watched the house and sketched, she tried to justify her anticipation. Calvin was a good-looking man. An interesting man. That was all. He might be available, but not to her. And just because he was interested in her art and happened to be the perfect gentleman, didn't mean she had needed to toss and turn the previous night, going over every word he'd said.

Someone came out of the Bevans house. Lucy straightened. It was a man holding a little girl's hand. Calvin was bringing Gwen over. Lucy hurried to the wardrobe and opened the doors. What she was wearing would not do after all. She pulled out two dresses fuller at the top and pinched in the waist and held them side by side. She chose the pale yellow with the scooped neck and no train, because the color brought out the gold tones in her hair and perhaps made her eyes less of a plain brown.

By the time Mrs. Yates escorted Calvin and Gwen into the sitting room, Lucy's hands were clammy, and her heart raced. She should have asked her mother to join them . . . having her there seemed safer somehow. Safer than letting herself stare at her male guest.

Gwen hurried toward her, still wearing her hat with a huge bow, holding up a sketchbook. "Look what Uncle Calvin gave me."

His face pinked, which Lucy found charming.

"It was my sketchbook as a child," he explained. "Very little used."

Lucy smiled as she leafed through the pages. The drawings were childish, similar to what Gwen had brought over the day before.

"As you can see, my family can do with your expertise," Calvin said.

"I love them all." Her heart thumped as his eyes seemed to see into her soul. She quickly turned to Gwen. "Ready to start? I think we should begin with this house, since it's a bit smaller than your uncle's."

"Can I use your colored pencils?" Gwen asked.

"Yes. Once you have the house sketched, you can color it in." She dared another glance at Calvin.

Soon, the three of them were outside, sitting on chairs Calvin had carried from the house. Clouds threatened rain, and the softness of the early morning had faded, but the darker sky gave Lucy a chance to instruct Gwen about color and shading. She hoped it all wouldn't be too daunting for the budding artist.

They spent the next hour sketching, shading, then coloring. Calvin even joined with advice of his own. When Gwen was happy with her first picture of a house, they walked to Quinn Manor.

"Did you ever finish my sketch?" Calvin asked on the WAY.

"I did . . . almost," Lucy said.

His eyebrows lifted, and he stopped walking. "Almost?"

Lucy stopped as well. "Everything is finished but the color of your eyes." And then she was blushing again, because those eyes were looking back at her. "I mean, they're an unusual color, and I've blended a couple of hues, but I don't think I've got it quite right."

Calvin's smile broadened. "Can I see it?"

Lucy glanced at Gwen, who had found the cat that frequented the porch. "Maybe later."

"Do you want to meet at Blackberry Hollow?" he asked. "Later?" His low voice seemed to touch her skin, and she suddenly felt hot.

"All right." She couldn't believe she'd agreed to something that felt like a secret meeting, even though Gwen had heard every word, whether or not she'd paid attention or cared.

"Sunset?" he said.

With his gaze on her, Lucy could only say, "Yes."

Twelve

One Week Later

"Trust me," Sylvia said as she leaned over a blueprint of the Bevans Estate on which she was marking her renovation ideas. "Be yourself, and she won't be able to resist."

Calvin narrowed his eyes. "Did you just give me a compliment?"

Sylvia looked up from the blueprint. "Maybe. But I'm telling you, let her know how you feel now, or it will be too late."

Three days. Lucy would leave for London in three days, and then she'd be on a ship back to America. They'd spent the last week together, caught up in one activity after another. When they'd met at Blackberry Hollow at sunset the week before, he'd nearly kissed her after seeing the drawing

354

she'd done of him. He couldn't prove it, but he believed she couldn't have done such a fine drawing without caring for the subject just a little.

And he had grown to care for her too. Calvin had even helped her with the tedious task of making inventory lists. When her mother had grown tired of the dust, they'd gone through the entire attic of Quinn Manor. They'd walked the property several times.

He'd been at the meeting with the auction house director. He'd listened to Lucy's doubts about selling the place and how she was considering waiting a year. She'd told him more about Robert, such as how he didn't want children for a while. Calvin had noted sadness in her eyes when she spoke about that. He'd read some of the articles Robert had asked her to read. She'd sat in his library while he drafted letters to his clients. And nearly every day, Lucy gave Gwen some sort of drawing lesson. The little girl was positively attached to Lucy.

And so was he. He'd spent hours watching her draw. When she was satisfied with finding the right combination of hues for his eyes, she'd given him the drawing to keep. She didn't know that it was on the table by his bed and that he'd probably never move it.

"I don't know how to be myself around her," Calvin told his sister, mostly speaking to himself. "Because I don't even know what I'm doing or saying half of the time."

Sylvia smiled. "Maybe that's a good thing."

Calvin shook his head. Sylvia was no help—well, she was actually a tremendous help, giving him courage when he probably would have given up by now. Sylvia had interpreted Lucy for him; it was nice to have a female confidante when navigating a man-woman relationship.

"You need to kiss her tonight," Sylvia declared.

Calvin snapped his head up. "What?"

"She must have time to think about what your kiss

means," Sylvia continued in a calm voice, as if her suggestion hadn't nearly stopped his heart.

"What if she doesn't want—"

"Kiss her, and you'll find out," Sylvia interrupted. She put her hands on her hips, her expression far from smiling. "Tell her how you feel. She'll have time to think about it as she gazes over Bevans Estate for her last few days." Now her smile was back. Cunning.

Calvin laughed, even though his stomach was a knot of nerves. "I don't know if that's the best advice."

"When have I ever given you bad advice?" Sylvia demanded.

Calvin thought for a moment, then conceded his sister always gave good advice.

Thirteen

Three days left, Lucy thought as she dressed for supper, having a hard time believing that she had so little time before saying good-bye to Quinn Manor forever. Good-bye to Mrs. Yates. To Gwen, Sylvia, and . . . Calvin.

Tonight the Bevanses were coming for supper. No doubt Sylvia would discuss her latest renovation idea, and Calvin would listen patiently. Then he'd ask Lucy about what she'd been sketching that day, even though he very well knew, since he'd been there while she was drawing. Later they'd play games until Gwen started yawning. They'd had plenty of comfortable evenings like this over the past week. Lucy would miss them.

Her mother was already asking questions . . . What would Robert think of Lucy sitting so close to Calvin? About her laughing with him so? Taking walks, just the two of them? Spending nearly every moment in his company?

Lucy heard the commotion downstairs of Mrs. Yates welcoming the Bevanses into the house, and her mother's voice carried up the stairs as she greeted them. Lucy turned to the mirror and pinned her hair into place. Her heart thumped when she thought of sitting across from Calvin at the dining table, of the way his gaze always seemed to find her no matter the situation.

Ready at last, she left her room and walked downstairs. She found everyone in the sitting room.

"There you are," her mother said, rising. "We were about to go in and eat."

Small arms wrapped around Lucy's waist, and she looked down to see Gwen. "Hello, sweetie," Lucy said.

Sylvia smiled her greeting, and when Gwen let go, she followed her mother and Mrs. Quinn into the hall. Calvin held back. He was unusually quiet, and Lucy looked at him questioningly. He took her hand, and brought it to his lips, pressing a kiss on her skin.

His expression was serious, as if he, too, knew they were losing time to be together. Fast.

Sadness flooded through Lucy, surprising her at its intensity. She linked her arm through Calvin's, and they walked to the dining room.

The conversation at supper was mostly between Sylvia and Mrs. Quinn. Lucy chimed in a few times, but Calvin remained quiet. She caught his eyes on her more than once, and her pulse quickened each time.

When supper was over, they moved to the sitting room, where there was a cheery fire. Gwen immediately begged to play draughts, and soon Mrs. Quinn and Gwen were playing in earnest. Sylvia had brought a sampler to work on and sat close to the game so she could offer Gwen advice from time to time.

Lucy's eyes followed Calvin as he walked to the hearth

and leaned against it, his hands shoved in his pockets. She went to join him, and when he looked up, their gazes locked.

"Are you all right?" she asked. "You've been quiet all evening."

"You're leaving soon."

"I know," she said, her voice falling to a whisper. Her face heated under Calvin's intense stare. Would she ever get used to him watching her that way?

"I'm not looking forward to it," he said.

She gave a small sigh; her stomach had tightened. She didn't know if she was ready for this—this talk of saying good-bye. "Would you like to walk through the gardens?" It was an impulsive suggestion. It was nearly dark, and the clouds had been ominous all day.

He gave a brief nod and straightened from the hearth. He told Sylvia where they were going, and she murmured something back.

Gwen and Mrs. Quinn were too absorbed in their game to notice much else. Once outside, Calvin offered his arm. Lucy took it—the second time that evening—and they walked slowly through the garden of roses. Most of the plants were fading with the cooling weather, and Lucy had a sudden desire to see what the gardens would look like in the spring.

It shouldn't have surprised Lucy to realize that they were walking toward Blackberry Hollow, as if their feet had their own minds. The sunset broke through the clouds, piercing the gray horizon with a deep orange.

When they arrived, Lucy reluctantly released Calvin's arm. "Have you eaten the blackberries here?" she asked to break the silence.

"I used to, as a boy," he said. "My mother made the most delicious pies with them. Her parents could never keep her away from the kitchen as a young girl, and she learned to make pies from the house cook."

"This place was probably a lot different when your

great-grandfather and Lucille used to meet here." Lucy turned to watch the mottled sunset. A breeze picked up, cool, and with the promise of impending rain.

Calvin turned to watch the horizon as well. "I think Blackberry Hollow is similar to how it was back then."

Lucy nodded. Standing here felt so natural, in the middle of England with Calvin, as if she'd known him much longer than a couple of weeks. She felt connected to him somehow. She didn't think that even Robert knew as much about her in their year of acquaintance as Calvin did in two weeks. Still, Calvin lived here, and she lived in New York.

"It's ironic, really, that we are standing here now," he said.

Lucy looked over at him. His eyes were darker beneath the cloudy sky—like deep pools of blue. "How so?"

"Because just as my great-grandfather wanted to kiss Lucille, I want to kiss you," he whispered.

Lucy's body heated, like it was on fire. "I don't know . . ."

He didn't move, didn't speak, just watched her.

Letting Calvin kiss her would change everything. It would make all that she had felt and thought about him real—no longer in her imagination or part of her dreams. It would mean he felt the same way she did about him. It would mean he wanted her. And it would prove she wanted him.

"I want you to kiss me," she whispered back, swallowing against the tightness of her throat. "But . . ." She inhaled. So many thoughts were tumbling in her mind, yet her body wanted to be near Calvin. To have him touch her, kiss her. Yet . . . there was Robert. He didn't make her think any of the things she'd thought about Calvin.

His hand threaded through hers with an intimacy she didn't know could exist from holding a man's hand. They were connected, a part of each other, although only their fingers were touching. Still, he waited; she both loved him and hated him for that. It meant *she* had to decide. Whatever happened next was her choice.

"Maybe just once," she breathed.

Calvin didn't hesitate to accept her offer. He released her hand and cradled her face, his fingers warm on her cheeks. Her eyelids fluttered shut because she wanted to feel every move, every breath. His lips brushed hers, barely touching them at first. Then he drew her closer, and she wrapped her arms around his neck, blending her body with his.

The first drops of rain fell, but she hardly noticed them. Calvin's mouth parted as he kissed her more deeply, and she responded, the intensity sending heat all the way to her toes. Lucy felt as if she were floating above the ground and burning up at the same time.

When Calvin lifted his head, breathing hard, he whispered, "Lucy . . ."

"Calvin . . ." This time she kissed *him*, pulling him against her again, and clutching at the curling hair above his collar.

There was no complaint from him, and Lucy couldn't imagine ever returning to Robert, or to any other man, after kissing Calvin like this. When they were forced to break off to catch their breath, Calvin said, "That was more than once."

Lucy smiled, holding onto his jacket, which was getting damp from the rain, because if she didn't hang onto him, she might not be able to remain upright.

"Before you leave, I need to say something," he said, his breath warm against her neck, contrasting with the cool air.

She wanted to kiss him again—to not talk about anything that might come between them, especially about her return to America or the man who waited for her there.

"I want to kiss you every day for the rest of my life," Calvin said, his lake-blue gaze holding hers.

Tears sprang to her eyes, and she blinked them away. "Calvin . . ."

His hand touched her cheek, wiping away raindrops. "I want you to stay here. I want to court you properly. And then I'll ask you to marry me."

Her tears wouldn't stop, and blinking did no good. The tears blended with the faster-falling raindrops. She tried to speak, but her voice refused to make a sound.

"I'm falling in love with you, Lucy," he whispered, resting his forehead against hers.

She closed her eyes and felt the warmth from his breath, the strength of his arms around her, the beating of his heart. She let his words wrap around her heart. A future with him would be completely different than anything she'd ever imagined, could ever have dreamed of. But he had stolen her heart.

She had fallen in love with Calvin Bevans III.

And now she had to tell Robert.

She took a shaky breath. "I must write to Robert."

Calvin stiffened, and Lucy realized he expected the worst. She continued. "To tell him I'm in love with another man and that I'm not coming home."

He kissed her neck, her jaw, and then her mouth.

She laughed, and when his kissing slowed, she said, "What are we going to tell my mother?"

He pulled away, his gaze soaking her in, his hands moving up her arms and resting on her shoulders. "We'll tell her you belong here, with me, and we'll invite her to stay."

Lucy lifted up on her toes and brushed her lips against his, tasting his kiss mixed with rain.

She had never expected to fall in love with Calvin—but now that she had, there was no going back. "All right, Mr. Bevans. Let's get inside before the rain makes us unrecognizable." She grasped his hand and tugged him toward Quinn Manor—and their future together.

HEATHER B. MOORE

Heather B. Moore is a *USA Today* bestselling author. She writes historical thrillers under the pen name H.B. Moore; her latest is *Finding Sheba*. Under Heather B. Moore she writes romance and women's fiction. She's a coauthor of The Newport Ladies Book Club series. Other works include *Heart of the Ocean, The Fortune Café,* the Aliso Creek series, and the Amazon bestselling Timeless Romance Anthology series.

For book updates, sign up for Heather's email list: hbmoore.com/contact

Website: www.hbmoore.com

Blog: MyWritersLair.blogspot.com

Twitter: @HeatherBMoore

Facebook: Fans of H.B. Moore

MORE TIMELESS ROMANCE ANTHOLOGIES

For more information about our anthologies, visit our blog at TimelessRomanceAnthologies.blogspot.com